Michael Dean

The White Crucifixion

A novel about Marc Chagall

Holland Park Press London

Published by Holland Park Press 2018

Copyright © Michael Dean 2018

First Edition

A CIP catalogue record for this book is
available from The British Library.

ISBN 978-1-907320-73-6

Cover designed by Reactive Graphics

Printed and bound by
CPI Group (UK) Ltd, Croydon CR0 4YY

www.hollandparkpress.co.uk

The White Crucifixion starts with Chagall's difficult birth in Vitebsk 1887, in the present-day Belarus, and tells the surprising story of how the eldest son of a herring schlepper became enrolled in art school where he quickly gained a reputation as 'Moyshe, the painting wonder'.

The novel paints a vivid picture of a Russian town divided by belief and wealth, rumours of pogroms never far away, yet bustling with talented young artists.

In 1913 Chagall relished the opportunity to move to Paris to take up residence in the artist colony 'The Hive' (*La Ruche*). The Yiddish-speaking artists (École Juive) living there were all poor. The Hive had no electric light or running water and yet many of its artists were to become famous, among them Amedeo Modigliani, Chaim Soutine and Osip Zadkine.

The novel vividly portrays the dynamics of an artist colony, its pettiness, friendships and the constant battle to find the peace and quiet to work.

In 1914 Chagall and his wife Bella made what was supposed to be a fleeting visit to his beloved Vitebsk, only to be trapped there by the outbreak of the First World War, the subsequent Russian revolution and the establishment of the communist regime, which was increasingly hostile towards artists like Chagall.

Yet Chagall kept on painting, and the novel provides a fascinating account of what inspired some of his greatest work. He eventually managed to return to France, only to be thwarted by another world war, which proved disastrous for the people he knew in Vitebsk, the people in his paintings, including his uncle Neuch, the original 'fiddler on the roof'.

The first virtue of a novelist is to be a liar.

Blaise Cendrars, poet, friend of Marc Chagall

Contents

PART I: VITEBSK, 1887–1913

On a highly auspicious day, the seventh day of the seventh month, I was born dead. I was brought back to life by the midwife holding me in a tub of cold water, then lifting me out again. I went from black to blue to pink. Then a fire broke out.

It started in a little house behind the prison on the outskirts of Vitebsk. Then it ripped and crackled through the *izbas*, the multi-coloured wooden houses of the poor Pestkovatik district. Many houses and shops burned down, though not the Shagal blue-painted *izba*, nor the little grocery shop my mother, Feiga-Ita, had started.

My painting of the scene, *Birth*, shows a claustrophobic single-room *izba* pressed down by a low crooked ceiling. By a red-canopied bed, a midwife is holding a baby. There is a proud father present, and a cow. There is a mysterious rabbinical figure at the window. The mother is naked except for a cloth round her middle and one sock. In front of her, by the bed, is a large tub of water into which they are about to dunk the baby, bringing it back to life.

The priority for the large Shagal clan, all present at the birth, was naturally to save the precariously living baby Moyshe from the fire and carry him off to safety. The bed with the helpless mother clutching her soaked baby son was lifted. Strong men trotted in step, carrying the bed out of the *izba* and away.

We finally arrived, rocking and bumping, at our beloved river Dvina. We had escaped the fire, but escape is not deliverance.

Down by the river bank, in the fire-lit darkness, they pricked me with pins to make sure I was still alive. It made me sensitive, sensitive to pain and the smaller pricks of life. I felt afraid and the fear never left me. My little *schwanz* – my penis – curled up like a comma between my legs, afraid to stand up straight. And so it stayed.

That is why I am hypersensitive, emotional, as feminine as I am masculine. I stammer and I am subject to fainting fits. I feel as if I have only one layer of skin and the sun shines through it. I am a weak man, in truth that is my strength. Power and self-assurance constrain the artist from the 'second reality' – that which is behind all things. He who wishes to master the world must first alienate himself from it. That essence is revealed to the weak man.

I am Moyshe Shagal, later known as Marc Chagall, from Pokrovskaya Street, Vitebsk. That's Pokrovskaya Street in the Pestkovatik district, in the run-down Small Side. There is another Pokrovskaya Street over the Dvina River, but that one is richer. As to my name, Moyshe Shagal, it has a meaning: Moyshe means Moses. Shagal is the past of the verb 'to stride' in Russian. So my name means 'Moses strode'.

My father, Khatskel – the name means Ezekiel in Hebrew – encircled my life like a protective fence. I did a charcoal drawing of him. Rearing upright in his *moujik* tunic and his peaked cap, with his bushy black beard and wild black eyes, he fills every inch of the grey paper as he filled every inch of my life.

Khatskel heaved and hefted barrels of herring for thirty-two years at a herring wholesaler's called Jachnin. At Jachnin, they used the Russianised version of his name, to make him less of a Jew. They called him Zakhar.

Schlepping herrings was not only Khatskel's life, it was also his death. He loaded a barrel of herring onto a significant lorry, one day, a lorry which reversed into him, running him over and killing him instantly.

My father would arrive home from work, his clothes glistening with herring brine, moving stiffly, face ashen, his whole body aching from the unremitting heavy drudgery. Each of those herring barrels weighed 80 kilos. I couldn't lift one of them without help, let alone heave them and roll them and lift them for ten hours a day, knowing there was another day of it tomorrow. And tomorrow and

14

tomorrow without end.

What had happened to so reduce him to a beast of burden? His family, my grandfather David's family, had had money, we could see that from the clothes in photographs. One of my uncles was put to work as a clerk – a decent job. How had father fallen into his fishy hell-hole?

He would gobble the evening meal – herrings, gherkins, cheese, butter and a big loaf of bread – occasionally showing his cat's teeth as he chewed. This used to fascinate me; it was the only time I saw through the thicket of his moustache and beard as far as his teeth.

Then there was time for us, our time. Children's time is different, everybody knows that. It's slower, usually. But because my father's time with his children was so vivid, it shut out much else, so taking time from other events.

While my tiny mother, Feiga-Ita, cleared the table and washed the dishes, we children sat and listened to father. We all used to sit on the timber-planked floor of the main room of our *izba*. There was not much in the room, a heavy dresser against the wall, a samovar on the table, a big clock whose face used to smile at me because I always ignored its hands.

The oil lamp was burning, casting a buttery yellow light, but outside it was bitter black. So there was a sense of our *izba* as the whole world, a world of light, of safety; with everything outside it chaos, elemental forest darkness.

I had six sisters; skirts for me were a place to hide. In the circle, legs tucked up, there was Zislya, Leya, Mania, Roza, Mariasenka and Rachel. There was also one brother, David. David was always coughing from TB. I painted him playing the mandolin, his face handsome but tinged with green sickly pallor. He died young.

I never painted the youngest sister, Rachel. Rachel was my guilty secret. I killed Rachel.

Father sat on a chair above us all. Not smiling, still looking worried, he would pull out little cakes and frozen pears, like a magician doing his act, and throw them to us children. Squealing with delight, we would catch the food and eat it.

Then he would tell us stories from the Talmud. The stories themselves were from the Mishnah, but how those stories evolved or came to be was in the commentary, in the Gemara. He would explain that to us, too.

So I learned early that there are no absolutes, only versions and variants. And nobody knows all the truth.

When we children were put to bed, father would read far into the night. He read the holy books and prayed, *davening*, rocking backwards and forwards, ululating. I wondered if he was praying for deliverance from his life.

My mother was the daughter of a kosher butcher in the nearby town of Lyozno. Without her, our family would have starved, as my father was paid a pittance – twenty roubles a month, for working like a mule.

Mother ran a small grocery shop, which brought in most of the family's money. She had been a ruler since childhood, having played mother to her own sisters, including the older ones. She was the nishoma – the active element, the prime mover, at times the only mover.

We were not hungry, at home – poor yes, hungry no. Riches are relative. We ate herring from the family grocery shop, bought on credit from Jachnin the wholesaler, herrings schlepped by my father himself. Only my father ate meat, a roast every Sabbath to keep his strength up.

On the Sabbath, the rest of the family had extra, too – stuffed fish, calves foot jelly, stewed fruit, white bread – just not meat.

So father ate like one blessed on the Sabbath day, but he was still pushed around by his little wife the rest of the week.

The high school in Vitebsk had already filled its quota of Jews, but it was mother who bribed the teacher with fifty roubles to get me in. This meant I crossed the bridge over the Dvina to the Big Side, where the richer sort lived. I was dressed in my Tolstoyan school uniform – a sort of peasant's tunic, worn with a tasselled cap. I attended *cheder* – Hebrew classes – too.

It was a day in May, fine and gentle, so we were out in the synagogue yard, us boys, no girls. We were *Yeshiva bocker*, boy students of the Talmud, learning the *drosche* – the sermons, preparing for our barmitzvah. There were eight of us, on benches brought out into the dusty courtyard. Osip Zadkine was there. If I was there, Osip was always there.

Dyadkin the *melamed* – our teacher – was a slight young man, sallow of face, fearful, nervous and permanently sniffling with cold. He wore a gabardine – a sort of Jewish religious frock-coat – and a high black hat. All that whatever the weather. He used to pinch our cheeks sometimes, bash our knuckles or cuff us round the head. Sometimes he bent our fingers back. Once, when he thought nobody was looking, he cuddled a boy and shut his eyes.

The *melamed* was teaching us about damages. Not damage – damages. Damage would have been more interesting, more philosophical. 'Damages' is about restitution, which is a form of revenge, which is small-minded and narrow, like the *melamed*. I had already apprised him of this fact – the small-mindedness – and been cuffed round the ear for my pains. Though most of the time I was a favourite because I was beautiful.

'And she, the cow, did strike the pitcher with her tail and did break it ...' shouted the *melamed*. He spun round dramatically, currant-eyes hard, fists clenched, as if about to chastise the cow for its behaviour, possibly cuff it round the head.

'Why?' a voice screamed. I realised it was mine.

'Why what?' The *melamed* was bewildered,

17

understandably so.

My stammer disappeared, as it does from time to time. 'Leave the poor cow alone,' I squealed, then burst into tears.

The *melamed*'s eyes shone as he cuddled me.

I was sitting bolt upright on the hard-strutted seat of a tram crossing Cathedral Square, in Vitebsk. I was coming back from *cheder* still feeling the *melamed*'s cuddles. I saw the sign out of the tram window – blocky white lettering, faded and grubby, against a Cerulean blue background, also faded. ARTIST PEN'S SCHOOL OF DRAWING AND PAINTING. Then the address.

As soon as I saw the sign, I knew. The sign was a sign! Even the weary old tram, worn out in richer countries before it even got to us, clanked its approval.

And my mother, bless her, got me in. Yury Pen was interested but not overly impressed by the drawings I showed him. Mother went to see Yury and talked and talked and talked until the shy teacher agreed to take me, mainly so Feiga-Ita would finally stop talking.

There was then a furious row between mother and father over the art school fees, five roubles a month, which ended with my tired and aching father throwing five roubles on the floor and storming off defeated, yet again, to bed.

In one respect, my teacher Pen was unique among men, in that he lived his life utterly alone. He had no lovers, of that I am quite sure, let alone a wife. He also had no friends or companions.

Yes, he would attend gatherings, exhibitions of students' work and the like. He would even attend parties thrown by students or former students. But he would stand in a corner, isolated, eating and drinking little, saying the minimum politeness dictated. Anodyne utterances, divulging no information of a personal nature – indeed there was no information of a personal nature to divulge. A life entirely devoted to art, then? Apparently so. He taught well, if a little didactically. If the view from the window facing Vygonnaya Street was just so – wicker fences, roofs, log houses – then it had to be painted *just so*. In the proportions of life, in the colours it was. All very literal.

His own artistic output was large, though not prodigiously so. There was nothing in it to indicate this lack of any emotional life.

I tiptoed into Pen's little flat above the school. The door was not locked. It was neat and tidy. There were no photographs on the bureau. Holding my breath, I walked lightly into his bedroom. No photographs there either, let alone any sign of illicit lovers as the prurient boy with his almond eyes was excitedly expecting.

On the walls, there were a couple of Yury's own paintings, nobody else's. The place was like a holiday flat ready to rent out to unlikely visiting tourists.

'Moysha Khatskelevich!'

'Aaaaghh! S-s-s … Sorry!'

Yury never showed anger, though this was as near as I had seen him come to it. The blue eyes bored at me harder than usual. He was wearing the formal garb he wore every day – a three-piece suit of good cloth worn even when painting. He wore that or a Jewish gabardine.

'Oh! Yury Moiseyevich! I … I was just …' It was obvious enough what I was just doing. I was snooping. I felt myself blushing. Hot flushes ran through me. My stammer, grown worse since I was bitten by the *cheder* teacher's dog, robbed me of coherent speech altogether. 'Yu … Yury …Moi … Moi … Please … I … I … There wa … wa … was … a … a view …'

'Would you like some tea?' He rarely smiled and he didn't then. But neither did he show a flicker of disquiet.

Although we students were strictly forbidden entry into

this inner sanctum of Yury's, he put the samovar on, made tea, even waved me to a chair. Then, while I sat in red-faced silence, sweating stickily, he held forth in a quiet, droning monologue on the importance of foreshortening and proportion to convey verisimilitude, taking his examples from my *Peasant's Farmyard* painting.

Then, when I had gulped down my brackish tea and stammered out a few platitudes, he saw me all the way back down the stairs, back into the school. And I was so frightened I never even thought about Yury's private life, inner life, emotional life, from that moment on.

Gogol Street, where Yehuda Moiseyevich Pen had his school, and above it his flat, was a wide thoroughfare, really more of a boulevard. It sloped gently down, then gently up again, with the school and the flat in the delve.

I walked slowly towards the school, which presented one whitewashed side to me on the left, with the other side facing the dome of the Saviour Church. You were never far from a church or a cathedral in Vitebsk.

I was a creature of strange wide eyes and tempestuous curls, striding powerfully along. I was at my most Jewish, I think. I even had *peyes*, those sidelocks sported by religious Jews.

Perhaps I just wanted to belong, to fit in. Certainly at that time I began my habit, which never left me completely, of mirroring whoever I was with. I talked like them, used their gestures, adopted their opinions, until that person left the room and the next person came along. A lot of artists do this. We shelter beneath the life-mimesis while our art is growing.

At the beginning, this mirroring provided cover enough. In any case, Pen was a Jew, and most of the other students were Jews, so I did not have far to distort to blend in. The other students included Lazar Lissitzky, the blank-eyed fanatic; Oskar Meschaninov, who Soutine later painted; Solomon Yudovin; Shmuel Jachnin, the son of the herring

20

wholesaler who was my father's boss; and Osip Zadkine, he of the lizard face, who followed me covetously all my life. Many of Yury's pupils went on to become famous. Vitebsk is a great art centre, I am proud of that. We even have our own hog-hair paintbrush factory. I am rather proud of that, too!

But I digress: the fellow-student I was closest to was Avigdor Mekler, known as Viktor. Viktor was one of the group I had known since school days, a group which also included Osip Zadkine and Lazar Lissitzky.

Viktor and I resembled each other physically: we were both dark, curly-haired, lithe-bodied beauties. Humankind is drawn to others like them physically, as well as in their personalities and qualities. So we circled round each other, Viktor and I, pulling quite close together sometimes, then a little apart but not too far, then closer together again.

Like Osip Zadkine and Shmuel Jachnin, Viktor was from the Big Side of Vitebsk, a world away from the poor Pestkovatik district, where our *izba* played host to wandering goats and squawking roosters, while splintering quietly from the outside and reeking of herring on the inside.

Viktor's father, the effusive but combustible Shmaryahu Mekler, had his paper factory – the most prosperous factory in Vitebsk – on the Small Side, near his workers, but his home was a three-storey stone mansion on the good bank of the river Dvina, right near the Uspensky Cathedral and within leaping distance of the birthplace of Vitebsk's most famous son, General Kropotkin.

Viktor and I stuck together from day one at Pen's, but all the Jewish students cohered as the cloud of pogroms, which never drifted far away, was lowering over us again.

Here in Vitebsk, we tended to get the more spontaneous, less organised, less planned pogroms. A bunch of drunken cadets ran down Vygonnaya Street. They got as far as Iljinskaya, the square at the end of my own street,

21

Pokrovskaya, smashing the windows of Jewish houses, beating up anybody on the streets who looked Jewish, molesting Jewish girls and women.

As students do the world over, we hungrily gathered shards of information about our teacher. Someone found out that Yury Pen was beaten as a child when he was caught painting. His mother beat him. It would have broken me if my mother had beaten me, I love her so much.

To our delight, Zadkine unearthed the damning fact that our teacher had failed the entrance examination to the Academy of Arts in St Petersburg. He had stayed on to try again, despite being, as a Jew, an illegal in the big city. He had paid a tribute – a bribe – to the yardkeepers, as they were called, not to go to the police.

'He was then …' Zadkine spluttered with delighted malice; we were all drunk in Lissitzky's room. 'Wait for it, he was then apprenticed to a housepainter.'

This got the reception Osip Zadkine hoped for, we all fell about laughing, feeding off each other's drink-fuelled hysteria. Yury Pen fulfilled the role of butt of student jokes rather well. He still wore his traditional Jewish clothes despite the risk of being beaten up in the street. He spoke very little Russian, which was unusual. All of us were stronger in Yiddish, but we students had been educated in Russian and were fluent, though not perfect.

Pen wanted to record Jewish life, which we respected, though we kept quiet about our respect, to each other. We also had to admit, though not too often, that he was less hidebound artistically than his narrowly Jewish persona would have led one to expect. His own teacher, Chistyakov, was international in outlook, looking to Russian woodcuts and even beyond, to France.

The early tasks at Pen's school stamped themselves in my mind, not least because we were testing ourselves against each other. To develop our still-life skills, Yury Pen placed a glass on a table and told us to draw it. With varying degrees of self-consciousness, we clustered around the newly significant artefact, and began its translation to paper in watercolour and its metempsychosis to art. I remember Osip Zadkine's lizard tongue sticking out as he imitated the postures and poses of an artist. I remember Lazar Lissitzky's sneer at the facile task, on view as he turned to encompass us all, as if about to make a speech – but then he always looked as if he were about to make a speech.

Most of us finished quickly, but Viktor was struggling. I surreptitiously helped him out with a couple of strokes of white, for which he shot me a rueful, grateful look. We ended up waiting for Solomon Yudovin and Shmuel Jachnin. Yudovin was confusing effort with purpose. Jachnin had screwed his first two efforts into paper balls and thrown them on the floor. Pen, with the raise of an eyebrow and an elegant nod, made him pick them up.

'All right, that's enough time.' Pen called a halt before Jachnin could destroy any more paper or Viktor suck himself down to the depths of despair, as self-knowledge shone brighter than the glass we were painting.

Yury Pen examined our efforts one by one in silence. You could hear us breathing.

'Only one of you saw the glass with his own eyes,' Yury Pen announced with soft finality. 'The rest of you didn't see it: you simply used your knowledge of what a glass is. Knowledge is accessible to all; vision is the mark of an artist.'

Yury paused while this wisdom hung over the room. I felt restless. My breathing was coming in gasps.

On he went: 'In young Moyshe Shagal's drawing of the glass there is a bit of reflected sunlight nobody else saw. It cast a small shadow that again nobody else saw. On the inner surface of the glass, there was a reflection from the table. The rest of you didn't notice that either. The glasses the rest of you painted are mechanical reproductions. Moyshe Shagal's glass is a work of art.'

The students burst into applause. I felt myself blushing. I hated this. I hated their attention, their crowd-approbation, the sheer mindlessness of it. But above all I hated my apparently artistic representation of a glass. It was all I could do not to call Pen an idiot there and then. This is not what I want. This is not what I want at all. Damn the reproduction in paint of a drinking vessel. No interpretation, no point, no purpose, no message, no soul. Damn it to hell!

Later that week, off we all shuffled to paint a townscape in the snow. There were about nine of us swinging our arms against the bitter cold.

This time I approved of our allotted task. Higgledy-piggledy houses of Vitebsk, above us on their hill; insecure, clinging to their hillside before they came tumbling down, as they surely would. We had a couple of hours before the light faded.

I painted a snowscape, showing a narrow path cleared of snow disappearing towards a hill where houses clustered higgledy-piggledy, blurring in the distance. It had a light Impressionist touch, like a Pissarro, except the *izbas* are unmistakably Russian.

My choice of title for the painting, *Yury's Hill*, is ironic – possibly arrogant, too. I meant I had climbed the hill of my teacher, mastering perspective and all the rest of it, and then gone further, leaving Yury Pen and perspective behind.

Yury Pen went from easel to easel, sometimes offering advice, sometimes remaining silent. It was obvious to everybody that those whose work he approved of were given tips and stratagems. Those he passed over in silence had already been placed beyond the pale. This latter group included my friend Viktor, who was next to me, clinging to me somewhat with a desperate look in his lovely brown eyes.

'Earth colours,' Yury Pen murmured in my ear, as I

24

worked, absorbed, no longer conscious of the numbing chill wind. 'Many good things here. Perspective good. Fading in the distance like the Impressionists. But earth colours only, please.' I nodded, stopping my work, standing stock still in defiance so he would move on. Yes, Rembrandt had used a restricted palette. Earth colours. So had Rubens. And yes, we absorb the greatness of the masters, we let their genius accrue to us. But we do not imitate them, not even as an exercise. There was only one response to Pen's facile, limited, blinkeredness. I mixed violet, there *en plein air*. I mixed violet and tinged it in as the wooden houses encasing the threatened people faded to sky in the distance. This painting marked my first use of my later so beloved violet colour. It is in the sky and it tinges the *izbas*. I love violet. Violet is my rebellion. I signed my painting in violet.

This time Pen collected in all the canvases, back at the school in the delve of the road. He kept them overnight in the studio before the verdict, next day. Then the paintings were paraded before their creators and the results announced. There were nine views of what we were all now mischievously calling Yurieva Gorka, Yury's Hill, the hill to the east of Vitebsk.

Viktor was pale in the face, Lissitzky was pre-emptively sneering, Osip Zadkine looked smug, Shmuel Jachnin had a frozen look, like icy armour. I prepared myself for more praise I did not want. And sure enough my painting was hoisted aloft on the large easel we were all looking at. There was my rebellious violet. Perhaps Yury Pen was even going to renounce his earth-colours-only theory, retract what he had said.

'Some colouring is questionable,' Pen intoned softly. 'This use of violet is spreading and should be stopped. But Osip here has produced a balanced composition which …'

I stopped listening. Yury Pen was droning on, but I

25

stopped listening. I moved forward a couple of paces. There was the signature on my picture. My own signature had been painted out. Yes, there was the signature. 'Osip Zadkine'.

Viktor was looking at me, his eyes were liquid-wide, alarmed. I tried to speak but only stammered. Weeks later, it occurred to me that Osip had gone back to the studio that night and changed the signatures on both paintings. And Yury Pen, limited Yury, had not spotted it. But then I just stammered. No words came out.

'I ... I ... my ... mine.'

Nobody heard me, not even Viktor.

'I can't do this, can I?' Viktor was pale, there were tears in his eyes.

We were sitting in the luxurious Mekler parlour, caressed by plumply prosperous armchairs. Viktor's effusive and ebullient father was out at work in his paper factory. His beautiful mother, who was always so sweet and feminine around me, was in the kitchen, brewing us tea and preparing little cakes.

I liked it here.

'Viktor,' I said, with self-conscious adult seriousness, 'I have no idea whether you can do art Pen-style or not. But do you want me to help you?'

I had this offer ready, because I knew he would ask. I wanted to be in a family, not my family, another family. This was not because I was dissatisfied with the family I was born into, far from it. Neither – and I must make this clear – was it the greater luxury offered by the Meklers.

It was partly the love of Viktor, partly the worship of his mother, partly the need to earn my way. And there was a challenge, too. Being born into a family was too easy; I wanted to talk my way into one, charm my way in, battle my way in.

'Help me?' Viktor smiled his beautiful smile. 'Oh, would you, Moyshe? I so want to be an artist, you see. But

papa wants me to join the family firm and make paper.'
Viktor gave a cultured pout at the very thought of it. 'So
there was a big argument and I won, and now ...'

Sarah Mekler came in with a tray of tea and cakes. I
blushed and started stammering. 'Can I he-he-help ...?'
Before my stammered offer was complete the tea and
cakes were being served. 'Oh, Moyshe, it is so nice to see
you again. Viktor has been full of stories of how well you
are doing at Pen's.'

Viktor frowned, taking his mother's remark as a slight,
a barb aimed at him. I frowned at Viktor, defending the
beauteous mother in my mind.

'I shall be helping Viktor, Mrs Mekler,' I said boldly,
all trace of my stammer suddenly gone. 'We are going to
paint together.'

'Oh, how lovely!' She looked me in the eye, that sweet
smile playing in her face. 'You can paint here, we've plenty
of room, haven't we, Vitoshka.'

Viktor did not even mind his baby name being used in
public, he was so thrilled about the lessons. 'What shall
we paint?'

At once, a picture came into my mind. It would be
flowers tied by bows, the sort of subject Pen would approve
of, quite meaningless.

'A still life,' I announced, gravely.

What emerged was not a typical composition; I painted
few still lifes. There was a rough-hewn hemp basket with
a fringed top, holding its shape because it is stuffed full of
lilies-of-the-valley. The basket had a wide pink ribbon on
it, which was drawn tight by two rosette-like pink bows.

The hemp basket and its floral contents were on a
table covered by a patterned thick tablecloth. Behind the
flowers, the room was visible, giving the composition the
depth required by Yury Pen, one of the classical aspects of
painting which I was soon to spurn.

And so the lessons began. I encouraged Viktor as much as I

could. I understood that the decision to give it all up, which surely must come, had to come from him alone, when he was ready. So I was as encouraging as possible while we both painted a *Lilies of the Valley* from our memories of these spring flowers.

At the end of the first session, he offered me a rouble a lesson in payment. This was exactly what Pen was charging, on top of the five roubles a month basic fee. It meant that my classes at Pen's would be free. And my family would be free of the burden of my studies, or at least part of it.

'No, no,' I said. 'I couldn't possibly accept that. I'm helping you because you are my friend.'

We hugged affectionately. 'I will pay you, Moyshe. Oh yes, I nearly forgot.' Viktor added, smiling. 'There's someone who wants to meet you.'

I was wary. People make me wary. 'Oh yes? Who?'

'Dr Brachmann's daughter. I see her at the Brachmann soirée every week. Last week she asked me to bring you along. She's heard of you. Everybody's heard of the budding great artist.'

'Dr … Dr Brachmann? What's the daughter's name?'

'Thea.'

I had never set eyes on Thea Brachmann, indeed I had never heard of her. I had few Big Side friends, apart from Viktor. But Viktor told me all about her, in such detail it was as if he knew our meeting, mine and Thea's, would be significant.

Viktor, I was sure, had no intimate relationship with Thea. (But why did I care? Why was I jealous? I had yet to meet her.) However, having passed Thea on to me, in a manner of speaking, Viktor's intensity towards me cooled even further.

I say 'even further' because he was now just playing a part during my art lessons. He was blankly imitating the earnest student lover of art. The key to Viktor Mekler was ambition. And because his ambition as an artist was being blocked by lack of talent, up bubbled ambition in another direction. He was resisting, he would always resist, a post in the family business empire, but to start up his own business, perhaps a rival to his father, that appealed to Viktor Mekler. Indeed, it excited him.

Such was the cooling between us, though with no open breach, it was no surprise to me when he suggested we make our separate ways to the Brachmann musical soirée, where, it was understood, I was to make Thea's acquaintance. So, scrubbed shiny in my best blue velvet suit, with centre-parted hair, I trod my way alone through the slush and ice towards the better sort, knowing, even then, that if I did not belong there now I soon would.

I heard the music as I passed the four Doric columns of the Big Lubavich synagogue where I once sang out my barmitzvah. But even as I thought that, the semi-musical memory was drowned out by a Beethoven sonata floating between the brooding clouds above and the grey slush at my feet, coming, surely, from the Brachmann place, which Mekler had told me was a few doors down from the synagogue.

I realised he had not given me a proper address, so I just followed the music. It was the *Pathétique*, in a good arrangement. I have always loved music. I play the violin and I have a strong sense of rhythm. I think that informs my painting, as colour-placement within a whole has a rhythm, too.

Anyway, on that evening I followed the tune, like a Hamelin child following the Pied Piper's flute, and it got me to the blocky pile of the Brachmann establishment.

'You must be Moyshe, the painting wonder. Viktor told me all about you.'

And there she was, in all her forceful glory. Thea was powerful; big and strong, though beautiful in a magisterial sort of way. She was wearing a long red velvet dress.

'Come on. I'll tell you who everybody is.'

And that is precisely what she did. The room where the soirée was held was a white and gold magnificence, a palace if you have been brought up in a wooden *izba*. The musicians playing Beethoven so competently were her brothers, it appeared. They were named first.

And then the most significant people in the room. Never letting go of my arm she nodded and encapsulated Vitebsk society: 'And there's the Governor, and there is Lengelfield and there is Alonov …'

Then came a pause for refreshment. She chose a glass of wine and dainties for me, holding the nibbles on their bone-china monogrammed plate while I ate them. She was feeding me.

I noticed Viktor Mekler, handsome, curly hair, making himself known.

'And there is Vinaver …'

It was my first glimpse of the Duma Deputy who was so mysteriously to become my benefactor. There were the iridescent eyes in the oval face, and the full beard that was the fashion at the time.

'And this is my father, Dr Brachmann.' Thea spoke with amused irony, very much in control, but the glance she threw her parent was fond, even cherishing.

'Hello!' Dr Brachmann was tall, with an unruly moustache, fleshy nose and strong jaw. He was an obviously sociable man, at ease with himself, at ease with others. When he visited his patients, so Viktor told me, he always stopped for a game of cards and a glass of brandy.

'I've been wanting to meet you,' he said, nevertheless speaking as if we had known each other for ages. He touched me, warmly, on the upper arm. 'I've known Pen for years. He's slow to praise. I've never heard him talk about any pupil the way he talks about you.'

'Thank you, sir.'

As Dr Brachmann glided smoothly away, Thea's mother made an appearance at her daughter's side. 'This is where I get my beauty,' Thea said.

'Thea!' Mrs Brachmann spoke with mock horror. 'She has her father's humour, that's for sure. And his irony.'

I usually like mothers, especially my friends' mothers, and I adored Mrs Brachmann on sight.

'Thea is obviously much blessed, on all sides,' I said, with solemn heavy gallantry.

Mother and daughter hooted with laughter at that, Thea tightening her grip on my forearm.

'You'll need to watch this one, Thea,' quoth Mama.

'I intend to, don't you worry,' Thea said, laughing a hearty, deep laugh which made her brown eyes sparkle. She gripped my arm with both hands, to emphasise my enslavement.

'Mind you, I'll have to let you go soon.' Thea announced that as her mother moved on, heading towards the buffet.

I took my cue. 'Must you?'

She laughed again, heartily enough. 'Come into the kitchen first.'

She let me go and strode off. For a dimwitted second I did not realise I was supposed to follow. I had to sashay through the crowd to catch up with her.

Along a corridor, her first then me, then into a kitchen that was bigger than our entire *izba*. A cook and a maid were drinking tea at a samovar on the table.

'Irena, Sonia, we need the room. Do you mind?'

The servants did not look especially surprised, leaving without a murmur, with the younger one, the maid, Sonia, giving me a curious appraising look, openly appreciative …

Thea leaned her back against the kitchen table. 'Now, then. Painter-boy.' She smiled.

I had kissed two girls, up to then, Anyuta and Olga, both of them school-mates. With Anyuta I had followed her for four years, sighing. I started lifting weights to get better muscles for her. Finally, I kissed her just as she started developing pimples. Then we stopped talking to each

31

other. With Olga, I was scared stiff of her corset, which she wore on purpose.

My stammer grew worse whenever I even thought of these girls.

Thea pulled my head towards her and we kissed. She opened her mouth, so I did. Our tongues touched. She pulled away.

'Not bad, painter-boy, not bad at all.'

'I want to paint you,' I said.

'Of course you do, painter-boy. I'm beautiful!'

'Indeed you are!'

'Do you want me nude?'

'Er … Ye … Ye … Ye …'

It was understood by both of us that I would paint Thea at her house, not at the Shagal *izba*.

Our place would have been too crowded, I said. True enough.

So was I consciously leaving our *izba* behind? Yes, I suppose so. I moved my easel and paints towards my destiny, with my mother Feiga-Ita's full support. My father was too tired to care.

Dr and Mrs Brachmann made a studio for me in a small room on the third floor which had once housed a live-in maid. It had north-facing light. They put a worn black horsehair divan in the studio, a divan full of holes. I guessed it was an old examining couch of Dr Brachmann's. It was almost as if they expected Thea and me to make love and wanted us to be comfortable.

They asked me, Dr and Mrs Brachmann, both together, if I had everything I needed. It was the first time I had been treated with respect as an artist.

Thea told me her parents knew the study of her was to be a nude. But I wondered if they realised the painting would not be a conventional portrait. That worried me, but classes at Pen's were so easy and I was riding so high there – even with Osip Zadkine stealing my work – that my self-belief as a painter grew in me, never again to waver. Thea was the first woman I had seen naked. I was painting my own desire. But the pose I got her to adopt, mainly with her back to the viewer, one arm on her hip, emphasised her size and strength as much as her beauty and womanliness.

Thea's face is turned away from the viewer, indeed it seems to have come off her shoulders. But as ever the colour is all. My passion for Thea is rendered in red. It is a boiling, unconsummated passion.

On the right, fading into the distance, are two doves of love on a white cloth with blue circles.

I assumed we would make love soon, that she would be my first. I knew Viktor Mekler had had lots of women. So had Lazar Lissitzky, but with him it was always prostitutes. (I was too poor for prostitutes, which was a relief, frankly.) Osip Zadkine had taken advantage of some poor serving girl at his parents' house, and boasted about it.

I was the only one who had not yet … Ironic, as I could not walk down the street or make a visit without unmistakable glances from women, even women of the better sort, women of all ages, all types, including my friends' mothers.

I told myself that desire for Thea would spoil the painting. We must finish the painting first, I said to myself, perhaps I even said it out loud to Thea. And after I said it, the stammering stopped.

Thea had her own aims and desires. She could grow deep-black sad for no reason known to others, though she recorded it all in the diary she kept obsessively, reliving her life and sometimes reshaping it more fully than she lived it. She told me she was writing about me in her diary. I came to fear that.

She could be tender with women, stroking their necks and faces, kissing them. With men she was quite direct. She would kiss tongue to tongue, sometimes in public, whenever she found a man attractive. She had been brought up surrounded by boys, having three brothers. She was at ease with men.

She would undress in her bedroom then come to our makeshift studio wearing only a robe. Then she would pose, as I instructed, seeming not to mind when I touched her. Once in pose, her demand was always the same: she wanted me to talk. Not just idle chatter, not just the rumours of the day. She wanted my secrets, my inner life. Sometimes I feared she wanted my soul. It was like a seduction, her seduction of me, while mine of her was on hold until I had finished painting.

Eventually, I gave in. I told her the secret I had never told anybody, the secret I *could* never tell anybody. The secret I was never to share with another living soul. The secret about Rachel.

I am alone in the *izba*, our family home. Father is at work, mother is at the shop, so also at work. All the others are away, at school, out playing, it doesn't matter, just away. I am at the beginning of that total absorption in creation which all artists attain, if they are to use their gift to the full. I am developing the concentration which focuses the talent. Without the concentration the talent fritters away.

I am drawing with charcoal. I remember every line of what I am drawing. I have some quite expensive grey paper and I am drawing a self-portrait on it. A self-portrait as a clown, with wiry hair standing on end, mouth all twisted, not handsome as everybody tells me I am.

You never really know when a drawing or a painting or an etching is good, but you sense when it is bad or you feel nothing, which is your inner self's rejection. This feels promising. It is feeding my sense of my own destiny.

Then comes a crying, a grating burbling screaming. It is coming from the girls' room. Oh no! They have left Rachel there. Rachel is ... what? Three. Four. I don't know and frankly I don't care. In a large family like ours nobody

34

says 'Look after this or that little one.' It just happens. Or it doesn't.

Rachel screams. She won't stop. My concentration, hard but new, is weakening. I am losing what I have gained. I *cannot* go backwards. This is *important*. I go through to the girls' room. I swear there is no premeditation but the charcoal is still in my hand. I break off a piece. I put it in the screaming Rachel's hand and guide it towards her mouth. Just to make her stop screaming. Just to make her be quiet.

It works a treat. She eats the charcoal; she stops screaming. I go back to my drawing. All is silent. The drawing is good. I hear somebody coming. When? I don't know when. I am concentrating. I go back to check on Rachel. She is on the floor in convulsions. I take the charcoal from her hand and put it in my pocket. I wipe her mouth.

Rachel dies later that day. Her eyes fill with heavenly blue, with dark silver. Her pupils freeze. Flies swarm down to her nose. The cause of her death is recorded as an epileptic fit.

That year, Thea joined us Shagals in our little *izba* for the *seder*, the Passover ceremony that celebrates the liberation of the Israelites from slavery in ancient Egypt. My mother had met Thea once before and given her the stamp of approval. My father and the rest of the brood had never set eyes on this, my new girlfriend.

Nevertheless, within minutes she had them all calling her by her intimate pet name, Theanka, as she insisted. Thea – Theanka – was a pearl that evening, a pearl to be cherished. Dressed in red again, though more demurely than at the Brachmann gathering, she charmed the Shagals and set us purring. Even my father, who kept dozing off, as he always did, at the head of the table, slept with a smile.

She dominated the *seder* night with tales of the poems she had written, the piano pieces she could play, stories of

35

the misbehaviour of Marquis, her pet dog, and some of her father's amusing medical stories. Then, with eye-watering cheek, Thea talked of the death of Rachel, so new and raw in our lives.

'I am so sorry about your tragic loss. I hope you will allow me to mourn with you, in quiet at home. One more set of prayers up to Rachel, in heaven.'

My mother left her chair to hug Thea. Even my father woke to shed a salty tear, running down curving into his beard. I tensed, wide-eyed, resolving not even to try and say anything. Thea was sincere, I believed that completely, but still it was an open bid to be part of this family – an open and strong bid.

I had not yet told her of my plan to go to Paris, to study art. Yury Pen had suggested it.

Thea burbled on about books she had read (Gogol, mainly), about her brothers' musical ability, about her father's visits to people we knew on the Small Side. She tackled the differences in riches, status and class between her family and mine with typical Thea clear-eyed directness. She acknowledged those differences, then moved on.

She held her own during the Hebrew Passover service, conducted by my father with David, the youngest boy, asking the four questions in Hebrew to which the entire service is a response.

Thea sang along with the service, she drank her wine at the toasts, then she insisted powerfully on helping my mother and sisters with the food, thus enabling her to whisper confidences over the cooker.

Then a miracle occurred: for centuries, a place had been left at the *seder* table for the Prophet Elijah, with wine poured ready for him. His arrival is supposed to usher in an era of peace.

This year he came.

As I was later to paint him, the Prophet Elijah flew over

Vitebsk, on his way to the Shagal household for the *seder*. Elijah flew like a *Luftmensch* in Jewish folklore, a poor man made of air with a belly full only of air, soaring above the snowscape, bent forwards with his sack of worldly goods on his back, his stick in his hand, his Russian cap on his head. I painted him as a traditional Jewish figure, a *moujik*, a peddler.

The Prophet Elijah had just flown past the Uspensky Cathedral, its towers in yellow and blue to the right. Below him, the snow was layered on thick. The Prophet will cross the Dvina River near the bridge and fly due east to reach the Shagal household. He will be there soon. He is on his way.

It quickly became clear to me that nobody else could see the Prophet Elijah, as he sat in the place left vacant for him. All around me the *seder* happily flowed. My favourite sister, Lisa, was just shyly offering to help Thea with dressmaking. David was sitting apart, plucking at his mandolin. My father was snoring. Everybody else was singing that song about animals eating other smaller animals until only the smallest was left. 'Chad Gadya', it's called. It's a very funny song.

The Prophet Elijah was sipping at his wine, which did not appear to diminish in any way. I realised I was having a visitation, witnessing a miracle. It made me feel tense. I did not want to do the wrong thing, disgrace myself. How was I supposed to behave? I waited for the Prophet Elijah to take the initiative; eventually he did.

The Prophet jerked his head, clearly motioning me to join him outside. I mumbled excuses but nobody was listening. They were all happy singing. I considered getting my coat but thought better of it. It would look odd.

Outside it was bitter cold. The snow was unusually thick for the time of year, more like winter than early spring. I shivered, my teeth clacking against each other. The Prophet was waiting for me, leaning against the *izba* wall, rubbing his hands together against the cold.

'That girl in there …'

'Thea?'

'Yes, Thea. She's not the woman for you, but she will lead you to the woman for you.'

'Er … right!'

'The France plan is fine. Go to Paris. There you will begin your purpose in life.'

'My … purpose?'

'Sure!'

'I have a purpose?' I was excited. Most people do not have a purpose.

The Prophet nodded, gravely. 'A purpose and a task. I have a job for you.'

'Go on.'

The Prophet spoke flatly, belying the horror of the words. 'Terrible times are coming for the Jews. Your task is to keep them safe.'

'How on earth can I do that?'

'What do you think? You are a painter.'

'You mean …?'

'There is one place and one place only the Jews will be safe: on canvas. You must put them there. When you get to Paris. Paint them.'

'All the Jews?'

'Yes. One Jew is all Jews. Past Jews are present Jews. Present Jews are past Jews and future Jews.'

I nodded. I swallowed hard. 'So what is going to happen? What will happen to the Jews?'

'Many Jews will die. Many. Many.'

'How many?'

'Eighteen.'

'Eighteen Jews will die?'

'Yes. When the Mal-e comes.' He pronounced it 'Marlay'.

'The Mal-e?'

'Yes. The Mal-e. It means the bad. The evil. It will

38

come in two waves and it will last for many years.'

I thought of all the Jews I knew. Eighteen. That was a slaughter.

'Will my teacher, Yury Pen, be one of them?' I don't know why I asked that.

'Yes. He will be murdered. He will be one of them. When the Mal-e comes. And after the Mal-e, worse. Worse is to come.'

'And is there anything we can do to stop this slaughter? This slaughter of Yury and the others?'

'No. There is nothing we can do. There never is.'

'And am I ...?' I stopped.

'One of the eighteen who will die? No, you are not. You will survive. You will be successful. But heed this well, Moyshe. You will do your best work in Paris. You will go to many other places. But you will never be as good again.'

'Will I see you there? In Paris?'

'You'll see me more often than you think. I'll be the man by the gate. But you won't recognise me. And you won't remember my visit today.'

'I don't understand. This doesn't make sense.'

The Prophet Elijah gave a dry chuckle, like bones scraping against each other. 'I will reveal things to you, in Paris.'

This I understood, from the Bible. 'You mean visions?'

'Yes. You can call it that. Visions. Magic visions.'

There was silence for a moment. Then I cleared my throat and babbled on. 'This era of peace we're told about. The one you're supposed to usher in.'

'Whadja mean, "supposed"? You sayin' I'm not doing my job right?'

'No!' I was freezing cold and I had had enough. They would be serving the Passover meal soon, and I was out here, missing it. I lost my temper. 'Don't be so touchy.'

'Who you calling touchy? Eh?' The Prophet clenched his fists.

Oh, this was all going wrong. The Jews have waited

39

for centuries for the Prophet Elijah and I was having a row with him. I heard my mother in my head. 'Typical, Moyshe! You let people walk all over you, then you get tetchy. Be firm in the first place, son.'

'I'm sorry … Please. Just tell me …'

'Yes, my boy. Yes, there will be an era of peace. But the world will go through the fires of hell first.'

'And the Jews … Will the Jews be involved?'

'What do you think? Just go to Paris and get painting, there's a good boy.'

Thea and I were in the studio the Brachmanns had created for me, the best equipped I was to have for a very long time. Thea was about to go and get undressed to pose for me. Would my whole life have been different if she had? Suppose she had returned to the studio, then slipped off her robe. Suppose I had then touched her, as a lover, for the first time. Surely we would not have stopped at that? Surely, we would not have received a visitor?

But that is not what happened. Such moments are the fulcrum on which our lives turn.

'Visitor for you!' Mrs Brachmann sounded amused, a touch arch, as if having a secret she knew would please Thea when revealed. She had burst into the room without knocking, as she habitually did, to make sure all was right and proper, despite her daughter's unclothed state.

'Mama, not …'

'Wait till you see who it is.'

Bella Rosenfeld swept into the room, all swishing Tyrolean green cape with a feather on it, jet black hair and enormous eyes. I just had time to think that a dark background would bring the cape forward, pushing it at the viewer.

'Not disturbing anything, am I, Theanka? So this is the painter-boy, the one you wrote to me about.'

'Bella!' Thea blushed.

'Very nice! No wonder you've been hiding him away

40

up here.'

'Oh, Bella! It's so good to see you.' Thea ran to her, embraced her and they kissed three times on the cheeks.

'Moyshe, this is my dear friend, Bella. She's been hiding away in Marienbad, pretending to study. Bella, how lovely to *see* you!'

There was much squealing and embracing and catching up of news, snatches of it in German, which both women spoke. Thea posing for me was completely forgotten. Then Bella appraised me frankly, as if estimating how much I weighed in order to sell me as meat. I managed to look back. She was exquisite, like porcelain, more obviously pretty than Thea, though not as voluptuous.

'Let's go for a walk.' Although the words were a suggestion, her whole tone and bearing indicated a command. We prepared to go for a walk. There was no question of not going for a walk; Bella had said we were going for a walk.

The sun was out, Thea and I did not take our coats. I was floating. Thea had found time to bring the Brachmann family dog, Marquis. I hate dogs, but even that did not spoil my joy. Thea and the dog walked behind, Bella and I were ahead, side-by-side, our arms just touching as we talked.

'What do you do?'

'I am an actress. Well, I want to be an actress when I have finished studying. But I have to act. I cannot *not* act. Do you understand that?'

'Yes. It's like me and …'

'I also want to write. Eventually. I love literature. And philosophy. But Viktor says I should do the acting first.'

'Viktor Mekler?'

'Yes. Do you know him?'

'Oh, yes. He's a good friend. We're at Pen's together. The art school.'

'That's a coincidence. I know Viktor well. He's very handsome.'

41

'You were talking about wanting to act.'

'Yes. So I was. But I have to earn the money to support myself while I act. That's the problem. My family has a jewellery shop. Rosenfeld's. It's by the Café Jeanne-Albert, you know?'

'Mmm. Yes.'

'The shop does well, but we aren't rich like Thea's family. I envy her, you know. Whenever I visit her, her brothers are playing Bach or Beethoven. And she has that lovely man for a father. I think, why haven't I got all that?'

'I'm … I'm sorry.'

She looked up at me and smiled, her eyes dancing. 'You are a handsome boy and no mistake. Almost as handsome as Viktor Mekler. What does your father do?'

'He works at Jachnin.'

'The herring wholesaler?'

'Yes. My mother has a small shop. A grocery shop.'

We had reached the Dvinski Bridge, the biggest of the wooden bridges over the Dvina River, as if there had been some sort of plan. We walked halfway across, then we stopped and leaned over the ornate iron balustrade. Our arms were just touching.

Down below, the water was churning pale green and white, running fast, tidal. I was conscious of the bulk of the Saviour Church behind us, then stared down again, into the water. This is where I had gone rafting with Osip Zadkine and Lazar Lissitzy while we were still at school.

'Just look what a little one he's got.'

There was a small boat in the distance.

'The water is the same colour as your eyes.'

We both turned at the same time, to kiss. When we stopped kissing, Thea and her dog had gone.

As I approached the office of the Duma Deputy Maksim Vinaver, my heart was going tyock-tyock-tyock like one of the clocks my teacher Yury so loved to paint. I had Vinaver's letter clutched sweatily in my hand. I knew

42

of him as a leading figure in the Jewish community, the editor of *Vokshod* (Dawn) – a Jewish magazine – and as a Duma Deputy. He was a *ganzer macher* as my father would say – a big shot.

I had seen him around twice, maybe three times, the last time that musical evening at Thea's house. His wife, Roza Georgyevna, made more of a mark than him. She looked as if she had stepped out of a Veronese. Then this letter from him had come out of nowhere.

In his office, there was a Levitan on the wall. Isaac Levitan was a *shtetl* Jew who painted great and glorious landscapes. Yury Pen had got us to study the one on Vinaver's wall (it was most likely a copy). It was called *Above Eternal Peace* and showed a huge brooding sky lowering over a bay with a house perched precariously on a cliff. It was in the romantic style. Imagine Caspar David Friedrich magnified by the vastness of Mother Russia.

Anyway, I stared at it, above Vinaver's head, as I twisted his letter in my hands behind my back and scraped my ungainly boots on his significant Duma carpet. He was writing at his desk but eventually he deigned to look up. He had iridescent eyes, with eyelashes that seemed to go up and down by themselves. They were framed by an oval face with thin, controlled lips and a chestnut-coloured beard. That whole noble profile I would have loved to paint, but was too shy to ask.

'Ah, Moyshe Zakharovich,' he said, using my Russian patronymic, not the Yiddish one, and speaking as if my appearance in his office came as a mild surprise, comparable, perhaps, to the cleaner turning up during business hours.

I nodded, confirming my existence, however tentatively. I started to say his name but my stammer plus a late realisation that I forgotten his patronymic reduced that to 'Ma – ma – ma' like a lost sheep or a small boy calling for his mother, neither being identifications I would have denied at that moment.

'I am told you wish to study art in Paris, Moyshe Zakharovich.'

'Yes. That is co-co-co-correct. Sir.' I still couldn't remember his patronymic. 'Sir' was probably too formal. I kicked myself with my ungainly boots.

Vinaver looked surprised. 'No need to grovel at this stage, young man. It's already in the bag. Yury Pen speaks very highly of you. He thinks you might be a second Antokolsky.'

I winced. 'Tha ... tha ... tha ...' Sometimes I think my stammer is a blessing from God. What if I had been able to say what came into my mind? 'A second Antokolsky? That sentimentalist? Mark Antokolsky with his *shmulzy* sculptures? Not worth a *grosh*. Please! It's bad enough we have one Antokolsky! I would not inflict a second one on the world.'

'Thank you,' I said.

'We can run to ...' he consulted a piece of paper on his desk. 'What's that? Oh, yes. We're paying you in francs. A hundred and twenty-five a month, apparently.'

'Tha ...'

'Oh, don't thank me. I'm just the middle-man.'

I'm just the middle-man. What in God's name did that mean?

Much later, I painted our leaving of Vitebsk not as it happened but as I dreamed it. In my painting, called *Over the Town*, it is not the Prophet Elijah who is flying over Vitebsk, not this time, it is Bella Rosenfeld and me. There is a Russian proverb, 'half the world weeps, while the other half leaps'; well, this is our leaping time, mine and Bella's.

I painted us flying above the Pestkovatik district. You can see Pokrovskaya Street directly below us, with the Shagal *izba* unmistakable.

I am smartly dressed in green trousers and a green check pullover for the flight. I am holding Bella firmly round the middle, between my legs, as we soar horizontally along

44

together, her head on my chest. I have painted myself as poised and confident.

Bella is relaxed though serious-looking, in a long blue dress fringed with lace and a blue check top. She has one arm extended, as we fly. She is waving goodbye to Vitebsk. So am I. We are youngsters leaving our childhood town for a bigger and better life, believing we will never return.

And that is indeed what we believed at the time. But we were wrong.

PART II: PARIS, 1913

My first painting in Paris was the *Self Portrait with Seven Fingers*. It shows Vitebsk and Paris together: Vitebsk is represented by a cathedral which, as a Jew, I was not allowed to enter. Paris is represented by the Eiffel Tower, a choice so stereotypical it is ironic. I painted myself with my back firmly turned to Paris. I am looking longingly at Vitebsk. 'I may be physically in Paris,' I am saying to the viewer, 'but my heart, my soul, my spiritual being, is in Vitebsk.'

And so they were. And so they always would be.

Paris. The 15th arrondissement, where the town meets the country. I was hurrying along back down rue Vaugirard to The Hive (*La Ruche*), the artist colony where I lived. The light here has a pure pale-blue quality. It is brighter than in Vitebsk, which for all its wide boulevards and open squares is dark with red brick and sooty.

It is violet dusk; the colour I love best. The blue flames of the gas lamps are making a dancing pattern, casting the edges of the wide boulevard into deep blue shadow. The French call this twilight time *entre chien et loup*.

I was coming from the Crédit Lyonnais office nearest to The Hive. It was in the rue de Lowendal, near the Invalides, almost opposite the military academy. I went there every month to collect my money, 125 francs transferred to my account by the Duma Deputy Maksim Vinaver, back home in Vitebsk.

As I walked back towards The Hive – nearly there now – I felt a frisson of fear. I remembered a letter from home. It was from Bella. Bella thought, she *thought* – she was not sure – that Duma Deputy Maksim Moyseevich Vinaver had been arrested. There had been huge pogroms back home, we all knew that. Had Vinaver been taken during these pogroms? So when I had asked for my monthly money, a few moments ago, I was no longer completely sure it would be there.

It was there. This time.

49

I made my way along the last stretch of rue Vaugirard. I saw the clock tower just before I smelt the blood. The Vaugirard abattoir has a clock tower; you can hear the hours and the halves and the quarters striking from the ateliers in The Hive. You can also hear the screams of the cows and goats before they die. On rainy days, the hard rain washes the gore from the abattoir along the gutters as far as The Hive. You can still smell it inside, in the ateliers.

I smelt the blood, it forced its way up my nose making my brain all red and misty. I drew level with the courtyard. You cannot help but look in. The scene stamped itself on my mind.

There was a cart on the left, behind it a slaughterman with a bristly black moustache, his white apron soaked in blood and gore. In front of the cart stood another slaughterman, a real giant with shaven head, black moustache and shoulders which only got thinner when they reached his wrists. His right hand was clenched. Round his massive middle was a leather belt holding a sort of holster which held the iron tools of his trade, all caked with gore.

The direction of his gaze led to a black and white cow standing rigid with fear under a sort of glass awning, with its back legs still half in the stable area. Another slaughterman in an apron, with the same toolkit round his waist as the giant, was swinging an iron bar with an axe-head in the air.

As I watched, the slaughterman swung the iron bar with the axe-head in an arc, down towards the cow's head, where it would smash just between her ears. I looked away but not quite in time.

I never painted The Hive's exterior, but at least three of the artists who lived there, known as *les abeilles* – the bees – did. One of them was Leon Indenbaum, primarily a sculptor, who was also from Vitebsk.

Indenbaum's painting shows the octagonal, beehive structure of the building, with caryatids on the outside. The artists' ateliers were like honeycombs inside the beehive shape. Indenbaum shows me painting in front of The Hive. I have on my characteristic slouch hat, for outdoor wear. I am wearing make-up, as I often did. I am painting a nude model, probably Margot. The grey figures behind the model are the Ostrouns, who looked after the maintenance of The Hive, as well as providing canvases and paint on demand. They could rustle up food at their little café, of a slightly more complex nature than the concierge, Mme Segondet's everlasting flow of free potato soup.

I stopped, blinking my made-up eyes at the complicated Odeon crossroads ahead of me. I could now see the rue Danzig, with the passage de Danzig, where The Hive is, opposite. Ahead of me was a green racing car, stopped by the kerb, a flashy Futurist object. I dislike cars.

The driver was sitting in it, wearing motoring goggles and a white silk scarf. The engine was running, making it belch with smoke like a snake with explosive breath.

The car had attracted a crowd of urchins, half admiring, half hostile. With a start and a blink I recognised one of them. I did not know his name, but he had chased Soutine all the way back to The Hive after one of his periodic bursts of temporary work, lugging crates at the Gare de Montparnasse.

Soutine attracted urchins like flies round dung. This one had waited under the skirting roof which covered the downstairs studios in The Hive. It had come on to rain and he stood there for ages calling after Soutine – 'Yid, Yid, Yid.'

I tensed but the car drove off, leaving the disappointed urchins to disperse. Fortunately, none of them noticed me, in my full make-up. Then, with relief, I noticed the large plate-glass windows of La Rotonde and the Dôme, the two cafés situated just in front of The Hive.

The wealthier of *les abeilles* – a relative term – like Modi, Amedeo Modigliani sometimes and Indenbaum

51

always, went there for a café crème or a croissant, as did Soutine when somebody paid for him. But I never joined them – well, hardly ever.

As I looked, their large plate-glass windows were reflecting and bending the shapes of passers-by. The *patron* of La Rotonde, M. Libion, came out to start tilting the chairs of the outdoor tables up for the night. He caught sight of me, giving me a spontaneous friendly wave and smile. I waved back, flooded with honey warmth.

I knew Libion only slightly. I used to write to Bella from the tables of the Rotonde, never from my room. I nursed a single café au lait for an hour while I was writing. Sometimes, not often, I sat with the other artists there, but never at L'Observatoire or Petit Vavin or the dozens of other little cafés and bistros where the better-heeled artists go to eat and mingle.

Then with relief I caught sight of The Hive. As soon as I crossed the road, I saw the familiar cement caryatids flanking the building at number 2 passage de Danzig. Outside the gates stood the peddler, as usual. He was a tall, broad-shouldered, very skinny man, with gappy teeth and a long beard. He was dressed in a much-worn Jewish gabardine.

I remembered bartering for bread at the Soucharewska Market, near the river in Vitebsk – all the panging memories of home.

Who was this peddler? I had no idea what his name was, even though he came here so often. We were not interested in names, we who created images, names even less than other words. Even Modi did not know what he was called, or anything about him. Indeed, Modi said he had never seen him, which was strange. Nobody else I spoke to had ever seen him, either.

The peddler regularly set up his handcart at the gates. He sold herrings, kasha, black bread, everything a man could conceivably desire. Well, everything an exiled Jewish painter living in Paris as part of the École Juive could conceivably desire.

I smiled at the peddler. The peddler smiled and nodded at me. He inclined his imposing head towards the herrings on sale. He indicated, with a wave of his hands, that what I had bought before was available again.

'A good herring is three kopeks back home,' I informed the peddler in Yiddish.

The peddler pointed to prices, scribbled in chalk on a flecked and worn blackboard. Herrings were twelve sous.

On the table, in a plate, in my atelier, there was a herring with some of its head and tail intact. It would do for this evening. I did not need another herring. I thought of my father, schlepping his massive barrels of herring for a living, too tired for anything except the Talmud when he came home.

I shook my head sadly to indicate I was not buying. To my amazement, the peddler embraced me, assuring me of his love without a purchase on my part. It never ceases to amaze me how much my fellow human beings like me and desire my companionship.

Here at The Hive I am an outsider, but only because I wish to be. I am bombarded with invitations and requests for my company, attend this café or that restaurant with me, come for a walk, go to a brothel, attend a ball. I say no to it all, well, most of it.

I returned the peddler's hug and made my way through the gateway, to The Hive.

Here it was, my run-down Eden. As I entered, I was flooded by a sense of fulfilment in my innermost secret *ruah* – the spirit. It was here I would fulfil my mission as an artist. I had not the slightest doubt about that. Such newly gathered honey flows inside me.

I am in the garden. I look at the first sculpture, standing there in the untamed long grass. The sculpture is human sized. It shows an angel with its wings pinned to its sides by a tangle of briar roses. The angel is sad but passive in the face of her plight. It is called *The Spirit Shackled*. It represents the free spirit, the spirit of creativity, shackled by the chains of reason.

I made my way across the grass, my spirit soaring. It was a wild garden. There were fruit trees, chestnut trees, linden trees and lilac bushes. The white hawthorn was out, drawing the eye. The garden is white in spring, from the hawthorn, vermilion in autumn, when the small berries pop out, and in winter dark like a hairy bush.

The foliage growing up The Hive building was lush at this time of year, too. And the wild grass, which nobody ever cut down, was tangled and luxuriant. I exulted in the manifoldness of nature and of life. One blade of grass does not resemble another blade of grass any more than a Raphael resembles a Rembrandt.

Goats, ducks and hens wandered The Hive gardens, trampling and eating the grass, in and out of the sculptures. There, in its familiar place tilted on its side in the long grass for ever was a bust of the Queen of Romania.

Why was a bust of the Queen of Romania here? Why did it exist? Why was it exactly *there*? And not *there*? No reason. It was gloriously meaningless. And did the Queen of Romania ever know her bust was tilted on its side half buried in the long grass in an artists' colony in the south of Paris, so she could see out of one eye only? What matters is that we do not know, cannot know and should not wish to know.

As I watched, a wandering duck waddled busily past and peed on the bust of the Queen of Romania. The Queen of Romania did not react, except perhaps for a little oxidation, becoming more tinged with green.

The female donkey was tethered out of peeing range of the statuary. Like the peddler, it did not have a name – as I said, we artists were not keen on names. It often brayed when Indenbaum played his guitar, so it was sometimes called Indenbaum's Ass.

As I walked, I believe the wind changed as I got a

powerful stench of blood from the Vaugirard abattoir, borne on the wind. With an effort of will, I summoned the odour of the lilac bushes and blotted out the whiff of blood. The paths and alleyways through the gardens of *La Ruche* had names like the Flower Drive, the Boulevard of Love and the Avenue of the Three Musketeers, though we hardly referred to these names.

The Boulevard of Love led to one of the many outbuildings, clustering round the main ateliers. I stared at one of these buildings, challenging it. It was the Exhibition Hall. We had arranged for the dealers to come here, all of them, well, most of them.

There they would stand. Vollard and Charles Malpel, Bernheim, Kahnweiler, Paul Guillaume, Netter, Laval, Cheron, Berthe Weill, the whole gaggle of them. All those faces and bodies I had seen through the plate glass of their galleries, never going in. All those shapes and sizes, all those deals and dealers.

I imagined them now, all fighting over paintings by Marc Chagall.

I walked towards the stone doorway of The Hive. On the left, as you enter the dingy corridor, is the lodging of Mme Segondet. On her door she has painted 'Mme Segondet: Concierge' in shaky and uneven black lettering.

The corridor darkened – there is no electric light here, just as there is no gas and no running water. Already my nostrils were wrinkling from the assault of the soap balls from Bon Marché, put down to kill the smell from the abattoir.

I walked on past the first studios, which being nearest the door are also the cheapest. Here is the Litvak Kikoine, then the bourgeois Indenbaum, my fellow from Vitebsk. Then next along the corridor, Avram Markovich. There is a sprawling pile of rubbish outside his door. Then the bitter Krémègne.

The beautiful Amedeo Modigliani – Modi – is now on

the ground floor, too, where all the sculpture studios are, since he made his wild decision to stop painting and be a sculptor.

I reached my door. I moved to this atelier only recently. I used to be next door to Modi, but the screams of ecstasy from his many lovers were distracting from both sleep and work. Faintly in the distance I could hear Kisling's phonograph playing tinny notes, just above the sound of my own breathing.

All the studios have a letter on the door. Mine is the letter A. None of the ateliers at *La Ruche* have locks. People wander in and out. Thefts of paint, canvases, food and clothes happen all the time. I hate that. I myself do not steal; I do not expect to be stolen from.

Every time I go out, I wind a piece of old wire round the door handle then jam it in the door jamb as I shut the door. It would only delay an interloper for seconds, I realise that, but most of the painter-magpie-thieves have at least a modicum of embarrassment about stealing from their fellows, so a few seconds hold-up, making their crime obvious to a passer-by, might be enough. Or so I hoped.

Sinking dread swept through me. The wire had definitely been tampered with – no doubt, no doubt at all. It was hanging down. I had not left it hanging down. I tried to persuade myself I had left it hanging down, but I had not.

I loosened the wire, put it in the pocket of my blue linen jacket and went into my studio. I saw nothing, because my eyes were shut in fear. I was even trembling slightly. I could smell the mix of linseed oil, turpentine and my own sweat which told me I was home.

I slammed the studio door shut behind me, as if to shut out the intruder I feared had already got in. I looked round wildly. The first check was always the brushes. Thanks to the Vinaver largesse, I could afford a couple of sable brushes. I also had a hog's hair filbert for close work, much envied by some.

They were both still there, still caked with paint, in fact, from the *Self Portrait with Seven Fingers*, the painting I was working on at the time. There was permanent white from my painted nose on the little filbert, cadmium yellow for the floorboards on the sable.

Then I lost myself for a while staring at my painting of *The Cattle Dealer*. The cattle dealer is sitting on a cart, being pulled by a horse. A cow is riding on the cart. The cattle dealer's wife is walking behind the cart, carrying a calf. The wife is painted as larger than the man and the cart because size means importance.

The cattle dealer is twisted in his seat looking back to where they have come from. The wife's head is also twisted, looking back. Even the cow on the cart is facing the way they have come, not the way they are going. Only the horse, the means of impulsion, is facing forwards.

This is what I am saying: Marc Chagall, the grandson of a cattle dealer, is being pulled forwards into his life in Paris but he and his beloved Bella are looking back to Vitebsk. The overall message, however, is a glorious pantheistic statement: the cow has the spark of the divine so is entitled to her place of honour and rest on the cart.

I breathed out, then breathed hard, steadying myself. I was sweating. *The Cattle Dealer* was untouched, I was sure of it. I lit the kerosene lamp and looked round the studio. Studios at The Hive were not called 'the coffin' for nothing; air was one of many shortages.

Everything in here is shaped by the hexagons which honeycomb together to form the basic hive shape of the building. Each atelier, each studio, is one such hexagon. To make the most of the natural light, painters who use it to paint (I don't, I paint at night) have to pose models at the summit of the triangle shape, below a 'metro'-shaped arch with a window above it. All the studios are like this, all identical.

My breathing slowed, although I could still hear it.

I could hear a distant train clatter past through the Gare de Montparnasse, too. Then the silence landed. I let my eyes sweep round my oddly shaped world, a world full of corners and angles.

The bed is upstairs on a balcony, where a bay overlooks the garden. Like everything else, it has been there for more than ten battered years. It is reached by a scuffed and scraped stepladder. I was the bed's sole inhabitant, a thought I did not let myself dwell on.

I was terrified of little Olga. 'Show me your leg,' I said. 'Up to there. Then I'll give you your ball back.' She did not. I gave her her ball back anyway, out of sheer relief.

Then that time under the bridge over the Dvina River. We were on a raft, floating on the churning turquoise stream. Three of us, all of us naked. Me and Lazar Lissitzky and Osip Zadkine.

'Just look what a little one he's got.' That was Osip. Osip, the yellow thief, the nasty boor, the masturbator. 'Just look what a little one he's got.' And they pointed and they laughed.

Eyes swivel – bang! – away from the bed, then. The kitchen is separated from the rest by a red curtain. You can see into the kitchen, on a table stained with paint, more stable but less romantic than the one in my painting.

There were some eggshells, two 2-sou soup tins and half a croissant, all from Bon Marché. (And excuse me, Paris, I know you think your food is wonderful, but the croissants are not as good as from the Gourevich bakery and pastry shop back home.) Sometimes I buy potatoes from the market for fifty centimes, or tomatoes for soup, but there were none there now.

Ditto sugar and tea, I'd run out. But there was a herring on a plate. There is always a herring on a plate. I ate the body of this still-life herring yesterday, leaving the head and tail for today, but now I did not feel hungry.

The four paintings I was working on at the moment are still disported around the atelier. Nobody had stolen them, but that was scant comfort. They steal my ideas, too. And someone had definitely been in here.

I took off my blue linen jacket, my blue linen trousers, my underwear and began to paint. I always paint naked. *Just look what a little one he's got.* When I work, I feel as if my father and my mother are peering over my shoulder – and behind them Jews, millions of vanished Jews of yesterday and a thousand years ago. They are all in my paintings.

I started to paint *The Wedding.*

As its background, *The Wedding* has the timber-framed houses with my mother's shop clearly labelled in Russian lettering on the far right. Against this background, the twelve figures of the wedding party, plus three children, are arranged in a V-shape.

The groom, in his long purple coat and high hat, is holding the bride's hand and gazing tenderly at her. He is Zussy Javitch, a close neighbour whose family house shared a courtyard with ours.

His bride, in traditional white with a veil and a bouquet, is Chaja Bejline, daughter of a *moujik*, a travelling peddler who drove a wagon with baskets of goods as far as Lyozno, as far as Yuhupetz, as far as … well, as far as his horse could travel without dying on the *moujik.*

The *moujik* himself, Chaim Bejline, is walking behind the bride and groom, dressed in fawn and brown, having left his horse at home. His wife and brother are just behind. The brother has a full beard.

On the far left of the picture, against two more blocks of colour of the same green and blue as the carpet, is Nicolas Antonowich. Although he works at Gourevich, the Jewish bakery and pastry shop, Nicolas Antonowich is one of the minority of non-Jews in Vitebsk. He has over his shoulders a balance with flour in the two weighing bowls.

In front of Nicolas Antonowich is a stout woman in red. This is Tanjka the Laundress, known as Tanjka the *gonif* – the thief. She is with her husband, in a blue suit. This is Moyky. There is nothing to say about Moyky. He is Moyky. That's it.

Ahead of them is my Uncle Neuch, my mother's brother, playing his fiddle. He is the fiddler on the roof, which inspired the folkloric musical *Fiddler on the Roof*, based on a story by the Yiddish writer Sholem Aleichem, which in turn was based on a drawing of mine of Uncle Neuch on the roof, playing the violin.

Uncle Neuch really did, on occasion, go up to the roof to play his violin. We boys from Pokrovskaya Street used to throw stones at Uncle Neuch until he either stopped playing or fell off the roof. His playing was terrible.

In front of the fiddler is Rabbi Paykine, reading aloud from the Holy Zohar, while walking along. The woman in orange is my Aunt Mariassja. Her three kids are gambolling round her. One stuttered, one was deaf and the third was simple. Aunt Mariassja is no doubt saying 'What have I done to deserve such children?', as she often did.

And then the tears came. They came in a gush, a torrent like the Dvina River in full flood in my sad and joyful town. Oh, Vitebsk, where are you? Where is Tanjka the Laundress (also a *gonif*)? Where is her husband, Moyky, about whom there is nothing to say? Where is Feiga-Ita, my mother? Should I put her in the picture? Where is Bella, where is Thea?

I howled and I howled in loneliness. And I only stopped howling when blood started dripping through the ceiling. Drip-drip. Big fat plop. Drip-drip. Plop-plop. Rich Cadmium red. Most definitely blood. It was dripping faster too.

I stood, heaving in a breath then roaring it out in one great blast of frustration:

'SOU-TINE!'

I pictured Chaim Soutine but his self-portrait was brighter than the picture in my mind: two bits of cheap linen have been gummed together and attached to a wooden stretcher. This is the canvas. The paint is thick, having been insufficiently diluted with linseed oil.

Soutine has made no attempt to prettify himself. A plain round face looks at first sight to be staring at the viewer, but on closer inspection it is looking past, giving him a slightly shifty look.

It is a Jewish face.

The blood dripping through the ceiling was plop-plopping faster. I sprang towards the door, then realised I was still naked. Moaning in frustration, I hunted around the cluttered, paint-bespattered atelier for wherever I had thrown my clothes.

I found the blue linen jacket immediately, but where had I thrown my trousers? I dashed up the stairs to the bed area, then dashed down again. Ah, yes! I had thrown them behind the old canvases when I put up the new canvas for *The Wedding*. Yes, there they were, tangled.

No time for underwear and God alone knows where my drawers were anyway. I struggled into my trousers. Then it occurred to me to make sure the dripping blood was clear of all my canvases. All was well in that respect. It was missing the upstairs part of the atelier, plopping directly on the lower *étage*, but nowhere near any of the easels, just making a rust-coloured puddle on the worn floorboards.

Attired as best I could, I dived for the door. Outside there was just enough light coming through the dusty windows to make a way forward. Despite the late hour, somewhere in the middle of the night, some artist was playing the trombone somewhere. One of the goats from the garden was bleating in response.

I passed the battered door of Emmanuel Mané-Katz, or maney-maney, as he was known – a terrible artist from the Kiev Pale. Someone had tried to kick his door in by the look of it, a discerning art-lover no doubt. Above the bashes and splinters, his door had the letter G on it.

My face dropped automatically into its sneer. Yes, I *know* I have a reputation for not valuing other artists, but maney-maney is like a breathing, not to say *kveching*, warning of what I will be if my painting fails.

All those sugary folkloric paintings of cute Jews going about their exotic, sighing, shrugging, Yiddish business with their palms out. Mothers anointing their children with chicken soup. Dainty rabbis, blessing. Acute cuteness. Terminal whimsy. I think he uses *schmulz* as a primer, under the paint.

I walked on, briskly. It suddenly occurred to me that I did not know where I was making for. Soutine had no fixed studio. As he paid no rent, he just settled in any empty atelier as long as it stayed empty. When somebody else wanted it, and could pay for it, he moved out.

I stopped. I rubbed my hand over my face. I pictured the dripping blood and the layout of The Hive. There were only one or two ateliers the blood could have come from. I walked on.

My nostrils were suddenly assailed by the stink of Argyrol. It was one of the characteristic smells of Paris – the cheapest antiseptic sold at Bon Marché. The cleaners very occasionally cleaned the studios, but never the corridors. Indenbaum's wife had been at work, then.

Indenbaum's wife was the only one who cleaned the corridors, plus Mr and Mrs Indenbaum's own atelier, plus on occasion even the café at the back of The Hive, run by the Ostrouns.

Up the spiral staircase to the upper floor, turn left. Past the Bolshevik Kikoine, past the bitter Krémègne. There was an empty atelier next to the Indenbaums. It had the letter F on the door. Soutine was in there. I could hear his voice.

Soutine, Soutine, Soutine. Oh, my Chaim Soutine! He was darkly depressed the whole time. He was sullen, he was as coarse, as rough-grained as his cheap linen canvases. He suffered permanently from TB, tapeworm and stomach ulcers, but frequently had flu and tonsillitis, too.

Plus he took ether. He stole it from the all-night pharmacy near Saint Lazare station, even though it drove him crazy. But he was crazy like a savage God.

The best of the many portraits of Soutine was a pencil sketch by Michel Kikoine, the jolly Bolshevik. It showed real insider knowledge, the work of a man who had known Soutine since they were students together in Minsk. Soutine's round face with its thick lips gazes steadily out at the viewer, full face. Kikoine has found Soutine's strength, his inner belief. This Soutine will not always be wearing rags.

But in a master-stroke – literally – Kikoine has drawn Soutine's arm across his chest, his large hand splayed, pointing at his throat. It is a gesture of vulnerability. The little boy beaten for drawing is still in there, still hidden, still frightened. But the man Soutine has the resolution and perseverance to overcome the boy – given the large dollop of luck, which is on the way.

I opened the door with my eyes closed, something I often do, out of terror of what I may find within. With my eyes still closed, I felt pity at the boy Soutine being beaten for doing his first drawing. He was beaten by his father. Drawing, all drawing, was held to be a blasphemy, a sin. The drawing was of the local rabbi. That did not save Soutine from the beating for blasphemy, although the drawing was so good, the rabbi bought it.

I also thought of the *am ha-aretz*. This is an archetype from Hasidic Jewry – the mystical, ecstatic Jewry I breathed in with the air in Vitebsk. It is the brand of Jewry which suffuses my art. With typical Hasidic complexity, the *am ha-aretz* can be an ignorant man, but also the simple unselfconscious man who has been chosen for God's work.

63

Soutine was the best example of an *am ha-aretz* I ever met. I never told him that, though. He would not have understood. Hasidism exists in concentrated pockets of Jewry. It was entirely absent from Soutine's birthplace in Smilavichy, near Minsk. Without Hasidism Soutine was deracinated, had no identity. He was an artist but not a man. He was nothing who painted.

But he resisted his fate as an artist. He resisted living. Any minor criticism of any aspect of any of his paintings from anybody would result in Soutine destroying the work, or occasionally throwing it out of the window. This delighted the street urchins, who gathered in the garden yelling 'Yid … Yid … Yid' at Soutine. The urchins would try to catch the falling paintings, which they would then oblige Soutine by destroying.

Or he would slash his paintings with a palette knife, or put his foot through them. Mme Segondet had already rescued several of his paintings, including some which are now worth millions, from slashed and trampled wrecks. She had then got M. Ostroun to restore them. A few of these had been returned to Soutine, but usually they were passed around the École Juive for safe keeping. I had three of them downstairs in my studio.

On occasion, we were called on to save not the work but Soutine himself. Chaim Soutine kept trying to kill himself. On the latest occasion, Krémègne had found him hanging, then cut him down in the nick of time. Krémègne never spoke to Soutine again after that. Soutine never understood why. Actually, I'm not sure that I do, though I suspected Krémègne, in particular, was jealous of Soutine's blaze of a mess of genius.

I opened my eyes in the middle of the room. Tableau. Still-life. Still-life with a living Soutine. Just. The boy doesn't eat. He just does not eat. As I tell him, you have to grease the axle, or the yellow wheels won't turn.

At The Hive, Soutine was known as 'Wild Man'

(*Sauvage*). Exhausted by his sordid losing battle with day-to-day life he was like a crippled madman.

He was naked, now, except for a disgusting, shit-caked, grimy, greasy coat. The *mecs* who slept over the gratings in the street would have disdained it. Soutine's clothes, like all his other possessions, were obtained from foraging in rubbish bins. He would then trade. The last one I recall was the attempt to exchange a cracked rubbish-bin boot for a herring (with me) or an egg (Indenbaum). Both attempted deals failed.

He was muttering to himself, like a *meshiganah*. He was wasting away like a candle. He waved his arms. His hands were covered in rat bites. His spavined genitals were peeping out of the flapping ends of the disgusting coat.

He did actually possess clothes, Soutine did. Though not many and they were characteristically bizarre. The last time he disturbed me, barging into my atelier, which he did about three times a day, he was wearing a pair of long johns, but he had stuck his arms into them. He was also wearing a leather belt as a collar. No wonder the street urchins mocked, then pelted him with ordure.

This was a man who had not mastered a single aspect of living. Modi by contrast had mastered them all. Maybe it was this polar opposition which made them so close they were conjoined spirits, forever together, brothers in all but name.

Soutine was painting. He was at his easel, applying colour to a worn, threaded canvas, far too rough from overpainting. He got them from the ex-boxer Soulie's shop at Médrano Circus for a few sous. Sometimes he sold failed paintings for a canvas value of a few sous less than he had paid.

He flapped away, with a brush. There was no form, no outline, no control, no draughtsmanship. I tried once, gently, to point out the advantages of form, draughtsmanship, structure.

'Cézanne had no draughtsmanship,' spluttered Soutine.

'Yes, but he was Cézanne.'

Soutine painted in a bouillabaisse delirium, every time. He painted like he lived – no preparation, no thought, no preparatory drawing or underpainting. Everything *alla prima*, splash colour at whatever you see out there. His paintings faded and rotted, their colour changing, because he did not prepare them properly.

I looked away from his canvas. Under the easel were some weeks-old copies of *Petit Parisien* he had scrounged from the Ostrouns, in a farcical attempt to inform himself of the doings of Paris high society. Some lesser spirits (like Osip Zadkine) found it hilarious that a penniless wreck and *tapeur* – always on the scrounge – like Soutine, sought to know of café society. Me, I found it touching.

The back copies were supposed to protect the studio he was squatting in from getting covered in paint – which they signally failed to do. Soutine's other attempt to keep whichever studio he was squatting in ready for a possible paying tenant was to sleep on a plank between two chairs, not use the standard-issue bed frame and mattress.

If a rent-paying painter was found for the studio, Soutine would offer to clean it before he moved out, then do the cleaning so badly Mme Segondet took it over. This happened time and time again.

A model was posed in the half-darkness, as the kerosene lamp borrowed from Indenbaum was running down. She looked exhausted, but smiled at me. I must say, I was half hoping it would be Kiki or Mado. Both lived at The Hive and posed naked for us for ten francs. But this was Margot, the dark-haired model who wore gypsy skirts. And she was dressed.

Modi would have painted her naked. Modi would have had her first. And probably had.

I had painted Margot myself, a chaste uneasy experience which made me nervous. I painted her on top of another painting, not one of mine, one I bought to paint over. So I used a thick impasto style – like Rembrandt – to obliterate what was underneath.

Margot, like a few of the models at *La Ruche*, did a spot of painting herself. So I showed her seated and painting a bright Expressionist-style landscape. I highlighted her long black hair. Her summer dress revealed some of her bare back and bare arms as she painted, holding the brush stiffly at arm's length, like an amateur.

Margot was originally from the provinces somewhere, not from Paris. She had a southern French accent. Nobody knew where she lived. She came in from outside now, though she used to live at The Hive. She had a toddler child. Nobody knew for sure who the father was. There was a rumour the child was half-Japanese, with Foujita the likely father. Margot would not say.

She supported herself by making puppets, which she sold at The Hive, as well as at the Paris markets. She modelled mainly at night, for more money. Unknown to Soutine, Mme Segondet was paying her for posing for him.

Margot had been passed from one artist to the other. She remained a romantic though, still calling the painters 'the heroes of my heart' without apparent irony. Like most of the models she was in love with Modi, but did not take her chances seriously. She was dressed as a waitress at the moment, that night in Soutine's borrowed atelier, or something like a waitress.

In the corner, on the table amid the other clutter, was a dead turkey-cock, white, like a murder victim. It was decomposing, dripping blood onto the floor and through my ceiling below.

'You *schlemozl*, Soutine,' I yelled out. 'You complete idiot.'

Soutine gave a vacant smile, stretching his round pasty face. There was some sort of insect nest in his ears. He was filthy. 'Hello, Moyshe.' He blew his nose into his hand then wiped the result down the flanks of the grime- and

67

shit-encrusted coat.

'Don't "hello Moyshe" me! That turkey is dripping blood into my studio!'

I caught sight of Margot, abandoning her pose, looking for somewhere to sit down. Soutine blinked. 'Oh, sorry. I'm going to do another turkey-cock. Then I'm going to do my own *Flayed Ox*. Light and transfiguration. After Rembrandt, you know?'

'Yes. I know.'

'I was at the Louvre this afternoon. I stood in front of *The Flayed Ox* for hours. It's marvellous, isn't it?'

I nodded, trying to calm myself down. The last time Soutine had visited the Louvre, he got into one of his rages in front of *The Flayed Ox*. The commissionaires ejected him. Soutine's transformative rages removed all vestiges of compassion, even towards himself. They were like epileptic fits – occasionally they *were* epileptic fits.

Being Soutine, he had not only forgotten I knew about his ejection, but had forgotten the incident itself. Soutine lives entirely in the moment, like a child – enviable in its way, I suppose.

'What are you going to do about that blood?' I said, into the silence.

Stupid question. He wasn't going to do anything. He never did anything about anything. I looked round the room for something to wrap the turkey-cock in. There were some old tablecloths, cheap paintings by others and bits of canvas, some of them sewn together, bought from the Cligancourt flea market.

I glanced at the painting of the turkey-cock and tomatoes on the floor. It was one of a number of studies of turkey-cocks Soutine produced, despite being terrified of most animals and all birds. His fascination with them and with blood, traces back to his childhood, that childhood which he could never face painting directly, because it was so awful.

This was before he did his famous homage to Rembrandt,

68

his version of Rembrandt's *Flayed Ox*. All the birds are pictured just prior to preparation and consumption. They are domestic, not wild.

This particular turkey-cock hangs from wires, plumb in the centre of the picture. He is being crucified upside down. To some this represents St Peter. Later, it was held to represent European Jewry. A dark brown background against the bird's yellow body pushes it out into the viewer's face, almost three-dimensional. The bird's legs are flailing; its hairless neck is white and stretched; its mouth is open, beak agape, contorted in agony.

I despaired yet again. He never – never – primed anything properly. With the cheap linen scrim he used, the weave shows through unless you prime it really well. That had happened with the *Turkey-cock and Tomatoes*. It was also beginning to saponify – dry out in bobbles and bits.

I nearly said something, but bit back my words. One negative syllable and he would destroy the painting, then and there. I wrapped the blood-soaked turkey-cock in the tablecloth. To my surprise, Soutine did not protest. He just stared at me, blank-eyed, glassy, the vacant smile half-abandoned at the base of his round face.

I thought how much I loved the materials I worked with: brushes, paint. I even love canvas – the unlaid-in bed. I love the feel of it. Soutine despises his materials because he despises himself.

'Get this turkey-cock dried out,' I said. 'Then inject it with ammonia.'

'What?'

'Ammonia. To preserve it.'

I found myself speaking slowly and clearly, as if to a child. The model, Margot, laughed. She cleared some clutter of canvases and rags and bits of cardboard off a chair and sat down. You would think Soutine had never had an art lesson in his life. In fact, he was a graduate of the École des Beaux Arts in Minsk, along with our neighbours, the bitter Pinchus Krémègne and Michel Kikoine.

69

Soutine had shared a room for a while with the bitter Krémègne. Krémègne was an autodidact by taste and temperament. A small gerbil-like figure with black hair and grey eyes who shrank when touched, wanted nobody in his room and who could conjure slights from the air. He wore brown corduroy trousers which matched his spaniel eyes in sadness. And a black beret which did not match anything, especially not the trousers.

He could be rude, he could be secretive, but the bitterness dominated all. His characteristic colours were blues, violets and greens.

Pinchus Krémègne's father was an artist – an artist with money. That financed the son's false start at the expensive business of sculpting – although Modi was to manage a similar false start on nothing. Like Modi, Pinchus Krémègne turned to painting when the light dawned, in his case during his studies.

Michel Kikoine was very different. He had a round face, round thin-framed clerk's spectacles, an aspiring pencil moustache and centre-parted slicked hair. He was jolly; he was a Bolshevik, although he came from a bourgeois background. He used to tell anyone who would listen that his father had seven violins hanging on the wall at home.

It was Michel Kikoine who told the story of how Soutine had turned up at three o'clock in the morning on his first day at Minsk Academy, five hours before the place opened. He then put his head down, worked his way through his hunger, slapping on paint with little thought of form. His tutors tried to train him, to tame him, yet he was still ignorant, still wild and uncontrolled in his art.

And he was still isolated. Isolated in Minsk, isolated in The Hive, even from the other Minsk artists. Isolated from everybody, except Modi, his gateway to the rest of humankind. Not only isolated and alone but actively unpopular, inside and outside The Hive. The influential Hanka Zborovski – wife of Modi's dealer – viscerally

70

loathed him.

Sighing, I looked at Soutine's work-in-progress for the first time. His portrait of Margot shows the model three-quarter length, facing the viewer. She is demure in a black dress with white lace edging at the throat, making her look, I thought, rather like a waitress.

Her hands are clasped tensely in front of her. Her expression is movingly sad, almost pleading. Her lovely down-sloping almond-shaped eyes are moist with the start of tears.

Soutine's own agony had something of Dostoevsky in it. Because of that, he painted pain with searing sincerity.

'Resume the pose, please,' Soutine said to Margot.

Margot sighed. 'I'm tired,' she said.

She gave me a most delightful smile, a moue, a shrug. 'Moyshe, will you come and have soup with me?'

Before I could say anything, Soutine threw himself to his knees, which exposed his genitalia still further, as the engrimed coat opened completely.

'Oh, pleeease!' wheedled Chaim Soutine. 'Please resume the pose. Please. Oh please. Oh …'

Soutine was always appeasing and timid, as only the truly arrogant can be. He was frightened. Yes, I knew he was frightened. But I have a life to lead, too, Chaim Soutine, and in particular I have a painting I wish to be painting.

So I put my hands over my ears. 'Shut up!' I bellowed at Soutine. I picked up a chair, ready to throw it at him. 'Shut up! Shut up!'

Soutine's eyes widened, flashing with that sense of his own greatness which never left him. The eyes were a degree of redemption from the tragedy that was the rest of his face. Those ruby lips in his self-portrait were invented – the sign of his need for sex.

I pictured my painting, in my studio downstairs. But all right, all right. My flash of temper over, I put the chair down.

Margot stood. She sighed. 'I'll resume the pose,' she said. And did so.

Soutine looked at her hard. 'Oh yes,' he said absently, still studying Margot's face. 'There is a letter for you.'

'For me?' Margot was amazed.

'No, for Moyshe.'

'A le-le-le-let ...'

There was no real system for delivering letters at The Hive. There was no real system for anything. There was a series of ever-changing tables outside Mme Segondet's room where incoming post was placed, but they were regularly stolen, as a prop or to use for firewood or even to use as a table. Anybody who saw a letter, delivered it to the right honeycomb. If they remembered to.

A letter! My darling Bella! I had been so worried that she hadn't written. I had been so jealous. A letter! How long had Soutine had it? Would I have got it at all if I had not by chance come to his studio? Oh, my Bella. My Bella.

Soutine had started painting. I saw a letter spattered with paint on the table where the tablecloth, the turkeycock and the bits of canvas were. The letter was addressed to me. It was from Thea.

When I got back to the sanctuary of my atelier, I glanced around warily. All was still. I let the familiarity calm me, trying to control my hectic breathing. I am cursed with a strong sense of smell. I could still smell Soutine's room on myself.

I had forgotten Thea's letter, even though I was clutching it in my hand. I threw it down unopened on the table, next to the skeleton of the herring, with its head and tail still attached. The herring's facing eye glared at me with blank aggression.

I took a new primed canvas, stuck it on the easel, throwing what was already there to the floor. I ran my hand over it, tenderly, voluptuously.

There was a timid tap on the door, so timid it was more

of a scrape with the nails. None of the École Juive artists would have knocked, not one of them. They would all have just come bursting in, as I knew to my cost. Oh, what does it take to be left alone? None of them were welcome, on random uninvited visits, except Modi perhaps. And even he only on occasion. I jumped to the door and let Margot in. She was nervous.

'I'm not …? I'm disturbing you, aren't I? You paint at night, everybody knows that. And it's … Well, it's late.'

But she made no move to go, just standing there, looking like Soutine's *Portrait of a Woman*, clasping her hands in front of her. Harsh words formed in my mind; I rejected them. I said nothing. But I knew from experience that a torrent would be released. When you say nothing people say your words for you, according to what they want your words to be.

She sucked in a deep breath, pulling in her stomach, then embarked on the speech she had rehearsed as she picked her way down the spiral staircase from Soutine's atelier to mine.

'I have a babysitter for …' she decided against naming him '…for my son. She will be there all night. Soutine wants to have me. He just tried to. I don't want Soutine and I don't want to go home yet. May I sleep in your bed?' She nodded up the ladder to my unmade bed.

'Yes, you can.'

She was speaking in French, I was speaking in Yiddish, an arrangement which always worked, somehow or other.

Margot smiled, holding out her hand. 'Will you come up to bed with me?' She tilted her head on one side, not so much coquettish as mischievous.

'I have work to do.'

She shook her head – that same rueful regret. 'Kiki said you would say that.'

'I said the same to her.'

She left without another word, slamming the battered door shut behind her.

I sighed, then resumed my painting.

Around dawn, I slept for a few hours, still dressed, still in my make-up, in my unkempt bed. When I woke up, shards of sunshine were struggling through the dusty window.

I had a sickening feeling something was wrong. I ran down the stairs and checked the brushes first, especially the expensive ones. I had forgotten to hide them properly before I went to sleep. But they were all there.

Something was missing, though. I know these things, I just do. I stared round the studio – paintings on easels, paintings against the walls and on the table. Drawings on the floor, against the walls. But I still knew which one was missing.

One of the jewellery shop series. It was gone. How can you be sure, Moyshe? There are so many of them. Did you not destroy it? Tear it up? And Soutine is not the only one who throws paintings out the window. You do, too. But it was missing all right.

The missing drawing was *The Rosenfeld Jewellery Shop, Vitebsk (exterior)*. The drawing of Bella Rosenfeld's family shop has the façade in the background, with lettering in Russian proclaiming it as Rosenfeld's Jewellery Shop. The café above the shop – where Vitebsk's brightest and best gather to see and be seen – is also announced in Russian script.

In the middle-ground is a typical Chagall *moujik*, a Jewish peddler on a little cart pulled by a pony. He is bearded and has a top hat. He is very much a passer-by in the bourgeois milieu of the Rosenfeld family shop, not glancing at the elegant façade as he drives past. Socially, this sums up the difference between myself and Bella.

In the foreground, to the right, there is a beautiful young woman, richly dressed with a wasp-waist, pursed mouth and furled parasol at an elegant angle. She is tiptoeing daintily in the muddy street, tilted slightly to her left for balance, perhaps just noticing the scruffy Chagall rooster and the sitting dog to her right.

This demurely elegant woman is not Bella – though she could be. She is Mrs Bishowskaya. Mrs Bishowskaya, all flower-scented and white-gloved, has just bought a diamond necklace in an elegant blue case from Mr Rosenfeld at the jewellery shop. The smaller stones were not of the first water, as Mrs Bishowskaya had just pointed out.

But having bought the necklace anyway, she passed the time of day, in a patrician sort of way, with Avram the apprentice and Rivka the cashier. 'How are you, my dear? And how is your poor mother?' Then she popped the diamond necklace in its elegant blue box into her black velvet handbag and tippy-toed daintily out into the street.

The drawing had been on the floor, next to that easel. Only one person would have stolen that drawing, that particular drawing. The serpent had stolen it. I roared out his name.

'ZADKINE! OSIP ZADKINE!'

I ran out of my atelier and along the corridor on the ground floor, breathing in the familiar dominant smells of Bon Marché Argyrol soap balls and cat piss, the latter left by The Hive's black cat, Matou, and his friends.

At the height of the day, The Hive cacophony had started up. The lowing of cows about to die from the Vaugirard abattoir, songs in Italian from upstairs to a guitar accompaniment, Archipenko, the Kiev averager, bellowing out his Russian songs from somewhere nearer.

The tethered ass let out a bray from the garden, on top of it all. I felt so stupid, I nearly brayed back. What was I doing here? I panged to go home, like a child, but fought it.

My face relaxed into an automatic smile as I passed Modi's studio. I walked along the row of sculptors, first Modi, then along the way, at the end, Zadkine.

With anyone else I would have knocked first. But not with him. Not with the serpent, Osip. I made to step inside.

75

But before I could, I filled with Osip.

Not memories, exactly, or not only memories. Not only impressions, not only experiences or knowledge of the man. The totality of the man would be somewhere near it. But the totality of the man inside me, a combination of me and him.

There was Zadkine's depressive delight in getting out of The Hive, which he hated and constantly compared to a chunk of Brie. He was always jumping on a train on the new metro line and travelling for the sake of it, mistaking forward projection for progress as so many do.

He could well afford these many journeys. He was rich, perhaps the richest of all of us at The Hive. His family, after initially wanting him to be engineer, had backed his choice of sculpture as a way of life. They were prosperous bourgeois. His father, Aron, a good man, was a lecturer at Smolensk academy, a far cry from my herring-schlepper father, God bless him.

Aron had been willing to pay for Osip's study in London. This apprenticeship was under a professor who specialised in the stone creation of fauns and faunesses. As a result of it, Zadkine sported English tweeds and narrow ties, smoked a pipe and told involved jokes in his excellent English, whether the person he was addressing spoke English or not – and most of us did not. He frequently mentioned that his mother was Scottish, or maybe was descended from Scottish people.

How had Osip got to this? The Osip who was at secondary school with me in Vitebsk. The Osip who followed me – he was always following me – to Pen's art school. The serpent Osip still taking me from my work, taking my work from me, envying and stealing everything I had.

I filled then overfilled with the essence of Osip, the very threat of him. I began to shake, like the ague, from head to foot in fear and loathing. I tried to remember if I had my make-up on; he would mock me if I had.

Taking a deep breath, I burst into his atelier. This unleashed a furious rattle of staccato barking. Zadkine's dog, Kalouche, a waist-high mangy hell-hound in indeterminate brown, the Cerberus of The Hive, stood with yellow fangs bared, poised to spring. The door swung closed behind me. I leaned against it, wheezing in terror.

I felt the *cheder* teacher's dog bite me all over again. I became the child the *cheder* teacher's dog bit. Dog bites can kill you. You can get rabies and die.

The fiend continued to growl but did not pounce. Zadkine, oblivious, chisel in hand, overalled from head to toe, continued his hewing from stone. He was working on a group of three figures, all turned in on each other.

Zadkine was very fond of groupings of three. *The Three Graces* were female nudes, two facing each other closely, touching, the third embracing the other two. We cannot see their faces, but they are indeed figures of grace.

Next to the graces, Zadkine's *Head of a Man* was a massive work of planes and lines, like an Easter Island statue. Upwardly diagonal slanting eyes are not so much sightless as hidden, as if the viewer is being watched from hiding. The narrow, wavy-lipped mouth is oddly like Zadkine himself. The overall effect, to me at least, was of a massive latent threat.

Zadkine broke off and dashed like a dervish away from *The Three Graces* back to the massive imposing stone head with its sinister letter-box eyes, all the more chilling for being so evidently human.

Then he dashed back, arms whirling, and attacked the trio again, splinters spiralling off it to the floor. Despite myself, despite my fear, my deepest aversion, I could instantly see the power and passion in what he was doing.

'Hello, Moyske.' The tones were honeyed-sweet, melodious. I never heard a sweeter speaking voice, as befits a serpent-tempter.

He did not break off from work. He did not look at me. I reluctantly approved. I would have done the same. And as to his name for me, 'Moyske' – he had called me that since we were at school together. How typical of Zadkine to find a name unique to him, so creating a bond I did not want. And how Zadkine-like that the name should be thoroughly irritating to me.

For a while, back in Vitebsk, when we were students, he managed to get both Bella *and* Thea calling me this loathsome name for weeks on end. I had to plead with them both on my knees, in tears, to stop it.

'Hello Osip.'

There he was, shock of floppy black hair over his face, going down to his jug ears at the sides. His straight nose was there to signpost the gaze down to that wavy-lipped duplicitous mouth from which his talk flew in a stream swimming with mini-serpents.

I had to look away from him, my eye alighting on that pipe on the table. Childlike looks and he affects middle-aged tweed suits and a pipe.

He turned to me, stopping working for the first time. He turned square on, imposing himself physically, head carried arrogantly. He was no taller than me but broad-shouldered. Powered talent. A madman who snapped at the wind.

My exercise book! My exercise book. It was in the desk. I was sure it was. All my school-work. I've only been a schoolboy a few weeks and all my school-work has gone. I tell Osip. I beg him to help. Even then I feel/intuit he has malign power over me. Some days later he returns the book. He claims he found it in some unlikely place – down by the river, I believe. Not even troubling to cook up a good lie.

'Osip, one of my drawings has disappeared. Give it back.'

The hell-hound Kalouche growled low. We were both

breathing heavily. Osip's mind was on his work, I could see that.

'What makes you think I've got it?' That was sharp for him, not as mellifluous as usual. Something was on his mind, plans were afoot. He read that, I read that. 'I'm expecting people.'

'Where is my drawing, Osip?'

'Answer my question, Moyske. What makes you think I've got it?'

'Because you always take what is mine. Give it back to me, or I'll search the atelier for it.'

Osip shrugged. With rhythmic sinuous motions he began to take off his blue overalls.

I glared at him. 'What are you doing?'

'I told you. I've got people coming. I need to change. You should stay, by the way. They want to speak to you, too.'

Osip was naked. His broad-shouldered flat sepia-coloured body was taut, with well-defined musculature. His circumcised penis was huge, much larger than mine, and semi-erect. His eyes were still holding my gaze. My mouth went dry.

'Go and search the room, Moyske. You'll feel better for it.'

I did as I was told, making a cursory search upstairs in the bed area, then the kitchen. This was paranoia, was it? The delusion that men and demons were stealing my things. I would return, shamefaced, to my atelier and find the drawing of Bella's father's shop tucked away somewhere. Oh, and by the way, there was no earthly reason why the exercise book should not have turned up by the bridge. We were down there all the time.

Even so, I did not expect to find the drawing of the Rosenfeld shop as easily as I did. It was under the bag where Osip kept his tools. I slid it out. It had not been treated very gently. Tears sprang to my eyes.

'Why did you take my drawing, Osip?'

By now Osip was dressed for his visitors in his tweed suit, boots, shirt and tie. He shrugged. 'I knew you would come and look for it. I wanted you to meet my visitors. Otherwise you would not have come.'

'That's rubbish,' I shouted. 'I could have come any time. And you could have just asked me to meet these visitors.' Except that Osip does not live his life in that straightforward way. And my curiosity was piqued, as he knew it would be.

Another shrug. 'Go if you want to.'

I looked at him, attracted, hypnotised. I saw him naked again. 'Who are they? These people. These visitors.'

'I'll make you some tea. Sit down.'

Still clutching my rescued drawing, I sat down.

They came in – these 'visitors' – almost immediately. Osip had planned it all, getting me here at just the right moment. But how could he have done? How did he know when I was going to wake up? Was Osip driving me mad?

As they filed in without knocking, without a word, one of them gave me a masonic sign. I replied to it as a reflex, then wished I hadn't. I had joined the Society of Russian Masons as soon as I arrived in Paris. That is so unlike me – joining anything. But I was lonely, bewildered, isolated into myself. Not to mention young for a person of ostensibly twenty-two years.

Three people trooped into Osip's atelier, two men and a woman. In my mind they were marching, thump, thump. They sat down in unison, too, in my mind, Osip having purchased a battered divan and an armchair at the Clignancourt flea market, making his atelier just about the only one in The Hive which could accommodate five people.

The newcomers were all Vitebsk painters, living in Paris, but not at The Hive – which shows you what a major art-centre Vitebsk was. What other town could boast such a collection in a foreign capital? Osip knew all of them well; I, inevitably, less so but none of them were strangers to me.

The two who sat on the divan were a couple, of sorts: Ivan Puni and his lover Ksana Boguslavskaya. I knew Ksana was betraying Puni, with Modi, as she was one of the loudest of his lovers, piercing into my concentration before I moved atelier to get some peace.

Ksana was wearing a long dress of cobalt blue with lighter blue sleeves. She had a rather pointy, quite pretty face. As she cupped her pointy chin in one hand, with Osip's green-painted wall behind her, the effect was rather Matisse-like.

Her cuckolded lover, Puni, glanced adoringly at her and lit his pipe.

Making up the trio was Lazar Lissitzky. He was another one, like Osip, who I had known since our shared boyhood in Vitebsk. Now, he perched on his chair, like a crow on a rock. Waiting. Biding his time.

Lissitzky was wearing a sort of buff overall, which on him looked like a uniform. And his puny slope-shouldered physique and short stature did nothing to mitigate his air of menace or diminish the aura that makes him the focal point of any room whose temperature he reduces by entering it.

There is not a kopek of humour in that pale strained face, the colour of weak Indian tea. Not only no humour, not a silver skein of compassion either, no mercy even. Yes, the domed pale forehead betokens intelligence. But the black eyes blazing at me now use the brain to bend the will of others, kill their spirit, distort their desires.

There is considerably less humanity in his blank face than in the planes and shadows of Osip Zadkine's stone *Head of a Man*, lowering at us from the corner.

Lissitzky spoke. 'Welcome to this meeting of the *Machmadim*.'

Welcome?? Meeting?? What meeting? Let me out of here! And whose room is it anyway? Not yours.

But Lissitzky is staring at me with those remorseless eyes. Me. Only me. 'Thanks,' I murmured. *Makhmadim*, I know, although I wish I did not know, is a Hebrew word which occurs in the Bible just once, in the Song of Songs. It means Beloved, or Precious Ones – though I can imagine nobody less precious than the terrifying Lazar Lissitzky. This movement, or grouping or whatever they are, of Jewish artists called the *Makhmadim* is publishing its own magazine. Lissitzky is pushing a copy at me now.

I took it. I didn't dare not take it. Is Lissitzky expecting me to read it, buy it, borrow it or swear an oath on it? The cover is awful – a bilious abstract in muddy colours, browns and greens. I am vaguely aware, as I avert my eyes from it, that Ksana Boguslavskaya has slipped from the room. Ivan Puni gave no sign of having noticed.

I leafed idly through the magazine, *Makhmadim*. It consists of folkloric illustrations on Jewish themes.

'We must all turn our art to the east,' announced Lazar Lissitzky.

'Our art must reflect our Jewishness so vividly that one glance will establish the creator as Jewish,' Osip Zadkine supported.

I thought of Jozef Israëls, Liebermann, Lily Joseph, Hageman, Solomon Alexander Hart; all great artists who happen to be Jews. That, one day, will be me. My influences are from Russian folk art – woodcuts – as much as anything Jewish.

'You mean we must all paint the same way?' I blurted out.

'Yes!' Lazar Lissitzky says.

Osip looked disapproving.

I got up, still clutching my drawing of Bella's family jewellery shop. The mangy waist-high mutt Kalouche growled low. I walked out.

I hurried back along the stinking, gloomy, din-filled

ground-floor corridor, intent on resuming my work, intent on leaving those who wished to talk about art to talk about art. I wished to practise it – I always have, I always will. And I must practise art alone.

I was some way from Modi's atelier when I heard the familiar sound of a female being brought to bliss by his ministrations. God knows, I knew it well enough. Through the cacophony of her ecstasy, I recognised the otherwise prim and judgemental person of Ksana Boguslavskaya, so recently perched on Osip Zadkine's divan, her shoulder just touching that of her erstwhile lover, Ivan Puni.

Matou, the black tom-cat, ran out of Indenbaum's studio, coming scrambling towards me on the greasy linoleum.

'Matou,' I cried in joy. He rubbed himself against me, purring.

I have always loved God's creatures, except dogs. All animate beings have a spark of God in them. I lost myself in Matou's pleasure as I scratched behind his ear and under his chin. He made that trilling sound in his throat.

As Matou ran off to play or hunt – perhaps the same thing – the door to Modi's studio opened. Ksana Boguslavskaya bustled out, straightening the long dress in various shades of blue. She treated me to a carnivorous glare as she bustled righteously past me in the narrow, piss-laden space, on her way to rejoin the discussion on achieving and enforcing uniformity in Jewish art.

Modi himself appeared in the corridor, cantilevered forward, wearing only a towel. Once again I pictured him not as he was but as he had pictured himself in his self-portrait. A clever angle of wall meeting screen shows us a seated Modigliani turned towards the viewer. He has given himself the characteristic 'long face' he gave all his sitters. His red coat is both opulent and threadbare, topped by a grey scarf to protect his weak throat.

Modi's technique with women was to invite them to his

83

room, then undress in front of them. The woman was then expected to undress, too. It had never failed, apparently. I was smiling at the very thought of him.

'Hello, Moyshe. I thought I heard you.' He grinned. Faultless Litvak Yiddish from a Greek God wearing a worn, and slipping, French towel. Who could resist that?

Where, how and from whom had he learned Yiddish? Yiddish belongs to the Ashkenazi Jews of the *shtetls* of Eastern Europe and Russia. Italian Jews like Modi are Sephardi – different tribe entirely. Yet Modi spoke Yiddish as perfectly as he spoke French and his mother tongue, Italian. His Yiddish had just a slight Minsk lilt, no doubt picked up from spending so much time with Soutine.

'Modi!' I shouted his name, holding my arms out wide. 'What have you been doing?'

We both screamed with doubled-over laughter, heaving in the corridor stench in glee.

'I've been sculpting,' Modi said. 'No, really. It's coming. It's coming.'

'Oh, Modi! If even the sculpture is coming …'

We screamed out laughter again.

'No, seriously. OK, a bit seriously. I'm getting on top of … I'm achieving this sculpture thing. Come and see!'

Modi pulled me into his studio. I could not tell if he did this by touching my arm or by the magnetism of his charismatic charm, physical beauty and sheer joyous goodness. But I ended up inside.

'Look at that,' Modi said, adjusting his towel. 'Coming along, isn't it?' He shook his shock of black hair, still tousled from loving Ksana Boguslavskaya.

I appraised the *Caryatid* quizzically. The pose of a woman holding up a heavy load is reminiscent of Modigliani's painting. The *Caryatid* was done in a ritualised, African-influenced style, although the whimsical expression of the naked woman's face is pure Modi, as are the beautiful, full breasts. She looked happy!

Modi loved women. He appreciated and cherished

them, preferred their company at all times to that of men. The fact that he was well-nigh perfect physically, and practice and variety made him an extraordinary lover, did his cause no harm, but it was his cherishing love and adoration of women that above all made them love him.

'I like it,' I said, truthfully enough, of the sculpture.

'She is eternal!' Modi shouted, as if I had suggested she was not. 'Women are eternal, God bless every last one of them. Look, she is speaking: "Nothing till I was made was made, only eternal beings. And I endure eternally."'

'Dante?' He was always quoting Dante, that was how I knew.

'Dante!'

I embraced his sculpture again, with my eyes. 'It's like that wonderful painting you did.' I hesitated. 'You know, you should ...'

'... go back to painting, Yes.' He gave a theatrical, Italian sigh. 'Everybody tells me that, Moyshe. I'll do that *after* I have achieved success as a sculptor.'

'Are you still giving the paintings away?' I meant the paintings he did in cafés. Sometimes he used them as payments for coffee, or he just gave quick sketches away anyway, especially to pretty girls.

He gave an Italian shrug. 'I'm a sculptor. *Basta!*'

I had been keeping my gaze away from Modi's beauty altogether, but then, for the first time, I noticed a cut near his mouth, a bruise on his face. There was a livid yellow-blue bruise on his arm too.

'Modi, have you been fighting?'

He laughed.

'Go on, tell me!' I sounded boyish, even to myself.

Modi eased himself into an armchair. He *was* bruised. He started to speak but then was convulsed with coughing, folded over, his muscles bulging and straining. 'Sorry! It's from the sculpting. The dust ...'

I hoped it was. We all feared TB so much nobody named the disease out loud. And Modi did not eat properly, any

85

more than the rest of us. One luxurious meal a month, after his cheque came through, then starvation. I pictured him at the luxurious meal – all velvet suit and elegant cravat, grace as well as beauty. Then I pictured him spitting blood from the tuberculosis he had had on and off since boyhood, retching, fainting from hunger. None of his women had seen him like that. Only Soutine and me.

Despite his beauty and brilliance was Modi *maudit*? That was one of the French words I knew, because Modi had taught it to me. It means accursed or damned.

'Do you know about the Beilis affair?' Modi said, his beautiful voice going thin, suddenly strained.

I shook my head, dumbly.

'A Russian Jew by the name of Menachem Mendel Beilis was accused of the ritual murder of a Christian boy, near Kiev. It's been a gift to the Camelots du Roi, here. You know them?'

'No.'

'They are anti-Semites. Do you know the work of a journalist called Édouard Drumont? He works for an anti-Semitic rag called *Libre Parole*.'

I shook my head again.

Modi was tense. 'I've never ... You see back home we don't get this kind of ... How dare they?'

'You got into a fight with them, didn't you? These people?'

'Yes. In the restaurant Spielman.'

'In the ... What were you doing there?' It was a very expensive place, even I knew that, from walking past it.

Modi grinned. 'My cheque from my brother had just come through. For a socialist deputy he's very generous.'

'So ... You were in this restaurant, and they attacked you?'

'Not exactly.' Modi grinned again. 'I was in the restaurant. And I attacked them.'

'Whaat?'

'I could see they were reading Drumont. I excused

myself to the lady I was with, left my table and went over to them. I said "My name is Amedeo Modigliani and I am a Jew."'

'Oh, Modi! How many were there?'

'Three. They tried to ignore me. So I said "Why are you reading this fascist shit?" Then we went outside.'

'What happened?'

'I beat them up. Well, two of them. The third one landed a few blows, before he ran away.'

I tut-tutted with exasperation. 'Modi, why don't you just paint?'

He grinned the lovely grin, like a peal of bells. 'Why don't you sleep with Margot? The poor *ragazza* desires your body, you know. You're a good-looking boy.'

I squirmed. 'Because of Bella.'

'And Thea?' He said it teasingly.

I squirmed anew. 'Yes. Maybe.'

I slammed the door to my atelier as far as it would slam. It did not really close properly. No wonder all humanity and Osip Zadkine could wander in so freely. I was still clutching the drawing of Bella's family shop, rescued from the serpentine wraiths of Osip.

I looked round the atelier as if I had never seen it before. Gradually, its familiarity reasserted itself, starting with the unique smells, the paintings themselves, their companion images in my mind ...

I stared at Thea's letter, unopened on the table. It stared back at me, wall-eyed, with one of Chaim Soutine's dirty thumbprints smearing just below the stamp.

There would be no peace now, no painting so no fulfilment, until I read it. I tore it open, ripping the envelope. Thea said she still loved me. She said Bella had grown close to Viktor Mekler, my dearest friend in Vitebsk and fellow art student at Pen's. She said Bella no longer intended to come to Paris to join me.

She asked if she could come to Paris in Bella's place.

PART III: PARIS, 1913

I was painting *Promenade*. In *Promenade* only Bella is flying; Bella in a fetching mauve dress, pretty and gamine, holding onto my hand, as her other hand disappears into the sky.

I am happy and smiling, but I am not looking at Bella. I am looking out, wide-eyed, clear-eyed, at the viewer, at you, my public. I am wearing a black velvet suit edged with white, reminiscent of a Rembrandt outfit which Yury Pen once painted me wearing.

My feet are planted firmly on the ground. Yes, I am in love, yes, I am happy, but I am and I remain an artist, a painter, first and foremost. I cannot lose the totality of myself in Bella because something of me must always remain outside and aloof from anything which is not my art. My feet are planted on the green chequered ground, fusing with nature, to keep me in touch.

The beds, up in the balcony of the ateliers, up the ladder, were all the same in *La Ruche*. They were narrow, single beds. But Indenbaum had his wife here with him, Lipchitz had his wife here with him. And the narrow beds were shared often enough, all of them were, except mine. Until now. But narrow they were, so I was suffering during my first nights in the atelier with Bella. I was not used to closeness.

I awoke from a light doze, stirring. She was tousled, naked, tucked into the crook of my arm. I smiled, but the smile wavered because she was pursed into a pout. She went up on one elbow, as best she could, her black hair falling over her face.

'Why won't you let me touch you? Eh? Why won't you let me touch your *schwanz*?'

I felt my little *schwanz* curling to frightened shrimp as it was named.

'I ... I ... I ...' The stammer was back.

91

Oh, that frenetic early time of Bella at *La Ruche*! The whole hive was abuzz anyway because the dealers were coming soon to judge the works of the Jewish painters, the École Juive. We were all on the *qui vive*, all jangling wild and pink-mist hysterical. We were all *fauves* – more wild than the wild ones – even if our paintings were not.

Sometimes, I caught myself wishing Bella had come at some other time, so I could get more sleep during the day. We were out so late at night that my painting time was getting nibbled into. And that with the dealers so close you could smell them.

But then I banished the thought as unworthy.

In any case, to be practical about it, if I had not got Bella to Paris when I did, I feared I would have lost her. Her letters had become less and less frequent, more distant, more full of Viktor Mekler, and possible futures involving acting and writing that could not include me.

And Bella was always influenced by her parents. Papa Rosenfeld, Shmuel Noah, the prosperous jewellery shop owner, waged a nagging war against me as suitor; Moyshe the herring-barrel schlepper's son from an *izba* in the *Pokrovskaya*, now a wastrel flâneur in Paris. Moyshe, who would steal his beloved daughter away to the gaping maw of the other side of the earth.

Although Bella never knew this, it was a close-run thing from my side, too. It was Bella I loved, not Thea. I knew that. But when Thea wrote, offering to catch the next train to Paris, when Thea said she loved me, missed me, wanted to be naked for me, and not just to paint. Well, what was a poor boy to do? I wrote back, not quite accepting but not quite saying no either.

I spun her round the town, Bella that is, on a dizzying good time screaming *this is what we want* inside, though it was not, and pretending even to myself that the pull of my painting, the massive desire to get back to work, was not happening.

I introduced her to Mme Segondet, an essential step as she would be living (rent free) under her octagonal roof. The concierge never disappointed. She enfolded Bella in a fleshy embrace. 'So beautiful, this one.' Then flopped onto a hard chair, complaining of her gout.

She asked me if I needed a 'holiday' from the rent while Bella was here. And when I smilingly said no, she leaned forward and embraced and kissed me. 'So handsome, this boy. You go well together. Beautiful couple.'

'Thank you, Madame!' Bella all but curtsied.

Mme Segondet launched into a familiar lament: *'Ah, mes artistes! Mes enfants du Bon Dieu! Mes pauvres abeilles!'*

Then she talked non-stop, gleefully peddling Hive gossip. Kiki the model was pregnant. Three of Modi's nude sketches had been seized by the police, but he did another three as replacement before the *flics* were out the door. The dealer Durand-Ruel had started buying up everything a painter had, not just one or two or three pieces. It had worked a treat with Manet. And Degas.

'Ah, Degas!' I said, following her lead into the gossipy mode. 'I saw Degas the other day. Almost blind. He was crossing Boulevard Pasteur, right near here. I just stood and watched. I felt awful afterwards. I should have helped him. Suppose he'd been hit by a car?'

In truth, I did not feel awful at all. Degas is a known anti-Semite, that is why I left him to his fate in the traffic.

'Oooh!' Bella actually stamped her little foot, as hard as she could, sitting down. 'He's always criticising himself,' she said to Mme Segondet. And then to me. 'Have some self-confidence, Moyshe.' She glanced sideways at Mme Segondet for her performance as helpmeet to win approval. 'And was he hit by a car? Degas? Was he?'

'No. There's not that many about, even in Paris. They all missed Degas.'

'You see!' Bella turned in triumph to Mme Segondet.

'I'm always telling him, if you talk yourself down, people will believe you. They'll take you at your own estimation. You should boast. Or at least put your best foot forward. Everybody else does.'

I shrugged.

'There he goes again! Have some self-respect, Moyshe! Tell him, Mme Segondet.'

Mme Segondet just smiled, refusing to criticise me. She launched into more seamless stories, brooking no interruption. Bella listened wide-eyed, all the romance of *la vie bohème*. I could have hugged Mme Segondet. In fact I did so, as we were taking leave, bending over her as the concierge was still overflowing her hard chair.

'She loves you, all right,' Mme Segondet whispered fiercely in my ear, as I folded over her. 'But she doesn't understand you. And she never will.' I nodded, she went on. 'Keep her. But keep painting. She will try to change you. Don't let her. Don't let her distract you.'

I introduced Bella to the Ostrouns in their café behind The Hive. They were feeding Soutine, at the time – a free meal. Bella's pretty little nose positively quivered with distaste. Soutine talked about the coming dealers excitedly, then beat a hasty retreat. As he left, he said 'Pleased to meet you. *Enchanté*,' offering a scab-ridden hand which Bella refused.

I asked M. Ostroun to get me some new frames, something that would impress the dealers, and gave him a list of colours I needed, but I cut it short as Bella was openly impatient and bored.

'Didn't you like them?' I asked Bella, when we had taken our leave.

She shrugged. 'They are like our servants at home.'

She was fine with Libion, though. The rasping-voiced, bald and burly *patron* of the Rotonde, the café just in front of The Hive, was a vital figure in the lives of *les abeilles* –

myself as much as any of them. As I told you, I used to write to Bella from the tables of La Rotonde, but I had not realised until I returned there with her just how much I had blurted out about her. Libion knew about the jewellery shop, about Bella's travels in Germany, about her skiing, about Thea …

But La Rotonde worried me, with Bella here: The Hive had no running water, as well as no electricity. So, many of the artists not only drank their morning café crème at La Rotonde, they used the toilet facilities and washed in the sinks in the café's toilets. It was that or not washing at all. Modi was an exception to this. He used the Restaurant Lutetia for his ablutions, the one with the best washroom in Paris.

Just after her arrival at The Hive, I broke the sordid details of our toilet arrangements to Bella with trepidation bordering on fear. But my unpredictable, beautiful will o' the wisp made me ashamed of my embarrassment. She burst out laughing, batting not a dark eyelash at carrying out her ablutions at the café.

Another surprise, she took to Libion on sight. She claimed to like playing on the slot machines in La Rotonde, which apparently involved constantly asking for his help and advice. Maybe it was just the louche atmosphere, but her flirting with the heavily built, though middle-aged, *patron* was becoming flagrant. Once she sat in his lap, when she had had a couple of pastis too many.

She was always smoking his free black-market cigarettes, then progressed to the under-the-counter hashish. Libion took to her, too, and often joined us at our table for a while, if the café was not too busy. She opened out to Libion about her writing ambitions. Sometimes she wanted to be a writer more than an actress; this was one of those times.

'I used to be a journalist,' she purred at Libion, batting her eyelashes. 'And a writer.'

I looked at her, quizzically. She had had some articles

95

published in a Moscow newspaper, *Ultro Rossii*, while she was a student. That was it, as far as I knew.

'She wrote some good articles,' I said uneasily but (I thought) loyally, to Libion.

But Libion was losing interest. He excused himself from our table and went to serve some customers who had just come in.

La Rotonde was our day place, we rarely went in the evening. This was partly because Bella wanted to explore Paris night-life, further afield. But partly it was the Night Blossoms, as they were called, who bloomed all over La Rotonde after dark. Bella never minded them but they embarrassed me, to the point of blushing.

One of them, a Scandinavian woman of a certain age, took to propositioning me in front of Bella, even during the day. Bella just laughed, but I hated it. Flattery from women just confuses me, though I suppose I am vain enough about my looks. I am certainly very aware of them. Since Bella arrived I no longer wear make-up, though.

Sometimes we trawled the poorer areas, looking for cheap food, cheap scents, bright colours and atmosphere: the rue Ravignan, the rue du Chevalier-de-la-Barre, the rue Gabrielle. Sometimes we went to a dance hall in the Moulin de Galette where you could dance away the night for four sous – which meant no painting at all, that night.

Oh, and so many more. Paris! Pa-ris! Azon's on the rue Ravignon gave credit to artists. At the restaurant Weber you could get a plate of York ham, a pint of dark beer and a hunk of cheese for two francs fifty. I used to ask Modi where to take her, then (I blush, I blush) play the *homme du monde* who had seen it all and pray to God I would not get lost on the way to one of these places I affected to know so well.

Then *she* found the Russian restaurants. There was one on the rue de la Glacière and another on the rue Pascal. Apparently. How had she found them? She teasingly

96

refused to tell me. In high dudgeon, I charged into Modi's atelier while he was sculpting and accused him of providing the information.

Modi took one look at my face and understood the seriousness of the situation.

'It wasn't me, my friend.'

'Honestly?'

'I swear. But … She comes to see me, you know.'

'No, I didn't know. When?'

'She's been a few times. In the afternoon, when you are asleep. She asks about Paris or she talks. I send her away when I am working.'

Modi looked concerned. I knew Modi would not proposition her. I trusted him. But I did not fully trust her.

So I let Bella lead me to the Russian restaurants, yes, she even knew the way. How? And we ate borsht or escallops with kasha. I was sure they greeted her as a returning customer. She denied it. I wanted to believe her. But it gnawed at me.

Finally, she confessed she had been there with a group from Vitebsk. 'I just wanted to talk about the old place.'

'You can talk about the old place with me. Why didn't you tell me? Why the big secret?'

She sighed, dramatically, like an actress. 'Because you would get jealous. Just as you are doing now.'

'Yes, all right. I am jealous. I admit it. But that is a good fault. It is because I love you.'

She looked bored. 'Yes, I know.'

'Who was there?'

'I told you. Everybody from Vitebsk. Lissitzky, Indenbaum. Osip.'

'Osip! Zadkine was there?'

'Not only there, he arranged it.'

'And where was I? At this time?'

'Painting.'

'And you didn't think to tell me? To invite me, in fact?'

'No. Osip said not to tell you. He said you would be annoyed because he had arranged it. And you are.'

The rules, the understood underlying rules of our lives together, Bella's and mine, changed after 'Osip's restaurant visit', as I thought of it. Bella arranged her own time, I arranged mine. Sometimes we met up, sometimes we did not. I knew Bella would be seeing others at *La Ruche* without me – Osip, Modi. But I resolved to rise above it. This was being mature, we both agreed.

And in any case, deep down, I cherished my freedom to resume my lone walks in Paris. With the dealers coming soon, I had the perfect excuse to wander from dealer's shop to dealer's shop, firing up my unashamed dreams.

There they were: Durand-Ruel, Bernheim, Kahnweiler, Uhde, Paul Rosenberg. It was like a litany to me. Sagot and Libaude were known to prefer unfinished works – cheaper that way. Charles Malpel was in the rue Montaigne, but the rue Lafitte offered richer pickings. Bernheim junior's shop was there and Diot, Berthe Weill, Sagot and Durand-Ruel. And so was the mighty Vollard.

Naturally, there was no question of actually speaking to any of these dealers – at least not yet. We had no language in common, and anyway I was not ready. They would be coming to *La Ruche* soon enough . . .

'See you soon, then, Ambroise,' I said out loud in Yiddish at Vollard's window, at 44 rue Lafitte, as the familiar bulk of the dealer squatted at his desk inside. He lived here, too. There was a little corkscrew staircase behind him, going up to his quarters.

There is a Renoir of Ambroise Vollard showing him as a bull of a man, with his biceps and shoulders pushing out his fashionable suit as he sits with elbows resting on a table, examining a statuette – the *Crouching Woman* by Aristide Maillol, whose legs and bottom Vollard cradles in large fleshy hands as he evaluates, ranks and rates her both aesthetically and in terms of value. Other statuettes lie on their backs on the table, submissively awaiting the great man's attention.

Vollard was forty-two when this portrait was painted. His round face with fleshy cheeks, goatee beard and balding pate is shown in profile, so his hooded eyes are half-imagined, raying in on the passive nude statuette, as her body grows warmer in his hands.

I had seen another Renoir, not as good as the Vollard portrait, in here on sale for 400 francs once. Four hundred francs! Now he had a Corot in, a Daumier, a Jongkind. I could see them all clearly through the window. As I watched, Vollard was caressing a statuette in his hands, just like in Renoir's painting. He was wearing the purple ribbon of the Palmes académiques. Modi had told me what it was – he claimed Vollard wore it in bed.

Two customers, an older woman and a younger, went into the shop, giving me a curious but interested glance as they did so. I watched them through the plate glass, eyeing a monotype by Degas. You could pick one up on the stalls on the quay for ten francs if you wanted to. Lord alone knows how much Vollard was asking for it.

They were in and out in five minutes, flouncing out in high dudgeon, all swishing skirts. Vollard was known for insulting his customers, shocking them. Modi had even taught me Vollard's term for it – *cochonnerie*, a term referring to pigs he had adapted from a bourgeois term of abuse for nudes.

Despite myself I smiled at the sheer brazen cheek of the man. Only Christians could ever have such self-confidence. And then, as I watched, Ambroise Vollard slipped into untroubled sleep, there at his desk, still holding the statuette in his hands. His fat cheeks blew out softly, bubbles formed at his lips. It was the sleep of excess, not the sleep of insufficiency, like my father.

I was throwing myself totally into my painting, working on the pictures I intended to show the dealers when they came. But I resolved to be a better husband – after the dealer visit. I resolved to redress the imbalance between my painting, on high, the main thing, and Bella, my love, but not the main thing.

I planned an evening of change between Bella and myself, a watershed, a turning point. I did not share this resolution with Bella. But when it came to it, I could not face losing painting time. Sleeping time, during the day, was expendable, though. So we walked out in our glad rags for lunch together, just my beloved and me, away from all distractions.

Bella was in blue, in a pale blue dress with small black and grey squares. I had by now run to a dandy's outfit: black velvet jacket, plum waistcoat, silk tie held firm by a stiff-starched collar. I could have been Modi, just after his cheque had come through.

A new persona had come with the outfit, another me, yet another me. I referred to the Boulevard Saint-Michel, along which we were walking, as the Boul' Miche, like an old *habitué*. I affected world-weariness; I affected *louche*. I did not fool Bella; I did not fool myself.

'That's where you see the night owls,' I drawled to Bella. 'I once saw one eating peanut shells out of the gutter.'

Bella nodded politely, following my pointing finger, even though there were no night owls to be seen, it being just past midday. She was lagging behind me, never being over-fond of walking, so we were walking in single file.

'Why don't we stop here?' she said, with a snap in her voice. 'There's a good place for mussels and onion soup over there.'

I shot her a glance, while shortening my stride to accommodate her slower pace. Had she been here before? With whom? Osip Zadkine no doubt. Mussels and onion soup would be typical of his anglicised view of typical French food.

But I could not let the new me of worldly sophistication slip by showing jealousy. I smiled glassily. It did occur to me to wonder, though, just what sort of woman would be impressed by this latest covering of new me. Some sort of doxy, cheap model, even floozy, whore. Bella was an intellectual, a reader, a linguist, far cleverer than me. So why was I doing this?

'We are going to Rosalie's,' I said, or rather drawled. I had planned it all; the lunch, my clothes, my persona, what I would say to impress her. There would be no spontaneous mussels or onion soup now.

As I spoke, a flurry of pigeons from the Luxembourg Gardens swooped down in front of us, then flew off again when a little train, on its way to Les Halles, hooted as it passed by. Two pigeons remained, pecking, circling each other, the male ruffling his feathers, cooing.

'Look, Bella, love birds. Turtle doves. Just like us.' I gave a false, hollow laugh to accompany this idiocy.

She appraised me coolly, pout in place, dark eyes hard. 'Aren't they the lucky ones.'

I had chosen Rosalie's for this lunch – this lunch which I had pre-loaded with pre-planned significance – because of Rosalie herself. Rosalie Tobia had been a model living at *La Ruche* until quite recently. As she got older and plumper, she started Rosalie's as her insurance against old age.

Rosalie was Italian. She had a fiery and furious relationship with Modi. Inevitably, they were lovers. Modi kept his drawings of nudes in her cellar and round the walls of Rosalie's. After their screaming, punching and spitting rows, Modi would take his drawings away, only to bring them back next day, as he had no other safe home for them. And naturally he always ate and drank without paying at Rosalie's.

For those of us who did pay, the place was cheap, even by Parisian standards – red wine was five centimes a bottle, champagne a few sous. Most of the École Juive artists went there, but after a few tensely discreet questions, I was sure Bella had not been there before, with anyone else.

101

You had to knock on the door to get in, it was that sort of place. If Rosalie did not like the look of an applicant (or supplicant) for food they were not admitted. On the other hand, the down-at-heel were often fed soup and bread without paying a sou.

I knocked on the door. A man from one of the half-dozen or so tables opened it, then sat down again. We went in. The place was packed, heaving with clients, noisy with chatter. Some people were eating standing up. You could hardly see the white walls, which had been left like that when Rosalie took over what had been a creamery. A waiter danced past, holding a tray of drinks on high in one hand.

'Excuse me, I want ...'

'Come back in an hour, *monsieur*. As you see, we are full.'

'Please tell Rosalie I am here. I am Moyshe Shagal. I ...'

He ignored me.

Bella was looking fed up, about to complain of being footsore. 'I am not walking another *step*, Moyshe. I refuse ...'

I caught sight of Rosalie behind the bar and waved. She looked delighted to see me. She had always liked me, as all the models did. She was another, like Margot, who had offered to share my bed, more than once. As with Margot I had said no, keeping myself for Bella, or so I told myself.

Rosalie eased her way through the crush. She threw her arms round me, which made
Bella's eyes widen. Rosalie was still attractive, with her round, open face, even if she was getting on a bit for nude modelling.

'Moyshe! Moyshe Shagal. How lovely to see you. And you must be Bella. I've heard all about you. You're a lucky lady. Follow me.'

Rosalie magicked up a tiny table for two, half under a coat-stand, right near the kitchen door.

'Will this do? If I'd known you were coming ...'

'It's perfect.'

I ordered sausages, sauerkraut and *frites* for two, chased down by a bottle of champagne.

Bella prattled away about Viktor Mekler. How *much* Viktor had helped her as an actress. He had been *so* helpful. *So* understanding. They were hoping to mount a production of *Three Sisters* at the Miniature Theatre. It would not happen now, as she had come to Paris. The chance had gone.

The mention of that theatre brought back powerful images of Vitebsk; the network of tiny squares and cobbled streets near Polotskaya; the markets, the mysterious dark shops, the peddlers – bearded *moujik*s with their carts of shabby wares – the meandering goats in the gardens, the wandering roosters.

I fell into a reverie, but Bella was still tinkling on, like a doorbell on one note with nobody answering. *Vik*-tor thought she had amazing range as an actress. *Vik*-tor thought she could be a second Olga Knipper, on the boards. With *Vik*-tor she floated on air, she was inspired. I did not respond. Eventually Bella ran out of sound.

We sat in silence, ducking out of the way as people came for their coats, until Modi appeared.

I was always pleased to see Modi, but never more so than now. I wanted to share the strain of entertaining Bella. I half-hoped Modi would do his 'restaurant trick', as I called it. He often undressed as he ate, the picture of insouciance, until every wide-eyed Anglo-Saxon girl was watching him – to the fury of their escorts.

Modi helped in the kitchen to pay Rosalie for his lunch, and to try, unsuccessfully, to stop his drawings being gnawed by rats. Indeed, he had just been peeling potatoes, having a half-peeled one and a wicked-looking small knife in his hand.

'I heard you two were here and dropped everything.' Modi grinned, like the sun coming out. Nature's abundance in creating his beauty extended even to his speaking voice, which was mellifluous and honeyed.

He was dressed in an outfit from a past generation: brown corduroy jacket, blue flannel shirt, red neckerchief tied flowing at his neck. At least he had taken the black broad-brimmed hat off to peel the potatoes.

'Lovely to see you,' I blurted out, trying not to sound relieved at the release of the tension between Bella and myself.

'Come and join us,' Bella said. She gave a tinkling false laugh. 'Squeeze in.'

I felt a flash of anger. I wanted Modi to join us, too. But I wanted to be the one to ask him. Modi was mine, not hers. I rebuked myself for my childishness.

Modi seized a chair from against the wall and edged in, shoulder to shoulder with me, half under our nest of coats. I grabbed a passing waiter by the arm and ordered the same for Modi as we were having. Modi did not demur.

As the grinning waiter removed Modi's knife and half-peeled potato, I noticed he also had his blue folder tucked under his arm.

I smiled at him. 'Show me.'

Modi looked serious, handing the nudes one after the other to me and Bella.

Modi's nude sketches of women have been called an aesthetic hymn to the beauty of the female body and so they are. With typical wit, Modi divided his drawings of nudes into *dessins à manger* and *dessins à boire*. The larger *dessins à manger* – drawings for food – he offered in the cafés where he had just drawn them in exchange for a meal. The smaller *dessins à boire* – drawings for a drink – were enough, he hoped, to exchange for a glass of wine.

Some of the nude sketches were pretty tame compared, say, to Egon Schiele, and I wondered quite what the Paris police were so worried about. Just one of them tiptoes a bit far across the boundaries of the forbidden: a woman dressed in a Basque that shows her breasts and a pair of elasticated stockings above the knee is holding her skirt up, so the viewer can see her sex. She looks rather sweet, as she is doing this.

The model for the drawing was a Hive favourite, known as Kiki of Montparnasse. Originally from the Côte d'Or, her real name was Alice Prin. Kiki means Alice, in Greek, apparently.

Kiki did not wear knickers. She said this was because the cafés did not have washrooms for women, so she had to lift her skirt where she stood to relieve herself. The effect was enhanced by her shaving of her pubic hair.

Our food arrived while Modi was passing the sketches around, but he ate distractedly, never taking his eyes off our faces, waiting for our reaction.

I liked the one of a woman with her legs and arms tucked up, as vulnerable as the foetus she suggested. I liked the plump, serious-looking nude who had one arm gracefully behind the back of her head – all the curving grace of a swan. I liked a pink and red nude with glowing flesh-tones. I liked everything.

'They're beautiful,' Bella murmured.

Modi looked grateful. 'You don't think they're lustful? Dante says the lustful are in circle two of hell.'

'I don't think you've got anything to worry about. This is great work,' I said. 'Stop giving them away.'

Modi shrugged. He knew he could do another, a replacement, just as quickly.

'You are a wonderful artist.' I smiled at Modi, who shrugged again in reply. There was a Modi cult in Montparnasse, led by the Belgian painter, Vlaminck, and I could see why.

'Your drawings are a hymn to women,' Bella said. 'You make love to us and celebrate us with the strokes of your pencil and pen.'

'Well said, Bella!' I was proud of her for that.

'Thank you, Bella,' Modi said. '"Love drew us onward to consuming death."' He spoke mockingly, quoting Dante as ever, but there were tears in his eyes.

I smiled at Bella. We were at one now, with Modi there. I simply wanted us to be at one when he left.

Rosalie appeared with the same food for Modi as we had ordered. She gave me a dazzling smile as she put the plates down, and was duly rewarded by a scowl from Bella. I put my arm round Rosalie's waist. She put her hand on my shoulder, then kissed my cheek. Serves Bella right, I thought. Serves her right for seeing Zadkine.

As we ate, there was a brief silence. Modi smothered his food in salt and pepper, as he always did. He could not stand the bland, in food, in books, in women, in life – although women and life were much the same thing to Modi.

When the conversation started up again, it turned into a familiar channel, the visit of the dealers and which pieces we were going to present. Now I felt at ease, not conscious of the person I was trying to be. I encouraged Modi to show the dealers his tender and beautiful nude sketches. Bella backed me. Modi demurred.

'I'm definitely going to include my portrait of Indenbaum and his wife,' Modi said. 'But after that, I don't know. I wanted to capture Indenbaum's caution.' Modi laughed. Indenbaum was a good man, indeed he was known as the Samaritan for helping his fellow artists so much, but he was more like a bank clerk than a painter.

'How can he be like that?' Modi once said. 'How can an artist be like that? Me, I want *une vie brève mais intense.*'

Bella translated it for me. 'A life that is brief but intense.'

'Yes,' Modi said. 'Not crabbed with caution. But what about you, Moyshe? What will you submit?'

'This dealer visit is my big chance,' I blurted out, without thinking. 'I intend to work every hour God sends. I need to sleep properly during the day. There won't be any more lunches, wasting time like this.'

The First Vision

I had no wish to go. I had no choice. We have no choice
in these matters. The Prophet Elijah appeared to me and
said I must 'visit' – his word – this sad event. It was as
simple as that.

My being, my essence, began to fill with Modi
– with Amedeo Modigliani. All my memories and
experiences of him accrued to me at once, so I was as
full as I could be of him.

With a few notable exceptions, like Baroness Hélène
d'Oettingen, who was Polish, Modi's lovers were
Anglo-Saxon women: British, American, Canadian, the
occasional Australian.

There was an English governess called Annie
Playden. There was Simone Thiroux, a Canadian
student who bore him a son. She wrote him a letter
from home, a heart-moving plea for a shard of affection,
promising to make no demands.

But more complex, more passionate, longer lasting
and more central to Modi's affections was the passion
with an angular, though attractive, brunette, a British
art journalist, Beatrice Hastings.

Kisling once asked – asked Modi, not her – if he
could paint Beatrice naked. Modi refused, although he
let all his other women pose naked for other artists.

Beatrice wrote for an influential art magazine called
The New Age. She was among the first to write about
Picasso, but Modi was supremely above using her to
further his career by writing about him, to her intense
fury. He refused it.

Not that she was without influence on his art itself,
far from it. During their rare interludes of tranquillity
and harmony, it was Beatrice who finally turned Modi
from sculpture back to painting. She was the only one

he would listen to, on that subject.

But there was not much listening going on, on any subject. Not much peace, or quiet, or reflection. I heard their loves through the walls of my atelier; I heard their screams through the walls of my atelier. Screams of love and hate.

They had some of the most erudite fights in Paris. They used to fight in verse. He would yell Dante at her. She would scream back Dante Gabriel Rossetti or Milton, who Modi especially detested.

The punching, the slapping, the scratching with Beatrice used to bring on Modi's snot streaming – he was always prone to snot-dribbles from the nose. I never knew whether this was from the hashish or a symptom of his TB. His coughing fits, too, grew worse at the height of his battles with Beatrice.

When he wasn't fighting her, he was fighting other men over her. There was a bloody fight in a café with the sculptor Alfred Pina who Modi accused of making eyes at Beatrice. Modi ended up sprawled on his back semi-conscious on the cobblestones.

Eventually, she fled from their incessant slaughter of each other; from the blows, from the raging their passion had become. She just disappeared off the scene.

As soon as he realised she was gone, Modi dashed off a nude pencil sketch of her. She is holding a towel just below her sex. Her hair is piled high on her head, ending in a thick plait falling to her naked shoulder. Her high small round breasts are as beautiful as only Modi could make them. Although her face is calm, Modi has emphasised Beatrice's engorged clitoris. He pinned the nude sketch of Beatrice in the middle of his easel in his atelier, vowing not to take it down or paint or draw another subject until he found her.

I have never, never, never seen Modi like he was then. None of the *abeilles*, not even Soutine, his unlikely spiritual brother, could console him or apply so much as a smudge of balm to his spirit.

Not me, either, me who admired and adored him so much. Nor the saintly calm of Samaritan Indenbaum, who helped everybody. Not Osip Zadkine, for even Zadkine loved Modi and behaved *almost* like a mensch with him.

Inconsolable, then, Modi ran from café to café the length and breadth of Montparnasse, then Montmartre, calling her name, bellowing out his agony like a stuck bull. To no avail. He never saw her again.

Modi's sanity and almost certainly his life was saved by the dealer Léopold Zborowski – known as Zbo – and his wife, Hanka. In Modi's portrait, the dealer is shown head and shoulders in an open-necked shirt. He is facing the viewer, but Modi has shown him with his almond-shaped gem-blue eyes hooded, as if he were blind – a gently satirical comment on art-dealers generally, rather than aimed at Zbo, who he loved.

Despite the hooded eyes and the characteristic Modigliani long neck, Zbo is shown in all his beauteous glory as the second most handsome man in Paris, after Modi himself. Interestingly, though, he has reduced Zbo's muscular power, making him more effete, even effeminate.

Nevertheless, this painting is a triumph. Modi once said 'The human face is the supreme creation of nature. Paint it and you paint life.' And there is the living Zbo, supremely created: full lips, sculptured-neat beard, long hair parted to the right to give a louche look. Even his nose is a ski-jump to glory. Like all Modi's portraits, it is an exercise in how far you can distort beauty and still retain beauty.

Zborowski was a middle-class, Polish intellectual poet, studying French at the Sorbonne, who had blundered into art dealing. After the break-up with Beatrice Hastings, Zbo and his wife Hanka took Modi in to their caravanserai on rue Joseph Bara, near the Luxembourg, where they lived with their dog, a stray they named Paddy (after Paderewski) who they fed on ham sandwiches.

They bought Modi canvases, paint, brushes. They made him take down the sketch of Beatrice to make his easel free again. They kept him away from the brandy and the ether. They made him paint. They paid him fifteen francs a day and all the models he could have. They even found the models for him, models who would make him forget Beatrice – there was Anna (one of his best-known sitters), Lunia Czechowska and Paulette – the girl with the ribbon in one of Modi's most famous paintings.

So Modi slowly began Life After Beatrice – which kept him in one piece until he went back to The Hive and met Jeanne Hébuterne.

Jeanne was surely the most beautiful woman in all creation – truly the female counterpart to Modi's male beauty. Her full lips were crescents of beauty. Her slightly fleshy nose was just imperfect enough to be perfect. Her eyes were the green of a glacial mountain stream. Her skin was ethereal, a translucent white. It was set off by the auburn tints in her dark, full, long hair.

Of all the females circling Modi, like bees round a flower, she was the brightest, the most suitable, the most natural. There was her temperament, you see: she was even and regular and calm, reassuring after the wild swings of Beatrice. She was of gentle spirit, with a sad dignity which held much in reserve, which any man would wish to explore, even aside from her beauty.

Her very proportions reassured Modi. Jeanne was petite, tiny in fact. She tucked into him, head on his shoulder, seeking protection. Beatrice had squared up to him. Almost as tall as Modi, Beatrice had been able to bloody his damaged nose and pummel his weakened body during their fights. But protecting Jeanne made Modi stronger, healed him.

Also, unlike Beatrice, Jeanne was no outside observer, not an art journalist who always put Modi on his guard, fearing betrayal. At times, Beatrice made him feel inferior to other artists, with her pointy intellect.

But Jeanne came from an artistic milieu, not an intellectual one. Her brother, André, was a Salon-exhibited painter. Jeanne herself was a first-water artist, trained at the Colarossi, a decent studio. I have always believed that if Jeanne's paintings had been by a man, they would have achieved recognition, even fame. Her oil of *La Ruche*, seen from a steep perspective through a winter tree, is superb.

Soutine, who spoke directly into Modi's soul, told him to marry Jeanne almost every day. Gentle Jeanne did not condemn Soutine and criticise him, as everybody else did.

For his part, Soutine worshipped her, adopting a doggish devoted persona in her presence. Serving up votive worship of Jeanne became one of the main pleasures of Soutine's life. He dreamed openly of a bourgeois wedding, white-dressed Jeanne and black-suited Modi, and himself, newly scrubbed, as best man.

The dream was shared by Jeanne, who was at heart a bourgeoise, too. But the very bourgeois-Catholic nature of her background put paid to it, even as a dream. Her father, Achille Casimir, objected to Modi on grounds of age – Modi was thirty-five, Jeanne nineteen, when they met.

Her even more hidebound mother, Eudoxie, loathed Modi as a talentless boor; a badly brought-up dauber. And a Jew, to boot. Eudoxie did not want her daughter consorting with a Jew and she said so, often, both to Jeanne and to Modi.

When Jeanne became pregnant with Modi's child

she broke off all contact with the pair of them.

Full of Modi, inside and out, I followed the Prophet, because I had to, because I had no choice. But it was still a shock, the sight of him, as big a shock as I have ever had.

Modi was below us, in a bed covered by a grimy brown blanket, so thin we could see through it. The tuberculosis – by now it had progressed to tuberculous meningitis and the booze and the hash had all combined and conspired to wreck his beautiful face. He was puffed up, full-bearded with a straggly and matted beard, accentuating his waxy complexion. His eyes were red-rimmed, the lids blinking constantly.

He was in agony.

While we were watching, nobody was tending him. There was a tin of sardines on the filthy floor, encrusted with flies. As we watched, the Prophet and I, Modi hauled himself up on one elbow to spit blood into a cracked and stained chamber pot. As we watched, the Prophet and I, Modi died.

We stayed there, still.

The generous and graceful Kisling arrived from *La Ruche* and took an impression for a death mask. Kisling and Indenbaum paid for Modi's funeral. Back at *La Ruche*, in human form, I stayed with Soutine for forty-eight hours, day and night, for fear he would kill himself from grief.

Bella was magnificent. She took shifts with me, watching over Soutine, when I needed to sleep or to work. (Yes, I continued to work on my paintings.)

A letter arrived from Modi's beloved brother in Lombardy: 'Bury him like a prince.' No special arrangements were needed for that. Modi *was* a prince, a prince among men. Yet still human bathos lowered. Modi's ID papers had been stolen. We needed help from our friendly policeman, Henri Zamoron at the *préfecture* at the rue Delambre, before we could get permission for him to be buried.

The dealers had been working together. Knowing Modi was dying, they held his paintings back. As soon as he died, they released his work in a glare of publicity for the romantically dead artist.

They made a killing from Modi's work, needing to pay him nothing.

But there was something more the Prophet wanted me to see. We flew to the rue de la Grande Chaumière. There, on the third floor, Jeanne Hèbuterne was at the window. As we watched, she jumped, sailing gracefully down, smashing herself to death on the cobbles below, with Modi's unborn child within her, dying with her.

Back at *La Ruche*, I was luminous with rage at the Prophet.

'Why did you make me see that? And don't say "Oh, you will forget it." I know I will forget it. But why did you make me see that?'

'Because you are an artist – a great artist.'

To my horror, I caught myself feeling flattered by the compliment, my rage subsiding, though not completely.

'You must know everything,' the Prophet continued. 'You must experience everything.'

I started to cry. The Prophet embraced me. I let myself be comforted.

I was calming. 'Was … is … was Modi one of the eighteen? One of the eighteen Jews who will die in the terrible coming times?'

The Prophet looked surprised, shocked even. 'Oh no! Modi will die of natural causes. You have just seen it, Moyshe! Seen it yourself. Silly boy. No, the eighteen Jews in the coming horror will be murdered.'

I was putting the finishing touches to *Dedicated to My Fiancée*, painting by daylight, unusually for me. It was painful to look at, this painting, I felt I was laying bare the disturbed state of my artist's psyche as I struggled to come to terms with Bella herself, with being forced up against Bella in the cramped impoverished conditions of the atelier, and with my jealousy of Bella with other men, which she fuelled so expertly.

A huge splash of angry red dominates the middle ground, most untypical of my work, screaming sexual fear of Bella. Against this background I have a disembodied female, a stockinged leg, the head of a horned bull, some hands and a palette whose every splash of paint is red, showing how Bella had infused my artist's life with lust and pain.

There was a polite knock on the door of the atelier. This was mid-afternoon, when there was strong northern light. Bella was out, God only knows where. I could not sleep. I was reading a week-old copy of *Le Figaro* I had borrowed from M. Ostroun in an effort to learn some French.

The knuckle-rap on the door was Commissaire Zamoron from the *préfecture* at the rue Delambre. It had to be. Nobody else knocked at the door like that.

'Come in, Henri,' I sang out, genuinely pleased to put aside the incomprehensible newspaper to talk with our favourite *flic*.

Commissaire Henri Zamoron strode in, beaming a broad smile, arms spread wide ready to hug me. We embraced in the French manner, then I steeled myself for the cheek kisses.

Zamoron was middle-aged, about medium height but stocky, his pale face dominated by a downward-drooping moustache which failed to depress his habitual good humour. Whenever I saw him, I pictured him in his office, seated at his solemn desk, in his suit with serious papers before him and behind him some of the best paintings in

Paris, covering every centimetre of the wall. His specialised in works by Utrillo and Foujita, but he bought anything he liked, including work by nearly all of us in the École Juive.

I met Henri Zamoron during my first week in Paris. He made it a point to greet all the new arrivals at *La Ruche*. With the invaluable Modi translating, he told me he had been given the job of reporting on Kikoine's wife, Rosa, who was listed as a known Bolshevik, though not an active threat.

Modi told me later that it was – inevitably – Osip Zadkine who had denounced her as a Bolshevik. Osip had hated Bolshevism since his time in London, a city which was apparently something of a hotbed of anarchism and Bolshevism.

Henri Zamoron, typically, regarded Osip as more suspect for the denunciation than Kikoine or his wife for being denounced. But he had signed up as a patron of Zadkine's, buying many of his sculptures, partly because he loved Osip's work (actually, so do I) and partly in order to keep an eye on him.

He had – literally – sat on the file on Rosa Kikoine, with her leftist leanings and Russian revolutionary contacts, keeping it under the cushion of his office chair. Most of Zadkine's lovingly compiled reports on the Kikoines did not even make it under the cushion, going straight into Zamoron's waste-paper bin.

Zamoron waved his arms. 'Modi ...' he said, and mimed 'coming, on the way'. I nodded. The policeman could buy one of my drawings or paintings without language, we simply wrote figures on a piece of paper while he cooed appreciatively. But for anything more than that we needed Modi to translate. How would we ever manage without Modi?

Modi appeared after a couple of minutes, towing the inexpressibly lovely Jeanne Hébuterne, with whom he had just been making love, judging by the warm, flushed, pink state of them.

With Modi translating, Henri Zamoron asked to see a specific painting of mine, called *Dedicated to My Fiancée*. I waved at it, up on my easel.

Ever the innocent, I thought he wanted to buy *Dedicated to My Fiancée*. My innate optimism hid from me the illogicality and impossibility of even this dedicated art-lover wishing to buy a painting he had never seen and, as I thought, never heard of.

'The lamp looks like a phallus,' said the policeman, with mock severity.

The lovely Jeanne was hooting with laughter before the translation reached me. 'Modi is much bigger than that,' she said in French.

Modi translated and added his thanks in French and Yiddish.

Through everybody's laughter, Henri Zamoron said that Osip had threatened to report the picture if it was included in the forthcoming private show for the dealers. Giving a perhaps deliberately stereotypic Gallic shrug, Henri asked if I would be prepared to alter the picture. With thumb and forefinger he indicated the small degree of alteration required, but in the present context the gesture sent Jeanne into fresh gales of giggles.

Modi could hardly translate for laughing. With a couple of strokes of the brush I rendered the lamp less suggestive. I gave it, in effect, a smaller one. Like mine.

'Good, that's that settled,' Henri Zamoron said.

The policeman nodded with mock approval at my corrected picture, *Dedicated to My Fiancée*. Then he made a moue, as if tortured by inner anguish. All of us in my atelier, me, Modi and Jeanne recognised this as a preliminary to more trouble. And sure enough ...

'There are a couple more things,' Henri Zamoron said. He had a naturally soft speaking voice, which he never raised. I had never seen him angry.

'About me?' I asked.

'No, you're in the clear, Moyshe. It's Modi here and

Soutine, I'm afraid.'

Modi laughed, no trace of fear. The lovely Jeanne, though, gazed at him wide-eyed with trepidation.

'Go on,' Modi said through his laughter. 'What have I done?'

Henri Zamoron looked mock grave. 'According to two gentlemen who came into the *préfecture*, you attacked them outside the restaurant Spielman. An unprovoked attack it was. They had gone there for an innocent political discussion.'

Modi took a deep breath. His smile was forced now, though no less handsome for that. He started to speak, but the policeman held a hand up.

'Unfortunately, the case has gone to my esteemed colleague, Commissaire Descaves, who is a sympathiser of the right. It was probably Descaves who encouraged them to complain in the first place.'

This conversation between Modi and Zamoron was naturally enough in French. So far I had understood one word: Descaves. It made me shake. All of us in the École Juive knew and feared Commissaire Descaves. We all knew the famous 'Descaves story'.

Descaves had offered the bitter Pinchus Krémègne eighty francs for his Expressionist-style painting of Soutine's mother, done while he and Soutine were art students together. The painting was reminiscent of Kokoschka and rather good. Descaves gave the bitter artist twenty francs, saying that was all he had on him. He told Krémègne to come to the station for the rest.

So Krémègne, all downward-twisted mouth, thick moustache and anarchic black beret, shuffled round to the *préfecture* at the rue Delambre. There, Descaves told him he had already paid the full amount. He threatened to have the bitter one arrested if he made a fuss.

The incident of the swindle over a painting of Soutine's mother had the paradoxical, and completely illogical, effect of making Pinchus Krémègne's bile at Soutine even worse.

The bitter one had fled the pogroms in Vilnius, escaped by a hair's breadth and established himself in Paris. He had unstintingly helped Soutine when he trailed in, some time later.

Nobody knew exactly why he later turned on Soutine, though Soutine's combustible mix of clinging, nagging helplessness and incandescent genius sparked fury wherever he appeared. Most likely, the gap in artistic ability between the two sometime fellow students becoming blazingly obvious was the simple cause of the bitter one's bitterness. His wince-making nickname in the art world, 'the poor man's Soutine', did nothing to reduce the bitterness.

And no doubt there was an inborn tendency to bitterness on the bitter one's part, which would have found him something to be bitter about in paradise. Certainly, Pinchus Krémègne's seemingly inexhaustible capacity for bitterness survived the happiest marriage at *La Ruche* – although his portrait of his wife in a cloche hat makes her look as miserable as him. Perhaps misery is what they had in common. The bitterness also survived a degree of worldly success.

I should perhaps declare an interest here: Pinchus Krémègne does not like me any more than he likes Soutine. (He loves Modi, though. Everybody loves Modi.) He interprets my frugality and lack of ostentation as meanness. He keeps telling Bella how mean I am, and I believe he is influencing her.

His feelings about me, however, are comparatively mild, a sort of afterthought-bitterness.

While I was dwelling on all this, Modi started to speak again but Zamoron spoke over him. 'Drumont and his friends on the far right will make sure they get a good lawyer. Descaves will help them. All I can do, I'm afraid, is keep you informed and find you as good a lawyer as I can, if it comes to that.'

By now, Modi and Jeanne were thoroughly scared. Modi licked his lips. 'There's something else, isn't there? You said ...'

Henri Zamoron nodded, also relieved to be passing onto firmer ground.

'Yes. You know Soutine's little trick?'

'Which one?' said Modi.

'The one with the paintings.'

Soutine used to sell a painting to a fellow artist at *La Ruche*, often somebody who was only buying it to help him out. He would then claim the painting needed more work – which it often did, but that was not why he asked. When the painting was returned, he re-sold it to someone else, telling the first buyer that the painting had been lost, stolen or damaged in restoration.

The main victim of this little jape, but no means the only one, was Indenbaum. Léon Indenbaum told me that Soutine had played this same trick on him seven times. By now, Indenbaum knew what was coming, but played along to keep Soutine from starvation.

'Who complained?' I asked. 'Who went to the police? Surely not Indenbaum. I don't believe it.'

'Neither do I,' said Zamoron, with Modi translating. 'It was an anonymous complaint, a letter ...'

Three of us said 'Zadkine!' in unison.

'I think not,' Henri Zamoron said. 'It's not his modus operandi. Osip would simply have complained to me. He knows he can do that. This letter was not addressed to any individual. Osip would have used his knowledge of the system and knowledge of us.'

We were all lost in admiration of Henri Zamoron's forensic skill, but he cut any compliments short with his traffic-stopping gesture. 'Fortunately, I found the anonymous letter before Descaves did. He doesn't even know about it. Yet. So I can sit on this one, too.' Zamoron gave an appropriate mime. 'But friend Chaim has got to stop this trick. Now.'

'I don't know where he is,' I said.

'I do.' Modi always knew where Soutine was. 'He's painting Indenbaum.'

Modi moved to the door, knowing he was needed to translate. Jeanne blindly followed Modi, as she did in life and unto death. I started to go back to my newspaper.

'We need you to come, too, Moyshe,' Modi said.

'Do you? I don't mind. But … Why?'

Modi smiled his gorgeous smile. 'Chaim respects you. He is even slightly afraid of you.'

'Really?' I couldn't imagine anybody being afraid of me.

'He regards you as austere and disciplined. The Monk of *La Ruche*.'

Jeanne giggled at that, clenched fist in front of her face.

'He is desperate for your good opinion of him,' Modi added.

This truly amazed me. If I had thought about it at all, which I had not, I would have said that Chaim Soutine was entirely indifferent to my opinion of him. Aloud, I said, 'I would have thought it was your opinion that mattered to him, Modi.'

'Not really.' Modi looked serious. 'Or not *exactly*. You see, he already has my good opinion. He knows that. I will always love him whatever he does. He has yet to win you over, so he is more likely to do what you want.'

'So much wisdom from one so lovely!' It came out before I could stop it. Young Jeanne giggled again.

'If *you* tell him to stop playing that trick, he'll stop,' Modi added.

I shrugged. 'All right,' I said.

If it had been work time, that is to say at night, I would not have gone. But now I had nothing to lose except sleep. So off we all trooped to Indenbaum's atelier.

Léon Indenbaum knew Zadkine from Vitebsk, but I did not meet him until he came to *La Ruche*. Many of the painters at *La Ruche* painted each other – Modigliani painted Soutine more than once, Soutine painted a striking portrait of a Hive denizen called Richard – a Christian, so not one of the École Juive.

Married painters were often painted with their wives: Modi painted a superb portrait of the sculptor Jacques Lipchitz with his wife, Bertha. Soutine started a portrait of his friend and fellow graduate of the École des Beaux Arts in Minsk, Moise (or Michel) Kikoine, with his wife, Rosa, the alleged Bolshevik, but never finished it.

Indenbaum, the Samaritan, however, was unusual in offering to pose for both Modi and Soutine only so that he could discreetly give them money. He wanted Modi to take longer over his portrait than Modi himself wished, solely because he was paying Modi by the hour and wished to pay him more.

Modigliani usually dashed off portraits in one sitting, if not in minutes or even in seconds as he did when he sketched in cafés. He was unused to taking as long as Indenbaum wished and, not entirely gratefully, claimed afterwards that slowing down so much had spoiled the portrait.

There is no evidence for this. Although a distinctive 'elongated' Modigliani head, the portrait of Indenbaum captures his solid decency. The receding hair, which has left a tufted island of erect black spikes stranded on a bald dome of skull, makes Indenbaum look highly intelligent, if not downright scholarly.

In Modi's portrait, Indenbaum is wearing a casual, pale green turtle-neck pullover. Soutine started to paint him more formally, in a jacket but with a more relaxed look. It would have been a masterpiece if he had finished it.

I am sensitive to smell. The smell of eau de cologne, turpentine oil and Argyrol hit me like a blow in the face as we all entered Indenbaum's atelier – Modi and Jeanne in the lead, then me, then Henri Damoron.

Chaim Soutine was as ragged and filthy as ever, but at least he had more than a coat on. He was at Indenbaum's easel, using Indenbaum's palette and paints, on a canvas supplied by Indenbaum – a seventeenth-century canvas, already painted on. Soutine complained the weave was too thin on any newer canvas.

The portrait of Indenbaum in a suit was coming along beautifully. Soutine did not stop painting, nor did he show so much as a flicker of embarrassment when asked by Modi to discontinue swindling his present sitter and others with a crude trick everybody knew about.

'All right. I won't do it again. Anything else?'

'Chaim, it wasn't me who complained.' Indenbaum was distraught, but everybody believed him.

'Keep still.' Soutine jumped up and down in frustration, splashing paint from Indenbaum's brush all over his unprotected filthy shirt. 'You'd think people who painted would make better sitters, wouldn't you?'

Indenbaum looked contrite. He loved *La Ruche* and everybody in it. It was Indenbaum who was always comparing life at *La Ruche* to a dream, from which we awakened only when we left.

I knew who had penned the anonymous letter to the police, denouncing Soutine. It came to me in a sharp picture of the perpetrator. It was indeed not Indenbaum, the main but not the sole victim; that was unthinkable. Nor was it Osip Zadkine, Damoron was surely right about that.

It was Pinchus Krémègne, Soutine's bitter friend from Minsk Academy, the one who had found Soutine hanging, saved his life, then seemed to regret it.

It was him.

The Second Vision

Once again I did not want to go. Once again I was part of an exterior force's purposes for me – but aren't we all? This time it was not Modi I was absorbing into my being but Soutine, and no doubt for the same reason.

We witnessed Soutine's transformative moment, the Prophet and I. We witnessed a Philadelphia industrialist, Dr Albert C. Barnes, whose fortune was based on Argyrol, seeing Soutine's masterpiece *The Pastry Boy* and having the exquisite good taste to buy everything Soutine had ever painted, within the hour.

And then the Prophet and I witnessed the change in Chaim Soutine, the terrible change. He instantly repudiated the genius early work of his time at *La Ruche*, the work which had so changed his fortunes. He destroyed many, many of his greatest paintings, slashed them with a knife. He replaced them with cluttered and hysterical landscapes of Céret, where he and other artists gathered, a place where prettiness pasted over the lack of all culture and tradition.

He metamorphosed from a living pile of rags to a dandy, but looked ill at ease in the fine clothes, like an acrobat wearing a suit of armour. He refused to speak Russian or Hebrew any more, but as his French was lousy, nobody could understand anything he said. He turned on his old friends, even Modi.

He smoked Lucky Strikes which made him cough, weakening his already poor health even further. The spicy food he loved made him ill, so he had to keep dosing himself with bismuth. He could have as many women as he wanted, but he could not enjoy any of them because his collapsing body left him impotent.

In short, all the sadness of Israel came over him, as the generous and elegant Moise Kisling put it when he painted him. Chaim Soutine was the most wretched, the most lonely success in all creation. Was he happier before Dr Albert Barnes? No, but it was a more fulfilling, more companionable kind of misery. And he painted better. (We all did our best work at *La Ruche*, not only me.)

It was his end, Soutine's end, we had come to witness. The Prophet had done it to me again, first Modi, now Soutine. O Prophet, why must I see these things?

The end was presaged by stomach pains. The bismuth no longer helped. All that hiding from the Gestapo was taking its toll, as was sleeping in the forest because any building at all had become dangerous.

By the time he was admitted to the Saint-Michel clinic he was doubled over in agony from inner bleeding, from peritonitis. He was dosed with medicaments – Papaverine, Laristin – which achieved nothing.

We watched him from the wall above his bed. He was chalky pale and writhing. We could see his morphia-dreams, we lived them with him. He dreamed up a white goat, right out of a Chagall painting. The goat danced attendance on him.

He was transferred to specialists in the 16th arrondissement, to the Maison de Santé Lyautey, followed by a white goat. At irregular intervals he would interrupt his own drooling, screaming and moaning with quite well-argued diatribes against Picasso and Braque. He also inveighed against the cows and roosters in my paintings.

For the first time in years, his days as an art student came back to him. We saw his thoughts, the Prophet and I. We saw him proud of his blue student uniform, back then. His landlady in Minsk was the widow of a railway worker. She walked with a limp. That fascinated Soutine, who wanted to convey the motion in paint. Not to convey rushing speed, like the Futurists, but to convey a limping old woman moving laboriously through life.

Soutine's first name, Chaim, means 'life' in Hebrew. But as we watched, Chaim had no more *chaim*. He breathed his last. His sadness was over.

Back in my atelier at The Hive, I asked the Prophet a

124

question: 'Is Chaim one of the eighteen Jews to die in the terrible coming times?'

'Yes, certainly. Chaim will be very ill. But he would not have died at that time if the Gestapo had not hounded him. He would have retained enough strength to overcome his stomach ulcers.'

'So that is Soutine and my teacher, Yury Pen?'

'Yes.'

'Sixteen more. Sixteen to go.'

I wondered who the other sixteen Jews were.

I was in Osip's room, looking at his sculpture of *The Three Friends*. Osip was not there. Bella was not there. I suspected that Osip and Bella were out somewhere together, but I did not know.

The three figures sculpted in bronze by Zadkine as *The Three Friends* are of indeterminate sex. The figures are shown in three-quarter length, from head to mid-thigh. The heads of two of them are touching. One of these has a hand protectively across her or his bosom. The third figure, whose head is apart from the other two, has a clenched fist.

The question is, who are the two who are together? Is it Bella and me or Bella and Osip? Is it even Osip and me, after all we have known one another since childhood? Similarly, the figure apart could be Osip or more likely me or even Bella.

I do not know if Osip completed this sculpture before or after he seduced Bella.

Next day, The Hive was throbbing, the loudening buzzing inside going all round the octagonal walls, into every crack and crevice, lifting the building into the air, for those with eyes to see it. The Hive was also shaking from the blows from Osip Zadkine's sculpture, to make sure I could never forget him.

Zadkine was an expert at making noise. When he wasn't hammering, his braying bellow of a voice was so loud while he told his anecdotes of his stay in England that he was called 'thundering Jupiter' by everyone at *La Ruche* but me. I still called him 'the serpent'.

Bella had suddenly decided she liked dogs, except for Thea's dog, Marquis, which she had taken to denigrating as ferociously as she now denigrated the beast's owner. In particular, Marquis was compared unfavourably to Osip Zadkine's dog, Kalouche. Bella became so fond of Kalouche, she took to accompanying Osip whenever he exercised the beast.

I truly could not understand what she found of interest in Osip. To me Osip Zadkine was nothing but a penny whistle, an empty shell which sounds when you blow into it. But there is no accounting for taste, at least not other people's taste.

So this exercise took place regularly, right out in the country, in the forest of Meudon. It involved Osip Zadkine, Bella and Kalouche catching a tram to the forest, often with a picnic. Osip's generous allowance from his father guaranteed the gourmet nature of this repast.

Osip Zadkine was an insomniac – as was at least one of the other École Juive sculptors, Jacques Lipchitz. Osip did his sculpting, and attendant shaking of The Hive, in the late morning, when he woke up. This was when I was most deeply asleep after a long night of painting. He would then embark on the picnic, nearly every afternoon, with his dog and my Bella both on a lead, as I thought of it.

Lately, they had taken to watching the occasional execution at the Santé together, as well – minus the dog on these occasions. And then lunch at Rosalie's. Jealousy is as cruel as the tongs of torturers, but without jealousy there is no love.

We quarrelled frequently, Bella and I, usually over my jealousy, which I did not bother to deny. After the quarrels, I absorbed myself even more completely in my preparations for the immanent art-dealer visit – my big chance.

But my suspicions continued to eat me from the inside.

I went to see Modi and asked him directly, bluntly. The look on his face was enough. I surrendered to my tears, leaning forward in my chair, covering my face in my hands, heaving sobs into my palms.

Modi came over to me, stroking the top of my head. 'You don't have to torture yourself, picturing them together. He only did it once.'

I looked up at hm. '*He*? Don't you mean *they*?'

Modi sighed his wise sigh, never more the oracle than now. 'He told her he loved her, when he seduced her ...'

'Where, when?'

'Out at Meudon. In the open air.'

'Zadkine hates the outdoors.'

'How little you know him, Moyshe. He picked up his passion for *le footing*, as he calls it, in England.'

'Oh, one of his English affectations. Does he smoke that bloody pipe while he walks?'

Modi laughed. 'They won't do it again. Osip thinks he's a character in a novel, usually a Russian novel. He's very self-conscious. Now he's riddled with guilt.'

'That's good of him.'

Modi laughed again. 'Osip told her it was a mistake.'

That made me angry on Bella's behalf. 'It's his way of getting at me.'

'That is not very gallant, is it? But yes, that's part of it.'

'I'll ...'

Modi interrupted, cut across me. 'No, Moyshe, you won't do anything. At least that's my advice. Bella will get tired of him. And soon. Pretend it never happened. Don't give Osip the satisfaction of knowing you know. That's what he wants.'

I nodded. I knew he was right.

We fell silent, both of us. But the silence was broken by a massive commotion outside. We looked at each other. Feet stampeded past the door, there was shouting from the corridor. We both knew what it was, from experience, from intuition.

Then somebody said the word, as more feet thundered past outside: 'Suicide'.

On, no! Soutine, Soutine. Did Soutine die by his own hand after all? Chaim, what have you done?

Modi and I ran out to the corridor and followed the throng. Through the open door to his atelier, I saw a sculpture entitled *Head of the Painter Foujita*. Léon Indenbaum had carved this massy mahogany head of Tsuguharu Foujita, one of the non-Jewish painters at The Hive.

As the door swung wide open I saw the Good Samaritan Indenbaum hanging from a rafter, Foujita was screaming next to his head carved in wood. Poor Mme Indenbaum was screaming with him, still smelling of the Argyrol with which she had been cleaning the corridor. Various painters and sculptors were yelling and crying.

Inevitably, it was Modi who knew what to do. He lifted Indenbaum's legs and bellowed for a sharp knife. Somebody fetched M. Ostroun, who provided a lino-cutting knife. Indenbaum was cut down alive.

Nobody ever discovered the reason for this apparently inexplicable action. During the course of his long and by and large contented life, Indenbaum never did anything remotely like this again.

Imagine a teenage dance with all the boys – the dealers – along one wall and all the girls – the painters and sculptors – along the facing wall. But instead of eyeing the girls as such, the dealers eyed their wares, in the form of paintings, drawings and sculptures. These were lined up on the floor or leaning against the wall behind their creators, some of whom were petrified rigid, some nervously pacing.

The École Juive artists present were Osip Zadkine (sculptor), Léon Indenbaum (sculptor), Jacques Lipchitz (sculptor) and the painters Moyshe Shagal; Chaim Soutine; Amedeo Modigliani; Emmanuel Mané-Katz; the generous and elegant Moise Kisling; the jolly Bolshevik Moise

Kikoine, who brought his Bolshevik wife, Rosa; and the bitter Pinchus Krémègne.

Jeanne Hébuterne turned up later, following her beloved Modi, as ever. Bella did not wish to come, which I found a relief.

This coming-together – I wouldn't call it a meeting – of dealers and artists was taking place in the Exhibition Hall, the large barn-like outbuilding which had been built at the same time as the ateliers of *La Ruche*. The roof had plenty of skylighting, to show the paintings and sculptures in a good light, though as nobody had ever cleaned it, it was begrimed with dirt and dust. Light filtered through with difficulty, shrouding the works in unintended chiaroscuro.

While the two groups were still apart, the artists standing by their wares, the dealers in a tighter convivial knot, Modi started to tell the artists who all the dealers were.

As painted by Pierre Bonnard, the dealer Ambroise Vollard is the epitome of satisfied middle-aged prosperity. He is shown in his plush sitting room, with a massy Biedermeier dresser and floral furniture. Art is represented by an empty Van Gogh chair and a couple of Cézannes on the wall.

The dealer is slumped Buddha-like in the envelopingly comfortable upholstered armchair, the dome of his largely bald head bent tenderly over the grey and white cat curled up in his lap. He cuddles the cat, embraces it to his bosom. He is somnolent, at ease; his only concession to action the steady digestion of his last large meal.

Rumour had it that Bonnard insisted on the dealer posing holding the cat to stop him falling asleep. Ambroise Vollard did not so much suffer from narcolepsy as embrace it. If ever a disease was an extension of a man's natural character it was Vollard's narcolepsy.

Despite the bourgeois trappings, Vollard was an aristocrat, originally from La Réunion, a French dependency between Madagascar and Mauritius. Although many artists have dedicatedly died for art, Vollard the dealer went one better and died *by* art – a Maillol statue fell on his head when his car crashed, killing him instantly.

Vollard, as yet blissfully clear of falling sculpture, was by far the dominant figure among the dealers who descended on The Hive to see the works of the École Juive. He was dealer royalty you might say. The man had discovered Cézanne; he was the dealer for Gauguin, Manet, Renoir and Picasso; he was the dealer for Les Nabis, a group which included Bonnard and (fatally as it turned out) Aristide Maillol.

Vollard was the arbiter of taste. If Vollard said that what mattered in a painting was 'finish' then what mattered in a painting was 'finish'. 'Finish' was demanded, presented, aimed at, sought after, yearned for without anybody knowing quite what the term actually meant.

It was Vollard who had started the dealer trick of buying up everything an artist had produced, thus completely controlling the market, although by the time of the dealer visit here described all the dealers were doing it.

Such was Vollard's dominance that it was not the case that his gallery was in Paris's main art-street, the rue Lafitte (he started at 39, then progressed to 44). No, the obverse was the case: the rue Lafitte was the *rue des tableaux* because Vollard was there.

Vollard's dominance of the art world of Paris rested not only on his illustrious clients, but also on his knowing everybody who mattered, despite not moving very far or very fast. His reach, his influence, was unrivalled and all-embracing.

The curator of the Louvre, no less, M. Migeon, would open his establishment out of hours when Vollard wished to see a painting. Vollard could get artists – the dealers actually called them 'amateurs', or sometimes 'dabblers' – mentioned or even reviewed in the *Journal des Artistes*. Get mentioned in the Journal des Artistes and you were made, your career on track, your life a success.

In the pudgy hands of a man like that rested the knife-thin difference between world fame and plenty for dinner, on the one hand, and the knowledge of utter failure followed by oblivion as the artist breathed his starving last, on the other.

It followed, then, that you did not cross a man like M. Vollard, the dealer. You did your best to please him.

I doubt that any of us painters and sculptors knew all the dealers, except Modi. Most of us, though, knew some or most of them. As to me, I knew who nearly all of them were, from my walks round Paris.

They were all there, that day, all the major dealers: Durand-Ruel, the Zborowskis, Bernheim, Kahnweiler, Uhde, Paul Rosenberg, Sagot, Libaude, Charles Malpel, Diot, Berthe Weill. Would one of them be my dealer by the end of the afternoon? I still had had no actual contact with any of the French dealers, only with Herwath Walden from Germany, who had made contact with me.

Modi, in his gregarious element, gleefully pointed out who was who: he told us about the Zborowskis, Léopold and Hanka, his own dealers. He pointed them out. The ever-generous Modi had tried to get Zbo and Hanka interested in the rest of us, but they were indifferent to me and had taken against poor Chaim Soutine, especially Hanka.

Then, to bubbling murmurs of excitement, Modi crossed the floor from our side to the dealer side and back again, towing a little fat man. I knew who this was: Guillaume Chéron, a former wine dealer. He had been Modi's dealer for a while, putting him up, paying him a per diem, before Modi had been taken up by Zbo and Hanka. It was typical of Modi that he still had good relations with Chéron even after he had left.

I had peered into Chéron's gallery, on the rue La Boétie, quite a few times. I had indeed peered at Chéron himself, but had not spoken to him owing to the familiar problem of having no language he could understand to speak to him in.

This mutual incomprehension unfortunately extended to art. Chéron walked along the line of artists, all standing in front of their wares like stallholders at a market, clearly making for me. I smiled at him. I was not wearing make-up, but I had combed my hair. He wriggled, clearly attracted to me. Then he looked at my work.

I had *The Cattle Dealer, Dedicated to My Fiancée, Self-Portrait with Seven Fingers* and *The Wedding* on offer, in my space, all leaning against the wall of the Exhibition Hall. I stood aside to let Chéron look. And look he did, standing back with his arms on his well-submerged hips.

His whole body began to move up and down, then from side to side. M. Chéron was laughing.

Chéron walked briskly back to the dealer side of the Exhibition Hall, still rolling with laughter. Modi put his arm round me, quickly distracting me from disappointment with gossip about the rest of the dealers.

There was the distinguished Paul Rosenberg. Heavy three-button coat open to display a three-piece suit thicker than the Exhibition Hall wall. His *private* collection included Ingres, Delacroix, Daumier, early Corot … The man was clearly a walking Louvre.

Paul Durand-Ruel, who dealt for many of the Impressionists, was the most significant dealer after Vollard. He too was a pioneer of the practice of buying up an artist's entire output cheap before they were known, then controlling the market.

Salvator Mayer was famous for the motto 'Goods are meant to circulate'. I did not understand what that meant, but pretended I did.

Another rue Lafitte dealer, Diot, dealt in Corot, Daumier and Jongkind.

Clovis Sagot was a former pastry cook. I knew Soutine had got wind of this, hoping to sell his painting of a pastry boy to him on the strength of it. Several dealers recommended painters to research a dealer's private life and interests, to make their wares more attractive, more of interest. Some even suggested choosing subjects to paint according to the dealer's interests.

Clovis Sagot was also known for the sign outside the Sagot Gallery, almost next door Vollard, at 46 rue Lafitte, offering 2,500 per cent gains for speculators in art. In an unintended topographical echo, Clovis Sagot and Vollard were standing in the order of their galleries in a line next to Bernheim, who was Matisse's dealer, and Durand-Ruel, their neighbours in rue Lafitte.

The dealer Soulié was famous for buying to order – meaning that if a buyer wanted a bunch of flowers to hang on the wall, Soulié would activate his artist contacts and get one. Picasso had picked up twenty francs for a vase of flowers, doing it this way.

The dealer Andry-Farcy, mainly based in Grenoble, was currently authenticating a Rembrandt.

Gérard was a dealer at the Boulevards.

Over there was the dealer Brame.

So many dealers. I stopped listening to Modi. Only one dealer was missing. Mine. Where was Herwath Walden?

I edged forward. Boldness does not come easily to me. But I edged forward and forward, hoping to be noticed. I could hear the dealers. Was my French improving? To some extent. I caught snatches of what they were saying.

'... the fricassee of rabbit cooked in wine. It's a speciality of mère Adèle at Le Lapin Agile.'

'The Portuguese oysters. Just eight sous a dozen, I tell

you.'

'The *boeuf mironton* ...'

'An excellent lunch at Larve's ...'

'Nipponese food. Has anybody tried it? Eels au caramel. Bean jam ...'

'The *canard au sang* at the Tour Argent. Incomparable!'

'The Café Voisin ...'

The dealers seemed in no hurry to cross the floor of the Exhibition Hall to us. While we awaited their pleasure, they moved from the subject of lunch and started discussing their artist-clients, all far better known than a group of exotic Yiddish-speaking Jews.

'Corot said the artist must be able to correct nature. *Ars addit naturae.* That's what Corot said.'

I needed Modi's help with the next one: '*Ne pas vendre la peau de l'ours avant de l'avoir tué.*'

'It means don't sell the skin before the bear's been killed,' said Modi, smiling benignly.

'And what the hell does *that* mean?'

Modi grinned. 'It means only buy when you know the work will appreciate.'

I went back to listening:

'These days, I refuse to deal at all outside the hours of twelve noon and two.'

'Only good for the Boulevard Clichy ...'

'I tried Guillaume's trick the other day. I persuaded some hayseed to let me keep the painting he was selling for half a day, for valuation. The second he was out the door, I phoned everybody, absolutely everybody, and quoted a basement price for them to quote the hayseed for the painting. When the hayseed picked up the picture, at the end of the afternoon, I quoted him a price above what I had told everybody else, but still half what it was worth. The hayseed said he would try elsewhere. I gave him my blessing. He was back next evening, footsore. I even told him the price had gone down since yesterday and he still sold.'

'Père Tanguy's little colour shop in the rue Clauzel …'

'For years I have avoided anything "neo" or "post" or "-ism" or "-ist". And then I thought, why not come up with one's own. So I started Gagaism, a genre for painters in premature senility; Mamaism, an over-preponderance of Virgin Marys; Baabaaism, a school of painters who follow each other like sheep; and then Tataism, for painters who have broken away from groups, as they seem to do with tedious regularity.'

'Monet is a Greek. I mean in the purity of his art. He looks at nature with the ingenious eye of a Praxiteles.'

'Take it to Chapuis' workshop, I said, that's all it's good for.'

'How is it possible to like both Delacroix and Ingres? Delacroix so full of fire, Ingres so cold?'

'Did you like the one about the connoisseur shut up as a madman for buying a Van Gogh?'

'I was stuck with this painting of a foot, had it for months. Then I hit on a wheeze. I called it *Rêve enchanté*. Sold it within the day.'

'A client asked me the other day which way up a landscape went. I told him it wasn't a landscape, it was a man playing a guitar.'

'The other day, I spilt my cup of coffee all over a painting. Sold it within the hour by calling the brown stain a "tone echo".'

'I paid ten francs for a monotype by Degas that I fished out of a box on the quays.'

'Drawings by Forain and Rops. Much in demand …'

'… a potential purchaser at Bercy …'

'… a fine Guys drawing for ten francs.'

The dealers were coming over, en masse, en bloc, like a phalanx of soldiers. Suddenly they stopped, midway between the far wall and our wall, where we had our wares displayed. As the de facto leader, Vollard rolled plumply forward first, clouded around with a miasmic smell of curried chicken.

'Has anybody got a painting of a Zouave?' Vollard boomed. 'I have a customer who wants a painting of a Zouave.'

Cue confusion while Modi attempted to render 'Zouave' in Yiddish. The nearest he could get, unfortunately, was 'Cossack'. We all looked at each other. There was bewilderment – Soutine, Indenbaum, Moise Kisling, Michel Kikoine. There was aspiration – Osip Zadkine, Pinchus Krémègne. There was churning nausea – me.

Mané-Katz stepped forward, just ahead of Osip Zadkine. 'I'll do it,' he said. 'I'll do you one. You'll like it.'

There was a buzz of mixed admiration – what chutzpah, what nerve! – and condemnation at this subversion of the pure flame of art.

'Maney always was a grocer.' I intended to mutter that, but it came out loud and clear. It's amazing how my stammer deserts me when I most need it.

'Why?' Osip Zadkine said, lizard smile. 'We should all follow the market. It's fun.'

'Following the market is like following a mirage,' Modi said. I could have hugged him. 'Nobody knows where the market will be next time you look.'

At this point, Mané-Katz and Ambroise Vollard took themselves off into a corner to discuss the customer's exact requirements for his Zouave. Next time I looked their way, Vollard had found a chair from somewhere and had fallen asleep. Mané was bending over him anxiously, clearly concerned in case his patron of five minutes' standing had expired.

The dealer Soulié, sharp-featured, swarthy and short, the one famous for buying to order, was talking to Chaim Soutine. They were both looking intently at a Bonnard-like piece of his, one I rather admired, called *Jug with Lilacs*.

'I have a buyer who especially likes lilacs,' Soulié

was saying. 'A Mr and Mrs Futter from New York. The gentleman, Matthew H. Futter, grows lilacs.'

Soutine's round eyes were growing rounder. He was foaming with hope.

'The trouble is,' Soulié drawled, 'they have only a small flat. How big is this?'

'I don't know.'

Soulié whipped a folding rule from his coat pocket and measured it. 'It's fifty-five by forty-six point five. Can you either cut a bit off or do another one, smaller?'

'Um ...' Soutine, who had not eaten for two days, looked about to expire on the spot.

Gérard, the dealer at the Boulevards, strode athletically over to me. He lifted my canvases on high, one after the other.

'*Self-portrait with Seven Fingers*,' he murmured, ironically. 'Why? Five per hand is enough for most people. What's so special about you?'

I laughed. 'It's ... There's a Yiddish saying, you see: "You can't thumb your nose if you haven't got fingers."'

'Meaning what?'

'I often paint Yiddish sayings literally. If you have seven fingers rather than five you can do a lot of thumbing.'

Gérard shook his head, exasperated. 'Yes, but as not many people speak Yiddish, they're not going to get it, are they? How do you expect people to understand this stuff?'

I shrugged. There was silence.

He stared again at my paintings, one after the other, peering up close, turning them this way and that.

'Look,' he pronounced. 'You're a fabulist. Transcendental meanderings. You've got talent, but I can't sell it. The market wants realism these days. I'm sorry Shagal, but people want to know what's going on, in a painting. They want it simple. Direct.'

And with that he paced gracefully away.

137

Then the dealer Brame lumbered over to me. A thickset, heavily bearded fellow, he looked more like a prize-fighter running to seed than an art dealer. The two wings of his coat had abandoned the struggle to meet across his paunch and waved at each other ineffectually, like parted lovers.

He looked carefully at my paintings. Then he looked at me. I looked at him. I could feel myself blushing. I hoped I would not stammer too badly. He dropped his gaze in a way I had seen before. It meant he was attracted to me. Hope, the gilded goddess, shimmered before me.

'I had a client once,' he said, slowly. He had a rich brown bass voice, I will never forget it. 'A lawyer he was. I sold him a painting of the Oise because he used to go for a walk there. Then he found out it was by Pissarro. Then he found out Pissarro was a Jew. He brought the painting back. Wouldn't have it in the house.' I nodded, just wanting him to go away.

He went on: 'Look, we all know you're a good colourist. But the trouble with this stuff,' he said gruffly into his beard, 'is the anti-Semites won't take it because it's Jewish. And the Jews won't take it because you send them up. You've got ability, my boy, you can paint. But I can't sell this kind of stuff. Research your market, that's my advice.'

And with that he lumbered off, as if looking for a tree to cut down.

I looked at the door, willing the dealer Herwath Walden to appear, like Elijah at the Passover supper. No Walden.

I could hear Osip Zadkine next to me. 'I want to develop a specifically Jewish art.' My God, how many times had I heard that, from him?

I stared with disbelief. To my utter incredulity, the dealers Zborowski, both Zbo and Hanka, were hanging on the serpent's every word. They were looking at the plaster version of *The Prisoners*.

138

This piece is a study of three figures. They are forced into what looks like a cattle truck by a trellis of struts. It is a journey of doom. The three prisoners are packed so tight you can hardly see there are three of them, even if you walk round and round the sculpture. There is no room to breathe. They are barred in, being hauled along to a terrible, inescapable fate.

The Zborowskis were agape with admiration at even this early plaster version, rougher than the later bronze. And I had to admit, so was I. This piece is Zadkine's redemption. How do you react when someone you loathe does something utterly magnificent? How good a person am I?

The Zborowskis were signing up Osip, adding him to their 'list', as they called it. I was pleased. Yes. I had found it in my heart to be pleased. Truly!

As if at a signal, and quite suddenly, the dealers started to act in concert, like an orchestra, all playing different instruments but to one end. Vollard had woken up. He was the conductor, the waver of arms.

Some of the dealers started to get hold of the artists, usually by the arm, and corral them gently into groups. The dealer Durand-Ruel seized Osip Zadkine from the Zborowskis. For a moment I thought they were fighting over Osip, but no. Osip was put in a group, standing next to Lipchitz and Indenbaum. All three were predominantly sculptors, exclusively so in Osip's case.

The dealers gathered round the sculptors, like butchers at the Vaugirard abattoir, deciding if the cattle were fat enough yet. An explosive popping of French plosives, a sizzling of French fricatives, a lulling of French labials all signalled the possible grouping of the sculptors for marketing purposes.

I did not need Modi's translation to follow that Lipchitz's *Europa*, in the version where Europa is stabbing the bull, could be grouped with Zadkine's marvellous *The Prisoners*. The dealers clearly felt there was enough correspondence to market the sculptors as a movement. Great excitement.

But then the dealers grew more ambitious. Chaim Soutine was seized by his bony shoulders and placed between the bitter Pinchus Krémègne and Michel Kikoine. They were clearly considering a Minsk School, based on them all having studied at the École des Beaux Arts in Minsk.

I was rather enjoying all this when I felt myself being forcibly seized from behind. I was frogmarched into the middle of the Exhibition Hall by the small, dark, cross-eyed figure of Berthe Weill. Two dealers acting in tandem, perhaps because they were both called Paul, Paul Rosenberg and Paul Durand-Ruel, seized Modi and Soutine. The three of us were placed in line in the middle of the Exhibition Hall, first Modi, then Soutine, then me.

'What are they doing?' I hissed at Modi.

Modi laughed. 'They are trying to position Soutine between you and me. It's a possible ploy to try to market him.'

At that moment, the inexpressibly lovely Jeanne Hébuterne turned up and burst into the most charming gales of laughter at the sight of her lover standing in line for marketing purposes.

Chaim Soutine, however, close to fainting from hunger, had not heard what Modi had said and had no idea what was going on. He was panicking at being touched, which he hated, even by women, let alone being shoved around and put in position. He yelled like a child at Modi to tell him what was going on.

Now, I love Modi as if he were David, my brother, but I have to tell you honestly I think he was at fault for what happened next. He could be mischievous, Modi could. Practical jokes were his sport. This is what he did: he deliberately mistranslated for Chaim Soutine. He told

Soutine that the dealers were ranking the painters in order of ability.

Soutine believed Modi completely. He broke away from his dealer market-position between me and Modi and ran screaming to the pile of his paintings. A palette knife appeared in his hand.

'Stop him!' I yelled. 'He's going to destroy his paintings.'

A contrite Modi reacted first, just as Soutine reached his paintings. He launched himself after his best friend, shouting 'No, Chaim, no.' Modi reached him just in time and seized and embraced him with one massive gesture. Chaim went limp. He was crying but calm.

'I'm sorry,' Modi said. 'I'm so sorry, my darling! I meant it as a joke. They like your work, they really do.'

But what really soothed Soutine was Jeanne Hébuterne gently easing him from Modi's grip and pulling his head down to her breast. Soutine wept softly into Jeanne's blouse. The Exhibition Hall was silent.

And at that moment Herwath Walden appeared.

Oskar Kokoschka painted Herwath Walden in three-quarter-length profile. Walden is portrayed as the epitome of the artistic intellectual. He has a massive domed forehead and sensitive wavy lips. Thin-rimmed spectacles shield weak bulging eyes.

The figure is boyish and slight, given a touch of bulk by an expensive, almost dandyish grey coat. The pose is hand-on-hip, elbow out, mannered even then. Tension is shown in the clenched hand.

Herwath Walden was from Berlin. His real name was Georg Lewin. The name 'Walden' was a nod to the Thoreau novel, *Walden: Or, Life in the Woods*.

German dealers were not unusual on the French art scene. There was Wilhelm Uhde and, even more importantly, Daniel-Henry Kahnweiler, a major dealer for the Cubists as well as Juan Gris. He held the first Braque exhibition at his gallery on the rue Vignon.

Herwath Walden was Jewish, although, like me, he did not want to be defined or limited by his Jewish identity. Though proud of our Jewish heritage, both Walden and I regarded ourselves as international, belonging to the world.

Yes, there he is! He is plumper than the Kokoschka portrait. High forehead, mane of blond hair, thick pebble glasses to correct acute astigmatism. He looks like a dreamy academic, physically weak. The chunky gold jewellery all over him is the heaviest aspect of his being. He is clumsy, badly co-ordinated and he chain-smokes.

I have not dared mention my meeting with him before, for fear of jinxing my luck. Even now I surreptitiously spit in my hand to ward off evil. The bitter Pinchus Krémègne sees me do it and smiles.

But what happened was this. My friend Blaise Cendrars, the poet, turned up at the atelier, towing this tiny elf who spoke German, which is close enough to Yiddish for me to understand him. The elf wished to see my paintings.

I was rigid with tension, all life in me ceased except my wildly fluttering heart. There, in my atelier, an international dealer, one Herwath Walden, put out his cigarette and held up one of my paintings, *Dedicated to my Fiancée.*

'Excellent!'

I was delighted, soaring. I decided not to tell him he was holding it upside down.

Blaise Cendrars knew; he gave me a quietly complicit smile.

But I did not mind. Truly! In fact, I never mind if my paintings are held or even exhibited upside down or the wrong way round – as this one was, in the end. My paintings can be read in any direction. I often turn the canvas upside down or sideways myself, when I paint. I am trying to overcome the limitations of space as well as time.

There was a wonderful stillness in my atelier – Bella was off somewhere with Osip – while Herwath Walden admired my painting.

'I'll come to the École Juive meeting with the dealers,' the little miracle said. 'I'm thinking of including you in an exhibition I am mounting of German Expressionist painters in Berlin.'

Walden was in a hurry. He dashed out of the atelier without visiting any of the other artists at *La Ruche*. I caught myself feeling pleased about that, then blushed with shame. I should have shown him Soutine's work. And Modi's. Ah well, too late.

When he had gone, I turned to Blaise Cendrars, all long chin and pursed mouth, his small frame extravagantly wrapped in a cloak.

'Thank you so much for the introduction,' I said.

'I can claim no credit, Moyshe,' Blaise said. 'Walden was looking for you. I ran into him. I simply told him where to find you and showed him the way.'

'He was looking for me? But how? Why? How had he …?'

Blaise shrugged. 'Search me. He knew your work well. He knew individual titles.'

Again, I had this feeling, this feeling I was afraid of, because it was too good, too wonderful. Was somebody looking after me? Did someone – or something – want me to succeed, to be a great artist? I fled from the thought because it was hubristic, tempting the Gods of fate and chance.

And yet. A benefactor I hardly knew was paying for me to live in Paris. Why? How? *He* had approached *me*! And now I am sought out by an international patron who somehow mysteriously knows all about me. How?

And on it went. Miracles lighting my path like fizzing flares.

Walden stood blinking in the doorway of the Exhibition Hall, his tiny frame sealed into a three-piece suit of English tweed. His upturned wing collar showed the lengths of his tie, below his turkey-neck. His hands were in his pockets in a louche pose, a cigarette dangled down from his lower lip, spilling ash on his waistcoat.

His even, quite handsome, features lightened at the sight of me. Ignoring everybody else, hands still in his pockets, he strode over to me. It was only then I noticed he had someone with him. I knew who this was from my wanderings around Paris from one dealer's shop to the next. It was Charles Malpel, a dealer with a gallery in the rue Montaigne.

Herwath Walden was again cordial, but again in a hurry. He glanced at the paintings I had ready for the dealers. He did not show any particular emotion.

Walden and Malpel began talking, ignoring me. I could understand, as they were talking in German. They were talking about framing. I could hardly believe it, but they were talking about framing *my* pictures, *as if for an exhibition.*

'Yellow frame,' Walden muttered. 'Plain ochre. Ideal for *Birth.*'

Malpel: '*Very black* frame of plain unmoulded wood.'

'Very yellow frame? Or sky-coloured? Hanging not in a small room, nor in shadow.'

'Yes, but not opposite a window with direct lighting.'

'Hang leaning forwards. It would be good if they were to one side of a window.'

And so it went on.

Finally, when I thought I was about to faint again, if not burst my *kishkas* all over the floor like a gutted Vaugirard calf – Walden the dealer actually addressed me, unworthy artist that I am, directly, face to face.

'I'll take these for my exhibition in Berlin,' he said. 'I must scoot off now. But I've brought you a local dealer. You need a proper regular outlet. Over to you Malpel. Toodle pip! Cheerio!'

I was too numb to reply.

Malpel introduced himself solemnly. He had an almost extravagantly ordinary round face, with features spaced out and tucked away modestly.

'I think we can run to two hundred and fifty francs a month for six small canvases, say fifteen by thirty-one.' It was the first thing he said. He said it in French. Modi reappeared by magic from calming Soutine and translated.

I nodded, dazed.

Charles Malpel went on. 'I'll take your entire output for say one and a half years and I will guarantee not to try to influence you. That will be in the contract. Come over to my home in the rue de Clichy and we can sign it. All right?'

'Yes. All right.'

'I understand you plan to go back to your home in Russia for a visit, before Berlin to see Walden?'

How did he know that? From Walden? 'Y … Y … Ye … Yes!'

'That's fine. I'll make my selection from your paintings when you get back.'

I had not stopped shaking when Commissaire Henri Zamoron appeared. He looked tense. I caught sight of the terrified faces of Rosa and Michel Kikoine, our watery Bolsheviks. They clearly feared Zamoron was visiting not for the paintings but for them. And indeed Zamoron went over to them.

But before he had time to break his beard in speech, there came a quite biblical thundering from the corridor leading from the Exhibition Hall back to the main Hive building. It was backed by a row outside. All activity stopped in the Exhibition Hall. We were all frozen. The miracle Walden had gone, but my other dealer – my God, my other dealer – Malpel, was still at my side.

For a second, Commissaire Descaves was framed in the doorway, nose in the air sniffing like a fiend pointing to hell. Then his *flics* – blue-uniformed footsoldier police – charged past him, about ten of them. The Kikoines were right to be afraid. The police made straight for them, seized them roughly and pinned their arms, over feeble, piping protests.

Then they called Modi's name. With a cry of 'There is the *cochonnerie!*' two of them seized his nude drawings from a pile of work stacked against the wall.

'Leave those alone, you scum.' That was Jeanne Hébuterne at the top of her voice.

Commissaire Descaves strode over to Modi. He was young, still in his twenties, all smooth-skinned efficiency and cropped hair.

'Amedeo Modigliani. Following a complaint made against you by M. Drumont, I am arresting you for an unprovoked attack on three of his followers in the Café Spielman.'

'What?' Modi said. 'Those fascists? They deserved it.'

Descaves took Modi by the arm. Modi burst out laughing. Jeanne Hébuterne joined in.

I watched Modi being led away. They had seized his drawings, too, by now. I watched Rosa and Michel Kikoine being led away. I felt sorry. I felt concerned. I loved these people.

But I was on the way. *I was on the way.*

I was on the way.

146

PART IV: VITEBSK, 1914

When I left *La Ruche*, I left the door tied up like a parcel behind me. I did not look back. I intended to return in a couple of months, after travelling first to Vitebsk, then on to Berlin for Herwath Walden's exhibition of my paintings at the Sturm gallery.

But the outbreak of war left me trapped in Vitebsk, unable to visit Berlin, get back to *La Ruche* or indeed go anywhere else on my three-month passport. What was foreseen as a 'flying visit' back to Vitebsk was to last eight years, at least partly because I was unable to obtain an exit visa.

Bella was with me, but all my paintings were trapped in Paris or – the ones Walden had taken – in Berlin. They were prisoners, hostages to war and the times, as Bella and I were.

My contract with Charles Malpel had been signed before I left Paris, but as I had no way of communicating with the dealer it might as well never have happened. I could only hope from afar that Malpel would look after my precious paintings.

And there was more news of my paintings. It was brought to me by Lazar Markovich Lissitzky, now known as El Lissitzky, the one who had witnessed my small one on a raft on the Dvina, along with Osip Zadkine, and announced it to the world when we were all boys together in Vitebsk.

Lazar (or El) Lissitzky, never shy of being the bringer of bad news, told me the following: my paintings and gouaches and drawings – my entire output except what had been left behind in my atelier at The Hive – had indeed been shown by Walden in Sturm's two scruffy rooms in Berlin, but they had simply been tossed in a jumble on trestle tables, as if at a sale of bric-à-brac. So much for that discussion on framing with Charles Malpel when the dealers came to *La Ruche*.

And, Lissitzky added in a delighted coda, for complex reasons of international finance and currency values,

Walden would be unable to pay as much as a kopek on any sales of the paintings, even if he wished to. There's an old Jewish saying, money is round, here today, gone tomorrow.

To Lissitzky's satisfaction, I burst into tears when I heard the news. Then I fainted, coming round in Bella's arms a good while later.

Then I painted *War*. We see an old tired eternal Jew. His life-weary body is hunched into a gabardine; he has an outdoor hat with ear flaps and plump slippers on his weary feet. His ancient's silver-white beard is etched in white lead, making the black holes of his eyes even deeper and more unfathomable. He is carrying his meagre belongings in a bag in the crook of his arm. This is everything he has got.

And behind him, understated, faint, seen through a window, troops march to war. It is 1914. It is *War*.

When Bella and I first returned to Vitebsk I was welcomed as a hero by Bella's parents, the Rosenfelds. At that point we still believed we could leave again. And by now I had earned some money from painting, enough, I briefly believed at the time, to support a wife in comfort.

Before I left, the Rosenfeld parents had not approved of me. It was not only that I was a herring schlepper's son from the Small Side. But also, incredibly, my orthodox, hyper-observant family were still not *frumm* enough for Shmuel Noah Rosenfeld, Bella's ultra-orthodox father.

Craven, craven Moyshe, I used to work my own family's religious credentials into the conversation with Shmuel Noah, before I left: there was my grandfather, the Talmudic holy man, was there not? There was my father's total knowledge of the Holy Books. Was there not? Mr Rosenfeld was not convinced.

Shmuel Noah Rosenfeld was a big, shapeless man with a small-featured, startled expression, as if permanently about to give vent to explosive indignation. He would shut his slate-blue eyes in perplexed exasperation, those eyes which peeped warily out above his nest of a Hasidic beard, like little ferrets wondering if it was safe to leave a sheltering bush.

He lived in fear of many things, did Shmuel Noah, but especially of the evil eye; shutting his own was a way of warding it off. Prayer, too, had this far from disinterested purpose.

Shmuel Noah, then, was in charge of his family's relationship with God, leaving Alta, Bella's mother, to do the ordering for the jewellery shop plus the vital task of displaying their wares. 'You can have too much in the window, you know.' Alta meant the jewellery shop window, though Bella laughingly used to say it was a maxim for life. Be wary, be cunning, don't show your hand, don't put everything you've got on display in the shop window.

Yes, be wary, be cunning, but also be fearful. Of what? Of everything, of life. On the face of it, leaving a light burning all night in the shop was a perfectly sensible precaution against burglars. But it reeked of fear, sought it out, the very watching lamp inviting the disasters it sought to prevent.

Shmuel Noah served customers in the shop, deferring always to Alta's knowledge of stock. But the basic division remained: Shmuel Noah did God, Alta did Mammon. Shmuel Noah did the sacred, Alta the profane.

Alta was a big woman. Her little mouth was always pursed as if permanently about to cry for help. *'What's so special about you?'* I used to scream at her in my mind. You run a shop, and so does my wonderful mother, Feiga-Ita.

But even as I silently screamed, I knew the answer to my own question. Shmuel Noah was a *ganzer macher*. He was so important he could cut his nails in front of you and burn the clippings.

The Rosenfelds lived on the Smolenskaya. The golden

151

road to heaven was the only road more sought after than the Smolenskaya, and even that did not run right down to a secluded bathing place on the Vitba River, not the Dvina, you note, the Vitba. Much more exclusive. And the shop. How can that one word 'shop' encompass both my mother's rough-hewn booth, still resembling its antecedent trees, among the wooden *izbas* of the Small Side, and the opulent Rosenberg emporium, gracing the Podvinskaya, the only boulevard in Vitebsk to rival the Smolenskaya, where they lived?

Above the Rosenberg emporium there is the Café Jeanne-Albert, with its elegant wrought iron-railed terrace garden. I used to sneak off there when I was at Pen's, usually alone but sometimes with Osip Zadkine or Lazar Lissitzky. I would order a French pastry, a cup of coffee ground from beans, a small glass of water. And I would feel like a fully formed human being. On the way down, to complete the experience, I would peer into the Rosenfeld emporium window, not to buy, oh no! not even really to look. Just to belong for a few seconds to that order of higher beings.

And now, on my return to my home town, a painter with contracts and contacts, a dealer of my own and an exhibition in a foreign capital, I was finally the equal of the Rosenfelds and their educated daughter who had studied philosophy abroad and spoke foreign tongues.

No wonder I was feted. No wonder the Rosenfelds finally accepted me as Bella's husband.

We stayed with the Rosenfelds, briefly, on arrival. But Bella felt trapped there, locked back in the box of her childhood. To get away, she spent hours in the women's bath-house, letting the attendants scrub her body and hair with caustic soap to the point of pain. Afterwards they served blue *kvass* to drink – blue with cold was the standard joke.

I enjoyed escorting her to the bath-house, a beautiful Romanesque-style building on a footpath right near the exclusive little river, the Vitba, even if it was just along from the madhouse. Bella didn't mind when I peeped in, as I usually did, catching tantalising glimpses of the women bathing, as in Rembrandt's *Susannah and the Elders*. It amused her.

To tame her restlessness, Bella worked in the Rosenfeld shop. There is a Yiddish saying, 'Like a queen among a hundred clocks'. With Bella that saying became a literal picture. The Rosenfelds sold hundreds of clocks: clocks on the wall, clocks on the table, clocks bigger than a man, clocks smaller than a watch. But maybe she was too much a queen, among the ticking clocks and the music boxes. Whatever the reason, her days there were not a success.

Avram the shop apprentice was by now Mr Avramel Bernstein, the Chief Clerk. This Mr Avramel Bernstein was an earnest, pale fellow who played third violin in the Vitebsk Symphony Orchestra and had a wife and two small daughters. He did not take kindly to Bella's frequent dreamy mistakes with money, which left the emporium short and chaotic at the reckoning at the end of the day.

There were rows. Mr Avramel Bernstein was no respecter of Bella's studies, her foreign tongues, her ability as an actress. All he cared about was that a music box had been sold for less than it cost, clock wrappings were left all over the floor and his books did not balance.

Bella's relationship with Rikva the cashier was no better. Rikva Romm resented Bella's assumption of friendship when it suited her, then playing the boss's daughter when it did not. At first, she ran Bella's errands with poor grace; a note to a friend, some shopping tasks, but later, especially when she realised Avramel Bernstein was on her side, she refused to do Bella's bidding.

Bella, seeking allies, as she tended to do, turned to Hershel Bronsky, the book-keeper, a desiccated figure who had come to resemble the paper they wrapped the goods in. His old shiny suit crackled when he moved. Hershel maintained a studious neutrality, so Bella was all the more

153

hurt when she learned it was he who had instigated the formal complaint about her to her father, made by all the staff.

Bella stopped working in the shop. As to me, well, when it became clear that I was trapped in Vitebsk by the war, I had to go like a supplicant to Shmuel Noah to avoid an army call-up. Shmuel Noah wangled me an office job, arranging army supplies in the Central Bureau for War Economy. I hated the work, indeed I could not do it to any level of ability, but it kept me from the front.

And I could still visit that honourable artist-toiler Yury Pen, whose self-deprecating irony was undiminished: 'My fame stretches from Peskovatik to Elaga.' (Yes, both parts of Vitebsk.)

But most important of all I could still paint. I painted *A View from the Window, Vitebsk*. When I first went to Paris, living at *La Ruche*, I saw Paris through the eyes of Vitebsk. Now, on my return, I saw Vitebsk through the eyes and with the experience of Paris.

In *A View from the Window, Vitebsk*, there is an unlit lamp in the foreground. Then you see plants, a paling, an empty garden, a fence and finally Vitebsk in the distance – tiny cathedrals and steep red-roofed houses – all at an oblique angle framed by a double window-frame.

Vitebsk is close to me but also distant, seen through a painter's frame, seen through glass, seen past an unlit lamp. I referred to the paintings of Vitebsk I produced at this time as 'documents' – I sensed even then that they were preserving what would one day be gone.

Obviously, Bella and I could not stay with the Rosenfelds indefinitely. We found ourselves a place on Offizierskaya. Chaya, the Rosenfelds' cook, came with us. Because of her, we had all the Vitebsk specialities I had so missed in Paris.

Chaya was built like a broomstick, with sharp eyes and

sharper elbows. Indoors, she wore a blue apron; outside, a wide, flower-trimmed hat which was supposed to land her a husband but never did.

She would bustle and battle her way round the Padlo market square and bring back booty of hard Gomel cheeses, like babies' heads, and *tsibulnikis* – pastry stuffed with fried onions. And waffles and carp and pike, and the *challah* sweet bread and golden pies with almond cream filling. They were the tastes of home.

And then there were the smells. The strongest smell of my home was the smell of fried onions – *grieben* we called it – when the onions were fried black. The Jewish pastry shop and the Polish confectioners were the only places in Vitebsk that did not smell of fried onions. And there was the background smell of herring, the herrings that my father schlepped.

Strangely, all the tastes and smells of home reminded me of the peddler at the gates of *La Ruche*. I missed missing home from far away, on my way into the atelier. The air was thinner in Vitebsk than in Paris. I can't explain it, but it was more difficult to breathe. I felt giddy more often. I fainted more often. I registered numbly that Paris, not Vitebsk, was my body's normal air.

There were things I had forgotten, too – aspects of life I had failed to preserve, no matter how much I thought of Vitebsk in Paris. For example, I have always hated rain, it unsettles me. But I had forgotten how rain made muddy the unpaved streets of Vitebsk's Small Side, pocking them with puddles. Efficient Paris with its modern underground drains had become my mind-pictured expectation. As I realised that, I felt I was betraying Vitebsk.

Life had split me down the middle. I was neither fish nor fowl, a deracinated Jew, not so much wandering as tossed hither and yon, trying to paint in his own way wherever he landed. I was Moyshe Shagal, was I? Or was I Marc Chagall?

Who?

The house, our new home, our first home, was Bella's grandfather's old place. A policeman owned it now, we rented it from him. Funnily enough, it was white with red shutters, like the white cap with red ribbon that policemen wear in the summer, when they come to arrest Jews.

It was in a street of white houses near Governor's Square, a square flanked by synagogues. It was the quietest street in Vitebsk, as if there were a dying grandfather in every house and everybody was tiptoeing around until he departed this earth. I had forgotten how low the houses are in Vitebsk, even old people have to crouch to get in their own front doors.

I continued to paint. I picked up the threads with Yury Pen and some of his pupils – Ilya Mazel, Lev Zevin, and some I knew from Paris who were back in Vitebsk, like Oskar Meschanikov and Paula Khentova. I saw Thea Brachmann again once or twice, too. I felt we were tied together because only she knew my terrible secret about my sister Rachel and the charcoal.

But that left us with the problem of what Bella was going to do. At first she tried journalism, picking up the threads from her Moscow days. She submitted some feuilletons to *Vitebsk Morning*, Vitebsk's journal, but they were not accepted.

Our parlour in the house in Offizierskaya boasted a green plush divan, Viennese chairs and a massy battered wooden table, covered with an oilcloth. We faced each other, smiling, at this table. We had been drinking tea with jam in it. We could see our happy faces, round, reflected in the brass belly of the samovar on the table.

She sat there poised, perching, balanced like a bird, elbow on the table, chin in hand, deciding what to do. All the flesh of her childhood had fallen away, leaving thin skin stretching over avian bones. Never had she looked more luminously beautiful to me; the gleaming white of that vulnerable skin, the perfect arrangement of her small features, the jet black of her hair. She was like a beautiful magpie, looking for bright things. ('And the Lord will satisfy thy soul with brightness' as it says in Isaiah.)

Bella was born in light. She was born on the fifth day of Hanakkah, the Festival of Light. As I was born in fire, so she was born in light. As I watched, fascinated, she stretched out an arm as elegant as a swan's neck and spun a lead top on the table. The top spun, blurring its four sides, each with its large black-printed Hebrew letter, *gimel, shin, he* and *nun.*

Gimel and *nun* appeared a moment, then blearily spun away. *Gimel* meant good, *shin* meant bad.

'I want to be an actress,' Bella said to the spinning top.

The top stopped then fell on its side. It showed the three graceful lines of the letter *gimel. Gimel* looks like a *moujik* walking forward but looking back where he has come from.

Bella smiled at me, shyly, like a delighted child who had completed her allotted task successfully. 'An actress it is, then,' she said.

I nodded, unable to speak, afraid I would faint. 'Y... Y ... Yes,' I said. It was all I could say, because at that moment I fell utterly and irrecoverably in love with her. And I painted my love in the *Double Portrait with Wineglass.*

There were many changes to my painting on my return to Vitebsk during the First World War. I found it difficult to obtain canvases, so many of my works were painted on pasteboard or paper.

There were also changes caused by my marriage to Bella and the sudden blazing fire of my love for her. My colours became softer, more lyrical and airy. I achieved total unity between the artist, the subject and the form.

Hasidic Jewish mysticism – perhaps all mysticism – aims at the unity of the subject and the object, achieved in spinning ecstasy by the ecstatic dancing on the festival of

Simchas Torah, when the very walls seem to be swaying to the rhythm of life and the empty ceiling moves the earth. Everything is unified. We dance, we Jews, in a circle to celebrate the closing of the cycle of the reading of the Torah.

I did a drawing of it, at this time: bearded men, tribal elders, jerking about in joy like the marionettes of the Lord. Even solemn, dignified Shmuel Noah, Bella's father, joined in, because the joy was God's will. I drew him, too, among them.

The love between husband and wife is a high principle of existence in the Hasidic book, the *Kabbalah*, because it embodies the highest union – the union of the male with the *Shechina*, the female aspect of God. Another Hasidic holy book, the *Zohar*, also says that a man and his wife make one soul and one body. I once celebrated this fusion in a portrait of Adam and Eve as one, their torsos emerging from a single trunk.

Now came an even more complete fusion. For me, there was no difference between myself, myself and Bella, and the paintings of myself and Bella. Bella had become the female part of me, but more, Bella had become all life that was not me. We were one, like Adam and Eve. I embarked on a series of paintings to exalt our love.

In *Lovers in Green*, our two heads are together, almost kissing. *Lovers in Blue* shows Bella holding my head in profile while tenderly kissing my cheek and mouth. Bella is shown as Columbine with me as Harlequin. In *Pair of Lovers*, my head is tilted back while Bella cradles me, her mouth gently kissing mine. In *Lovers in Pink* we embrace, and her head in profile is blocking mine so the viewer can see only my bubbly fair hair. She has a lovely, Madonna-like profile.

However, the most sensuous and joyful of all my love paintings with Bella, the one that completely encapsulates our loving bond, is the *Double Portrait with Wineglass*.

In this painting, reminiscent of Rembrandt's *Self-Portrait with Saskia*, Bella is shown full-length in a white bridal gown, slit to show one leg painted vermilion. Bridal-Bella is carrying me, sitting on her shoulders, one leg dangling behind her and one in front. Above our heads floats and hovers a lady angel in red with red wings, waving benison on the ecstatic couple.

Once again, I have painted a Yiddish expression literally – or taken it even further. The expression is *'Si trogt im ouf di hent'* meaning she carries him in her hands. She is supporting him, completely. My utter need for Bella is there for all to see.

I have painted myself in brilliant red, bubble hair bubbling, grinning gleefully, holding aloft a celebratory glass of red wine. At Bella's feet is the Dvinski Bridge, the bridge where the raw Moyshe Segal made the defining decision of his life, choosing Bella over Thea; the river Dvina, where little Moyshe went rafting with his schoolmates Lazar Lissitzky and Osip Zadkine; and the blue-domed Ilynsky Cathedral, surrounded by lion-coloured fields of grain, which stands for Vitebsk, as it did from afar in Paris in the *Portrait with Seven Fingers*.

Unusually for me, the couple's ecstasy is rendered as sexual, as well as emotional: Bella's bridal dress is pulled down, her breasts are visible to just below her nipples. This was the most sexual period of my life, as this painting clearly shows. But overall the mood is one of delirious, life-affirming joy through love, giving and receiving love, achieving union through love, with sex playing its part in that.

When my darling Bella found a path in life her happiness was mine. This path was being an actress on the stage. She had studied under Stanislavsky in Moscow, before she came to join me in Paris, so there was nothing new in her interest. But I knew she had found his ways demanding. There had been many tears.

But a new impetus presented itself, right on cue. Tucked away among the lively and developed theatre scene in Vitebsk there was the Purim Players. Every year, this little group played out the Purim story of Esther and her cousin Mordecai and how they (but especially Esther) saved the Jews from the wicked Persian king, Ahasuerus, and his even more wicked vizier, Haman, who wanted to kill all the Jews.

Not long after we arrived back in Vitebsk, when we realised we were trapped and unable to get an exit visa, the Purim Players played out their tale in the Rosenfeld's luxurious household in Smolenskaya. We had all exchanged the traditional Purim gifts. Chairs had been placed in the parlour, where we all sat in rows, except Bella's father, who presided from the head of the table in a long silk coat. His beard had been combed and buffed like a horse's mane, until it shone. Shmuel Noah beamed at the world. Bella and I beamed at each other.

The players burst in: 'Happy holiday, Reb Shmuel Noah. Happy holiday everybody!'

We all wished each other Happy Holiday, then they started the play. Esther, looking like an angel in a white dress, was played by Thea Brachmann. Mordecai, all jester bells and riding a white stick, was played by my old friend Viktor Mekler, now the successful owner of his own rag and paper business and no longer dabbling in painting. And Ahasuerus, the Persian king, was embodied in the stately presence of Maksim Vinaver, my benefactor, no longer a Duma deputy but free from the charges which had led to his arrest.

Bella watched with shining eyes as Esther revealed her secret to Ahasuerus – she is Jewish. Esther then reveals Mordecai's services to the Persian Empire, implicates the wicked Haman in a plot against the Jews, including her, and generally triumphs. The evil Haman is hanged.

The audience, which included my old teacher, Yury Pen, sitting alone, as ever, thundered their applause.

Shmuel Noah poured brandy for the Purim Players. Bella clutched me tightly. I did not need her to tell me, as she did when we arrived back home, that she wanted to become an actress.

Yiddish culture deals in types – the saint, the madman – which does not mean we are not interested in individual quirks and foibles, far from it. The jobs in the village become archetypes into which the individual fits – the matchmaker, the tailor, and famously, Tevye the milkman from the Sholem Aleichem story, *Fiddler on the Roof.*

The people in my paintings, and the animals too, are timeless archetypes, which is exactly why they are not symbolic of anything else. They already stand for something – themselves and all others like them, throughout time.

My friend Viktor Mekler, it occurred to me, was not quite an archetype in his own right, more a sub-archetype. He was a thwarted artist, which is a sub-group of the artist archetype. Life came easily to Viktor. He was handsome, clever and industrious. He could get men and women to do what he wanted them to do.

It was all so easy for him that, being still a young man, he took what he had achieved for granted as soon as he had achieved it. Come out from one's father's shadow? Achieved. Tick it off. Set up one's own business? Naturally. Watch that business quickly become one of the leading enterprises in Vitebsk? A shrug of the shoulders.

But all Viktor wanted was to be some sort of artist. He was conscious of a lack, a void inside. Bella, with her fine-honed neurotic's intuition, apprehended this. She used to say Viktor was like 'bitter chocolate' – disappointing expectation.

When I tried to help him with painting, back in those early days at Pen's, all I managed to do was clear the clutter, so making his limitations clearer to him. I am no teacher. I seek my own aggrandisement too much to subsume myself for the sake of others. Teachers are self-sacrificing. That can never be me. I give to the world in other ways.

So Viktor had abandoned painting and taken to acting in plays, but still more to the writing of them. He lit another artistic candle within himself to guide himself to some meaning in life. And the way Viktor saw it, with that inborn clear-headed practicality he was always denying, was that writing offered him a greater chance of success than painting.

After all, there was only the one painting school in Vitebsk, Yury Pen's. There were three theatres, one of them specifically for Jewish plays. The Jewish Theatre, near the railway in Vygonnayaskaya, puts on plays in Hebrew.

'It's about a woman possessed by an evil spirit,' Viktor said, waving his play at us. He was lounging on our green plush divan, soft as butter, imported from the Rosenfeld establishment. He stared Bella in the eye, twinkling. 'I immediately thought of you.'

'Thank you very much!' Bella was speaking in a girlish voice, with exaggerated clarity. Her laughter – genuine enough – had a high, girlish, gurgly giggle in it.

Bella was one of those people who creates a new persona for everybody she comes into contact with. So for Shmuel Noah, her father, she was clever and cutting. Thea got tears (for some reason) as well as the lofty grace of the victor over the vanquished. With Viktor Mekler she could be kittenish, but anguish was never far away – a kitten that had lost its ball of wool. Viktor was tacitly expected to find it.

'Come on Viktor,' I said. 'What is going on here?'

Viktor looked pleased that I could see through him – we were good friends, after all.

'I want you to star in my play, Bella.'

'Oh, Viktor!' Bella clapped her hands together to one side of her face, transformed into an actress already. 'You're an angel!'

The newly seraphed Viktor beamed.

'Come on then, Viktor,' I said. 'Tell us all about it.'

He suddenly became serious, even shrewd, the underlying paper manufacturer showing through like a palimpsest. 'It's a play about the false messiah, Sabbatai Zevi. Title: *Satan in Vitebsk*. You know the old saying "Do not give Satan an opening"? Here, they do. But Bella is Rachele, Rachele to the rescue; a holy woman who vanquishes the false messiah.'

'Oooh!' Bella gave a girlish scream and clapped her hands again.

'What happens to Rachele?' I asked.

'She dies. But she has a lovely deathbed scene.' Viktor added the second part quickly.

'It sounds MAR-VELLOUS, Viktor.'

'I hope so,' said the playwright, modestly.

I started sketching Bella in the play before rehearsals had even started. *The Abduction* is a sketch for my painted backdrop to the Vitebsk Jewish Theatre's production of *The False Messiah*, by Viktor Mekler. Bella is shown playing Rachele, the saviour of the town, symbolically carrying off the seventeenth-century false messiah, Sabbatai Zevi, who claimed to bring hope and redemption before joining the devil.

Zevi, played by Lazar Lissitzky, is shown being lifted bodily in his blouse and pantaloons so he is parallel to the ground in an impossible but symbolic feat of strength by Rachele/Bella.

Viktor Mekler's visit ushered in a time of happiness, even bliss, at our new home in Offizierskaya. Even the lack of an exit visa, meaning we could not leave the city limits, not even to go to Lyovno, the next town, made Bella and me feel cocooned rather than trapped.

I had embarked on the sequence of *Lovers* paintings, starting with *Lovers in Green*, with Bella all bright-eyed bird happiness as she posed for me. But with this fulfilment as an actress, she grew round and glowing with inner joy.

I started on *Lovers in Blue*, putting myself in Harlequin costume and portraying Bella as Columbine as a kind of secret joke about her acting. Bella really felt as one with me, here in Vitebsk, she was part of my mad inventions in colour. They never seemed strange to her.

And as she was part of my work, I became part of hers. The play was bringing us such happiness. We rehearsed her part together, though sometimes she went off to see Viktor to discuss her character and rehearse with him. She and Viktor took to going for long walks together along the Dvina towpath, to discuss her role and anything else they might wish to discuss.

I found *Satan in Vitebsk* rather good, and I was happy to tell Viktor so. The further removed from my own work any form of art is, the easier I find it to give praise – given that there is some heart and soul present in the work, or I cannot praise at all.

Viktor's play is in essence a story of religious hysteria – a desperate grab for exaltation by embracing false gods who embody false ideas. The story opens with a pogrom by a Cossack hetman, Bogdan Chmelnicki, which is supposed to presage Armageddon.

Out of the bloodshed, the birth pangs of suffering, should come salvation. There are portents of the second coming of the messiah. Signs are found in the Zohar. The new messiah will lead newly transformed people to a new form of living.

Rachele – played by Bella Chagall – is the wife of the handsome Rabbi Benish Ashkenazi – played by Viktor Mekler. She has visions. Her visions tell her that the coming Sabbatai Zevi is a false messiah. Rachele is visited by Satan and tempted, but she keeps to the path of righteousness.

Rabbi Benish, too, the loyal husband, denies the coming messiah but the town is divided. The letters S and Z appear everywhere. Sabbatai Zevi's supporters use his kerchief to help a woman give birth with no pain. Evil spirits are exorcised from a house where they had dwelt for years. A child who has been frightened by a black dog and has not spoken for years speaks again.

More and more of the townsfolk await their promised messiah. They are waiting with intensity, with a passion, suspending all other life. There is an ancient Hebrew saying, 'May you live until the Messiah comes.' This is the transformation in lives and fortunes that is spaced out in millennia.

But Rachele's visions, stronger and ever more frequent, tell a different story. She hears voices. She sees the Prophet Elijah who tells her this is a false messiah. Rachele tells the town of her visions but only her husband, Rabbi Benish, believes her. Rachele is arrested as a witch and cast into prison.

Sabbatai Zevi makes a triumphant entry into town on an ass. The people exult. A coronation is planned when the false messiah will be garlanded and crowned. The people believe they will pass to the Promised Land by underground tunnels on that very day. Their sufferings, their long, hard sufferings, will be over. Their enemies will be vanquished.

Rabbi Benish frees his wife from gaol. He takes her with him to the synagogue. It is the night before Yom Kippur, the holiest day of the year. Rabbi Benish is to conduct the Kol Nidre night service, the taking of vows witnessed by the souls of the dead. Rachele makes her visions visible to the congregation at the height of their ecstasy. She shows them Sabbatai Zevi embracing the devil.

Sabbatai Zevi enters the synagogue. He cries 'I am your God, Sabbatai Zevi.' But the people no longer believe him. Sabbatai Zevi is cast out from their midst.

Then one day, when Bella was away at the theatre for the dress rehearsal, Viktor Mekler burst into our home, dishevelled, half in costume as Rabbi Benish Ashkenazi, half in day clothes. I was painting *Lovers in Blue*. I was just dabbing at Bella's pale blue dress with its small black and grey squares. My eyes opened at Mekler. Was Bella dead?

'There has been an accident. At the theatre.'

Was Bella dead?

'Bella is in hospital. She has hurt her ankle. She wants to see you immediately.'

Bella had fallen off the stage at the Jewish Theatre. I ran to her at the Jewish Hospital, next door to the railway station. Over the hoot of trains, through the stink of urine and formaldehyde I spoke to doctors, then to a wan and tearful Bella in a bed in a peeling once cream-painted ward called Women's Medical.

Her left ankle was badly sprained. She would make a full recovery but not in time to play Rachele in Viktor's play. She howled with rage and frustration, there in her hospital bed. I held her hand. I soothed with animal noises of love as much as words. She kept saying she did not want to know who would take over from her as Rachele. She never wanted to know. I was on no account to go and see the play. I promised that.

On the way out, a young doctor took me by the arm, pulling me to one side in the green and yellow-painted corridor. In hushed and reverential tones he told me Bella was pregnant.

I painted Bella and Ida. Bella is lying in a dressing-gown on a bed next to baby Ida, in swaddling clothes. Chubby baby Ida's face is puckered in sleep. There is a dummy in her mouth. Bella is lying on her side, turned towards her child. Her face in profile is serene. Her arm is bent in tenderness towards Ida, her fingers just touching the baby's face.

At the top of the picture, to the right, we can see my hand, just my hand, no more. My hand and splayed fingers are resting on Bella's hair.

How much love there is in this hand, its protection running through Bella, along her arm, to the sleeping baby Ida. Here is no warrior, no clenched-fist fighter. Here is a gentle open caressing hand of eternal love and care. It is a hand unmoving, which will stay in its place, playing its part in the love which drives us.

Father, mother, baby. There is something of the eternal about it.

PART V: VITEBSK, 1917

I was ecstatic. I was exultant. The whole world was singing hosannas and lifting Marc Chagall with its breath. I swung my Bella through the air. We were both flying like *Luftmenschen*. The Jews were free, suddenly free. The Pale of Settlement, our corral for centuries, was gone overnight. The fences were down. The Jews could live anywhere. I could live anywhere. We were full citizens of Russia for the first time. We had rights. We belonged. We were equals. We were allowed to practise Judaism in synagogues with walls as tall as cathedrals.

Just think, I could go into a church, if I wanted to. I could travel to St Petersburg without permission. I could do anything I wanted to do, go anywhere I wanted to go. I could fly.

No wonder we embraced the new order – at first.

In joyous celebration, I dashed off the only political painting I was ever to paint: *Peace to Huts – War on Palaces*, it was called. It celebrated the Russian Revolution as a muscular triumph. A stocky Russian peasant with a full beard, dressed in a red tunic, strides over a hill holding a palace aloft in his extended arms. The peasant is roaring. He is about to smash the palace into the ground.

The peasant, in my own mind at least, was not a Jew. The revolution was a triumph for all mankind. All mankind would now be happy in a just and equal society. That is what we thought, that is what we all thought – at first.

And there was more. Was my new-found luck to have no end? It started like this. There was a Marxist exiled in the west who lived at *La Ruche* for a while. His name was Anatoly Lunacharsky. I never took much notice of him at *La Ruche*. He was just there, around, like one of the cats. Who knows who will be important in your life? Who knows?

But anyway, this Lunacharsky is suddenly a *ganzer macher* in the new regime. He is the Head of the People's Commissariat for Enlightenment (my God!) known as

NARKOMPROS, which runs cultural affairs in Vitebsk, reporting to Moscow. Anyway, it seems that, unknown to me, this Anatoly Lunacharsky not only knows my painting, especially *Peace to Huts – War on Palaces*, he likes it enough to recommend it. Recommend me.

We live in an age of reports, now, this new age. I was shown Anatoly Lunacharsky's report on my work: 'His crazy canvases with their intentionally childish manners, their capricious and rich fantasy, their typical grimace of horror and considerable share of humour, provoke the spectator's attention.'

Oy! Is that me? Thank you, Anatoly Lunacharsky.

I was summoned to Anatoly Lunacharsky's office. I felt like I did when *former* Duma Deputy Maksim Vinaver mysteriously gave me 125 francs a month to go to Paris. That was in the old world, the world before the revolution. But my feeling was the same. What the hell was I doing in this office, rolling about inside the best clothes I have got?

The address I was given for Lunacharsky's office was Bukharinskaya 10, which I had never heard of. It turned out that the old Voskenskaya had just been renamed after some sort of revolutionary, who again I had not heard of, called Bukharin.

The new People's Art School, where Lunacharsky had his office, turned out to be a beautiful old building, white-faced with a lovely portico, formerly the private house of a banker called Ivan Vishnyak.

Anatoly Lunacharsky told me what I was doing there, in his office in the lovely house, now a school. I am the commissar of all art activities in Vitebsk Province. I am head of the Vitebsk People's Art School which NARKOMPROS will finance.

'Throw yourself head first into the sea of revolutionary art,' Lunacharsky told me, stroking his goatee beard. 'Give yourself wholeheartedly. Put all your faith in it.'

I nodded, vigorously. I wondered for a second what he

meant by revolutionary art. 'Very good, sir,' I said.

Yesterday, I was nobody, a painter who wonders where his paintings are, in Germany, in France. Today, I'm a *ganzer macher* – an artistic pillar of the revolution.

I went home. Bella was a little down, a little sad. She still limped from that sprained ankle. She still wanted to be an actress.

'I'm a commissar,' I told her. 'I'm the head of an art school.'

'Oh, Moyshe!'

'I'm more important than Viktor Mekler.'

She laughed.

I kissed baby Ida, there in her little cot. 'Your daddy is more important than Viktor Mekler. More important than Maksim Vinaver, now a former Duma deputy.'

'What's happened to him?' Bella asked, concerned. 'He was good to you.'

'I know. I know. He got out OK. He's in the Crimea, I think.' I went back to baby talk with Ida. 'Goo-goo! You wait till your grandma hears about this. Feiga-Ita will have no more worries.'

'If only your father had been here to see it.'

'Yes, if only.'

He would have schlepped his last herring, and all because of me. But too late …

Our little family, Bella and Ida and me, moved into two rooms in the school I was going to run, on the top floor at Bukharinskaya 10.

'You can employ your old teacher,' Bella said, proudly. 'Look how far you've come.'

I shrugged. 'Maybe,' I said.

I had not thought of employing Yury. I thought back to all our disputes: perspective, classicism. I thought his values were old-fashioned even then. Now, I am supposed to be running a school where we throw ourselves head first

173

into the sea of revolutionary art. I do not know what that means, but whatever it means, it does not mean Yury Pen, with his stolid, pedestrian representations.

But enough of that. I looked tenderly at Ida, on Bella's knee. I was responsible for this miniature person who had the same number of fingers as me. Seven. When you are responsible for another human being you are not the same person as you were before, believe me. You are a person with a happy load.

'Ida, you know what I heard? Somebody is writing a book about me, about my paintings. Two people, in fact. Tugenhold and Efros, they are called. A book! About me! You are going to be so proud of me.'

Ida gurgled, opened her mouth, kicked her little pink legs. Proud already.

The school on Bukharinskaya had rooms on the second floor, above the Party Arts Administration offices. I showed Bella round my new domain.

We had an art library, not large, but it had shelves, it had books. We had a joinery workshop. We had painting and sculpture studios, and a shop for materials with nothing in it.

A gallery was being set up for student work. And I had my own office, as Director of the school. There was no sign on the door, but somebody had put a disintegrating old desk and a chair behind it, a chair which did not match the desk. I made a sign in balsa wood, in curly letters: *Marc Chagall School Director.* I brought Ida in her crib to watch me fix it on the door.

Vitebsk has not changed, I thought, as I hammered in the nails proclaiming my success. At least not that much. It is still a place of lamp posts, pigs and fences, with animals in the streets. But already there were fewer animals. Already the shops were emptying. Already, it was not as easy as before to get some types of food.

I pretended not to notice. I received a typed formal

memo from Anatoly Vassilyevich Lunacharsky, telling me we had 150 students enrolled. I wondered about teachers. I did not have long to wonder.

I kept running into Yury Pen, streaks of grey in his beard and hair now, face interestingly creasing in new places. He was hanging about the place. He made small talk about the past. He talked about his painting, he asked about mine. He asked after Bella and Ida. He said everything but what was on his mind. Until finally he came out with it.

'There's a rumour going round about teachers for the school.'

'There are always rumours going round, Yury. A new one every day. A time of change is a time of rumours.'

'People are saying teachers have been appointed, for the school.' Yury was dragging out each word. It was costing him to talk like this. I tried not to take pleasure in it. But he had bullied me. Or had he? No, he hadn't. All right, he had been domineering and tried to change my style. I swore I would never do that with my pupils.

'Teachers appointed?' I said. 'First I've heard of it.' And then. 'Look Yury, I don't think this is for you. Not at the moment. Once we are established, modern ways, we can maybe carry somebody who represents the past. But not now.'

Tears sprang to Yury's eyes. He walked away without a word. I saw him in my mind going back to that single man's flat I knew so well. In one of two rooms he would relive what I had said, but he would not share it with anybody else, because there was nobody else to share it with.

I fought back tears of my own. I no longer wore make-up, but out of habit I wiped under my eyes where the mascara would have run. I who had so much had spurned my old teacher who had so little. As School Director I was right to do so. But was being right so important? What did I feel? I knew what I felt. Ashamed, is what I felt.

And guess what? Yury was right about teachers having been appointed. He knew more than I did. And I was the Director. The next day another of these memos appeared on my desk, long, formal, I didn't bother to read it all. But buried in the formal Russian was the phrase 'new teaching staff'.

On a hot rush of rage, I ran upstairs to Lunacharsky's office. You know, when I look back on it I think I was lucky. What I was going to say was better not said. But when I burst into his office, with its pleasant view of cathedral spires and the river bank, Lunacharsky was not there. Other people, however, were there.

Ivan Puni was there. And Ksana Boguslavskaya, who I had last seen on her way from Modi's room after they had made love. And El Lissitzky, the Lazar Lissitzky of my boyhood.

'We are the Teachers' Committee,' Lissitzky announced. 'Welcome.'

'Thank you,' I said, dryly.

'Come, there is a lot to discuss. We must waste no more time,' said Ksana Boguslavskaya, in a tone of mild rebuke, as if I had just come from a day's rafting on the river.

We all sat down, some on the few chairs in Lunacharsky's office, the rest on the floor. I sat on the floor. There was still no sign of Lunacharsky himself. I felt as if I had wandered into another dimension of existence, another life.

'We wish to develop the Society for the Encouragement of Jewish Art,' said Ivan Puni.

We could have been back in Osip Zadkine's room at *La Ruche*. Once again, we were establishing societies, committees and groups. Once again, the group was speaking with one voice, as one entity, as a devouring Group. It did not matter who said what. Sometimes I imagined the three bodies with one mouth. And one brain.

'Another item on the agenda ...' this was Boguslavskaya but, as I say, it could have been any of them '... is the monuments to Karl Liebknecht and Karl Marx.'

176

I was ambushed by my own flippancy before I could stop myself. 'I've never heard of Karl Lieb ... whatever. All I know about Marx is that he was a Jew with a white beard. Mind you, so was Abraham.'

There was a deep silence. Then Lissitzky spoke. Lissitzky is the only man I have ever met whose smile makes him look more serious. 'Actually, technically Marx was a Protestant.'

'Technically?'

'He was born a Protestant.'

'And his beard was black.' That was Boguslavskaya.

The troika resumed their serious work after my trivial, flippant interruption. I felt as if I should stand in the corner, like a naughty pupil, not the School Director.

'The monuments to Liebknecht and Marx are to stand outside the school,' said one of the troika (as I say, it doesn't really matter which one).

'They will be made by our own students, here in our own workshops,' said another one.

I nearly said 'Until a moment ago they were my workshops.' But I choked that back, as it sounded so childish. I must work with these people.

'It is good that we all know each other from *La Ruche*,' said the committee.

'Yes,' I said. 'It means we all know what to expect.'

I could almost hear Zadkine's dog barking mocking assent, all the way from Paris.

But what did the committee matter? Work, my all-important work, my life-blood, work was going well. The Society for the Encouragement of Jewish Art gave me my first commission, the first since my return to Vitebsk. It was a public commission, to decorate the Jewish secondary school next to the main synagogue with a series of massive paintings.

I suggested the three themes: 'Visit to the Grandparents', 'The Feast of Tabernacles' and 'Purim', but Lanacharsky

177

had the final say and for reasons unclear to me, the troika of Puni, Boguslavskaya and Lissitzky had the final say on what went to Lunacharsky for consideration. However, as I excitedly told Bella, I got everything I wanted out of the commissioning process and I was thrilled and energised by the thought of starting work.

I began with my painting of *Purim*, which shows Esther and Mordecai from the Purim story placed against a Vitebsk background.

I was in a state of high excitement, near delirium, as winter came. In our main room at the school, which was studio-cum-living quarters-cum-Ida's bedroom-cum-everything that was not our bedroom – mine and Bella's – I dashed about between the three huge paintings for the Jewish secondary school, working on all of them at the same time, breaking off quite frequently to cuddle Ida, change Ida's nappy, sing to Ida.

Then there was my job, my new job at Vitebsk People's Art School. Bella even called me 'Mister Director' and there were a lot of directing jokes like 'Direct the bottle into Ida's mouth, please.'

Bella did not want to breast-feed. She was permanently tired, she still limped from the ankle injury, she was fractious, skittish and moody, if I'm honest (which I try to be). She missed not only the transportation-into-otherness of acting – which I understood very well – but what she imagined as the camaraderie, forgetting perhaps that when she was part of the acting company there were many, many quarrels.

And what of me? As to actually doing the job, as opposed to being it – being a director – I had to work with the dreaded troika: Lissitzky, Boguslavskaya and Puni.

But then, to be honest with myself, I reminded myself that I had made a complete mess of my one and only forced foray into administration, in the past – arranging army supplies in the Central Bureau for War Economy, that job Shmuel Noah had found for me – so I had to sup with the devil, so to speak.

I arranged a meeting to discuss the school's recognition as an Academy of Higher Learning, which the troika rearranged, and after discussions so boring I went numb, they went through Lunacharsky and through various other committees to Moscow. After that, I am a little vague about what happened.

More congenial to me was the finding of more teachers and more students for my Vitebsk People's Art School. There was a new revolutionary newspaper in Vitebsk, *Art of the Commune*. I walked to their offices in Freedom Square and after only three hours of procedural discussion – mainly about who was going to pay and how – I placed an advertisement asking for teachers.

As for pupils, I felt fully, excitedly, in tune with the revolution's call for art for all. As the first snows came, I stopped passers-by in the street, telling them about my school. Most of them shivered on their way – there was already a shortage of coats – some laughed, but one or two enrolled.

Talking of coats, I had not got one, at least not a proper Russian winter coat. I had a threadbare coat from Paris you could see through. But money was short. The big news among our friends, Bella's and mine, was the Tugendholds buying some new shoes. I had not been paid anything yet – Mister Big-Shot Director. Our savings had run out, so we were living on handouts from the Rosenfelds.

Scraping together what cash we had, I went to Royak the tailor to get my coat patched.

This was at the tumbledown wood annexe to his *izba* tucked away in the rabbit warrens of the Small Side, not far from my late father's factory.

'Ah! Director Moyshe Shagal,' said Royak the tailor. He was a lanky man with a long, lined face, wearing a brown leather cap, a calico shirt worn colourless with washing and a worn leather jerkin. He was sitting cross-legged on the floor, sewing away at a lady's blouse.

'Hello, Royak. How are you?'

'I'm at your service,' he murmured, still concentrating on his work, not looking up. 'What can I do for you?'

'This coat, you see? There's more hole than fabric.' I took it off and held it up.

Royak finally looked up. There was a silence. 'Oy vay! You're not joking, are you? I can't make clothes out of air. And you got plenty of air there, Moyshe.'

'Can you put patches on?'

'Where? It would all be patches.'

'Just the biggest holes.'

Royak the tailor sighed, took the garment and shook it impatiently, as if expecting bugs to fly out of it. Then he examined it minutely, stitch by stitch.

I fell into a reverie while he was doing this. Then jerked awake. Behind the tailor, on the wall, there was a home-made notice board. It had lists of when various tailoring repairs were due, plus the tailor's copy of receipts. But to one side, there was a drawing. It showed the shoe repair shop next to the tailor's, an ordinary *izba* but done in the style of a traditional Russian woodcut. It was good. It was very good.

'Who did that drawing?' I said, nodding at it.

Royak the tailor replied without taking his eyes off my coat. 'My son, Efim.'

'I'd like to enrol your son as a student in my new art college. I think he's very good.'

A wheezing sound emerged from the chest regions of Royak the tailor. Without pausing in his assessment of my coat, his shoulders started to heave. Royak the tailor was laughing.

'Efim is ten years old,' the tailor said.

I blushed. 'Doesn't matter,' I said, defiantly. 'I want the best in my new art school. No, Royak, that's not completely true.' The tailor looked up for a second at that. 'In this new world every man can be an artist. And every woman, too. I am going to help them. We are in a new era now, after the revolution. This is the dawn of a time of universal harmony, liberty and beauty.'

As I spoke, I remembered that Yury Pen frequently took boys and girls as young as ten for his art school. The thought made me angry on two counts. There would be nothing new in my brave new revolutionary policy. And secondly, the thought of Pen made me angry because I knew in my heart I was not treating him fairly. Never mind, the revolution will inevitably create casualties.

The tailor looked up from his work, the half-smile buried under his unruly moustache gone.

'You mean it, Moyshe? The boy loves his drawing. He would love to draw in your school.' Then his long face fell, creasing along its many horizontal lines. 'But we could never afford it.'

'Forget it!' I said, magnanimous *ganzer macher*. 'With his talent, the boy gets the lessons free!'

As I said that, an image of the troika rose up in my mind – Lissitzky, Boguslavskaya, Puni. Even at this early stage, before the school had even opened, I realised I would have to tell them of my noble offer to the tailor, clear everything with them. Their stone-blank, judgemental faces grew bigger in my mind. I shivered with apprehension.

'Thank you,' said Royak the tailor, quietly. 'But I can't …' Royak the tailor held my coat up with a helpless gesture. For a second I thought he meant he couldn't repair it, but then I understood.

'We barely have enough to eat,' he said quietly, with amazing dignity.

I blushed again, tears sprang to my eyes, as I understood him. 'Royak, I will pay for the repair to the coat,' I said, having no idea how I was going to do so. 'You don't have to … give me anything in return for your son's lessons. It's a pleasure! The gift is greater for the giver, as they say. It's a blessing.'

Now, the tailor too had tears in his eyes. 'Thank you, Moyshe,' he said.

In a self-portrait I dashed off at this time, I portrayed myself as a warrior for the revolution. The *Self-portrait with Kris* shows me all bubbly ginger hair and smile, dressed in black in fencer's pose, waving a sword which, despite the title, is too long to be a kris. I knew that but didn't care overmuch.

Meanwhile, I and the Committee of the People's Art School, Vitebsk, found teachers, all with impeccable revolutionary credentials, to head up each department of our new school.

I myself was in charge of the Painting Department, as well as being Director of the school. Lara Radlova was in charge of Drawing, because of her studies of workers working. Ivan Tilberg headed the Sculpture Department. His speciality was concrete busts of Lenin and Marx. These were held to be inspiring socialist art, even if they did tend to melt in the rain. And there was also Nedezhda Lubavina, heading the Preparatory Course, a woman whose dealings with the revolutionary authorities has been exemplary, as she had denounced five people already, all of whom were in camps as a result.

So, at this point, I had sound revolutionary heads of department and a beautiful building. What I did not have were very many canvases, and no ready primed ones at all, which the preparatory class would need; or any paper whatsoever; or any materials the students could sculpt with, other than a little old and hard modelling clay.

I was about to make my first speech as Commissar for the Arts and Director of the People's Art School, Vitebsk.

The school was packed for the official opening ceremony. I had rehearsed my speech, as the new Director, in front of Bella, who had smiled, and baby Ida, who had gurgled appreciatively at it. Bella did not want to come, that evening. That did not surprise me, greatly. She gave the excuse of needing to look after baby Ida, but her parents, the Rosenfelds, could have done that. No, Bella craves the limelight, centre stage. She cannot settle for a place in the wings.

So behind me on the stage in the school hall, sitting precariously on motley broken chairs, dressed in their best, were Anatoly Lunacharsky and the heads of Drawing, Sculpture and the Preparatory Course. Also seated there was the Committee of the People's Art School, Vitebsk. The committee had expanded, comprising not only the troika – Ivan Puni, El Lissitzky and Ksana Boguslavskaya – but eight people altogether, three women and five men.

I had been given notes about Karl Liebknecht and Rosa Luxemburg, so I would say the right things about these people, who were apparently fallen heroes of the People's Revolution in Germany. As well as the local Vitebsk newspapers, there was a reporter from *Isskustvo kommuny* from as far away as Petrograd. There was another one from *Izvestia*. I did not want to make any mistakes.

My voice shaking only slightly, wearing my best suit, I addressed the rows of upturned moon-faces. Speaking from the heart, I spoke of the importance of artistic development for the proletariat and the new art, to be created in this building, which must have wide scope for development.

I spoke of the fundamental differences between the way the artistic development of the masses was carried out under the old regime and how it will be carried out under the dictatorship of the proletariat. As I said that, I looked out for Yury Pen, but I could not see him anywhere.

My speech had been rewritten many times by all eight members of the Committee of the People's Art School, Vitebsk, especially by El Lissitzky. It resembled the written pronouncements about art they were putting out almost daily. Saying it out loud, I experienced a strange

183

feeling of restless ennui. I really just wanted to go home to Bella and Ida.

'In the old days,' I said, 'art existed for the benefit of the happy few. For the working masses, every one of them an artist, the doors to the temple of art and science were tightly closed. Only by a miracle could one of their number gain entry. But now the doors to the scientific and artistic holy of holies have been well and truly opened.'

Then, as peroration, I announced the opening of a new Museum of Art in Vitebsk, headed by myself, as Commissar for Art. There would also be a Communal Studio, for the fulfilment of all commissions in the town, for theatre sets, cinema posters, frescos and signs. All must be passed by the Committee for the People's Art School, Vitebsk.

There was a thunder of applause. I left at the end of it with people shaking my hand.

Swollen with righteousness, I would have helped any worker, anywhere in the world, to do anything. I was looking round for workers to help. I was holy in my comforting conformity.

But to my amazement, the newspaper reports the next day were mixed. The local press, *Vitebskii listok*, was fulsome in its praise. I had opened up 'a little corner of culture in Vitebsk'. I basked in myself as I read that out to Bella, who was silent at it. But *Izvestia* noted to their 'great surprise and chagrin, there were no workers present at the opening of this proletarian institution'.

I was, I must admit, a little annoyed at the distraction from my own paintings, the ones commissioned for the Jewish Secondary School. I was deeply absorbed by those three paintings: *Visit to the Grandparents, The Feast of Tabernacles* and *Purim*. I was still working on them simultaneously and they had become part of me. It was difficult to wrench mind and body from them to struggle through the cold to teach art to small groups of students *en plein air*. But I did.

At least it was not snowing, but it was numbingly cold as we all struggled outside the school with our art materials. The whipping wind blew spitefully through the darns tailor Royak had made in my coat, then through the brown Russian blouse I was wearing beneath it, to look every inch a revolutionary commissar. The silent group of eight people looked wanly to me for a lead.

Pied Piper-like, I led them out of town and up to the hill on the outskirts of Vitebsk which I called *Yurieva Gorka* (Yury's Hill). So here I was, back at *Yurieva Gorka*, with me as teacher, not pupil, and Yury, my teacher, somewhere in the town, at home presumably, painting alone.

I looked round at my charges as they set up their easels, pressing them down in the snow, trying to protect their paints from freezing. Two of them had been house painters before enrolling at the school. They were Mikhail Veksler and Ilya Chashnik.

Chaim Zeldin was one of the many ex-Red Army who had enrolled – former cavalry, Fifteenth Red Army, he told me proudly. You could see his khaki jodhpurs below his long coat. I don't know if he still had his pistol at his waist, under the coat. Most of the ex-revolutionary soldiers stayed armed all the time.

These three, Veksler, Chashnik and Zeldin, were protégés of Ksana Boguslavskaya who, even more than the others on the committee, wanted to bring the workers to art, as well as art to the workers – indeed that was her favourite slogan.

Chaim Zeldin was only two years younger than I was. Ksana had praised the quality of his roof painting, interior painting and signboards to me.

Then there was Lev Zevin, a skinny, girlish boy who looked even younger than Chaim Zeldin. His teeth were chattering as he set up his easel. I think his parents knew El Lissitzky.

The other men were Lazar Khidekel and Moyshe Khunin. I knew little about them but Lazar Khidekel was a burly, fierce-looking fellow who looked as if he was spoiling for a fight. Bella knew Moyshe Khunin's family and did not approve of them. She said his father was a *gonif* who had embezzled money from the synagogue.

But the one I was most aware of, as the wind eddied the top dusting of the snow round our legs there at the bottom of the hill, was Anastasia Ivanovna Berberova. She was the only woman and the only non-Jew.

Her family knew the Jachnin family, which owned the herring wholesaler's where my late father had worked. It had been nationalised by the revolution. Bella said Anastasia had had an affair with Shmuel Jachnin, the son, even though she was married. But at any rate, she was now making great big goo-goo eyes at me. It reminded me of Margot, the model at *La Ruche*. And Kiki and all the others, come to that. This may sound arrogant, but I often wished I had been less well-favoured in face and form, less attractive to women

They started to paint, all of them, while I went from one to the other. Lazar Khidekel was slapping paint about with brisk, childish confidence.

'Hey!' I said to him, peering over his ham of a shoulder, 'Slow down! You're not painting a roof now!'

He wheeled round, clenching the fist not holding his paintbrush, waving it under my nose. His tortured face was all burning brown eyes and stubble. I wished I could have painted him as Christ.

'OK, OK,' I said, stepping back. 'Take it easy. It was just a joke!'

'Not a very funny one,' growled the house painter, his voice gravelly in the wind.

I hastily moved on.

It occurred to me then that I have never been interested in the 'dirty work', as I thought of it, of producing a picture. The planning, the preparation. If you think about it you destroy it. All I am interested in is reaching the finished version. I resolved to be more circumspect, if only to protect myself from the fury of my pupils.

I stopped behind Anastasia Berberova.

'Not bad,' I said unconvincingly, as some shaky houses thinly dotted her canvas. 'But you must work more quickly. *Alla prima* painting has to be done fast, before the paint dries. Think of Monet ...'

She stopped painting and smiled up at me.

'Show me,' she said, offering me her brush.

'Well ... all right.' I made a few brush strokes on her painting, with her brush, and then stopped. I stared at the painting. 'Look at that ... What is that colour? It's the new cadmium red, isn't it?'

She smiled up at me but said nothing. I gave her the brush back.

To break the awkward silence I cleared my throat, shivering in the cold, shivering with nerves. I plunged in without thinking. 'Matisse would never have used that colour, for a start,' I said, falling into that horrible jocularity that had just failed so completely with the house painter, Lazar Khidekel. I jabbed my finger at the too bright red. 'It's like a whore's lipstick.'

She looked at me with mock reproach, head on one side. She was a petite, gamine brunette with short hair and a boyish figure, a physical type I have a weakness for. Our eyes met for a second. Then she wordlessly offered me the brush again.

I could not resist taking it. For the next fifteen minutes I lost myself in improving her painting, with her standing close to my shoulder, occasionally touching my body with hers.

I was happy enough doing this, though pangs about my own paintings kept breaking through the trance I fell into while painting Anastasia's. But then, suddenly, as if at a signal, the little group all started asking questions.

'How do I capture the cloudy sky?'

'Must I have a vanishing point?'

'Look, have I got this path through the snow quite

187

right?'

'Be quiet! Be quiet a moment,' I shouted at them. And then a white mist clouded my mind, formed of frustration and impatience in equal parts. I shouted out something that had not even consciously occurred to me before.

'You are all using too many colours,' I yelled into the wind. 'Look! Just look at the scene. Red, blue-green. A quiet red. Some white for the snow. That is all you need.'

'Now he tells us,' shouted Mikhail Veksler.

That started them all off. 'What's the point of letting us get so far and then ...?'

'What do you mean? You're not being clear.'

'Leave him alone!' That was Anastasia.

I put my hands over my freezing ears to drown out their din.

Chaim Zeldin, Mikhail Veksler and Ilya Chashnik complained to Ksana Boguslavskaya the next day. They made much of my 'incorrect' attitude to proletarian strivings. Ksana came to see me at home. Privately, she was sympathetic. She was warm with Bella, expressing concern about my wife's new fears of leaving the house, something which had suddenly come upon her. She was sweet to little Ida, even bringing her a home-made wooden toy, a diabolo.

She asked to see what I was painting at the moment, so I showed her: propped up on an easel in our bedroom was a painting called *The Martyr*. As in *The White Crucifixion*, my most famous painting, a Christ/Chagall figure is shown wearing a *tallith* – a prayer-shawl – in his martyrdom. But in this painting the full-bearded figure of Christ/Chagall is tied to a post, not a cross.

He is wearing a cap, just like the one I had seen on Royak, the tailor. His arms are tied behind his back. His legs are tied to the post, so he is off his feet. A Magdalen figure in a veil clutches his legs. This is Bella. Just in front of him, a Jew with a moustache and beard reads from a holy book. This is Bella's father, Shmuel Noah Rosenfeld.

Behind the tied Christ/Chagall figure, as background, Vitebsk is in flames. Uncle Neuch, the original fiddler on the roof, is playing his fiddle to the Christ/Chagall figure's right. A red flying cow gives succour; a rooster flies on guard above the figure's head.

Ksana Boguslavskaya stared at the painting in fixed silence. Then she looked quizzically at me. Suddenly, it was clear to me what I had done, or what the artist in me had done. My fears for Vitebsk were laid bare, in colour. And to fear for the future was to question the revolution.

But Ksana said nothing, so, naively, I thought her visit had settled the matter of the complaints. But she reported the complaints about me to the Committee, even asking for written statements from all the students. It was a pattern I was to experience again and again in my time as Director of the School and Commissar of Art for Vitebsk.

I also thought at the time that she had not mentioned my painting, *The Martyr*, to the Committee, but she had.

I was striding, marching along, long legs along the middle of the road, which was clear of the snow banking on the pavements. It was dusk, the light fading fast, lamps popping alight in the distance, the cold growing thicker. The faint light was violet.

I was on my way to collect Bella from the baths. I was pleased to have got her out of the house at all. Her fears, her anxieties, her terrors were growing all the time, paralysing her or inducing fits of screaming. What worried me most was that she seemed to embrace these fears, these hours, now days of panic. She saw something creative in them; she felt she was growing by them, being shown another world.

When the fears took her she was incapable of looking after baby Ida. Chana the cook had left us; we could not have paid her anyway. Right now, Bella's sister, also called Chana, was visiting every day to help. Sister Chana was

189

the only person, aside from me, who Bella would entrust with Ida.

I could hear the river gurgling and plashing in the background, though I could no longer see it. The violet had turned black. The noise still reminded me of rafting in the summer in my boyhood.

Suddenly, I saw two figures coming towards me very slowly. It was a man and a woman. Even from here, in such poor light, it was obvious the woman was with child. They were laden with baggage, both carrying cases. He had something strapped to his back. It looked like a cross.

I stopped, peering at them as they came closer to me. As they approached, I felt a clammy chill which had nothing to do with the weather. Words flashed into my mind, words from nowhere: 'And the darkness he called night.'

'Hello!' The man called out to me as they approached.

More words flashed in my mind: 'And the days draw near that Israel must die.'

Here was a skinny goat tethered by the riverside. Behind the couple, in the road, a withered black cock suddenly let out an almighty crowing. I shivered, more in fear than cold. When the hour of judgement comes, the black cock will crow.

'Hello,' called the man again. Now the couple were closer I could see that the struts strapped to his back were not a cross, they were an artist's easel. 'We have just arrived in this town, from the station. I fear we are lost. I am looking for Bukharinskaya 10. There is a school there.'

'Yes, I know it.' My voice was weak, my teeth chattering.

'Good. Then perhaps you know El Lissitzky? He was supposed to meet us at the station. There has been a misunderstanding, perhaps.'

'Yes, I know Lissitzky.'

'Excellent! Lissitzky has invited me to teach at the school. My name is Kazimir Malevich. This is my wife. We are to live at the school, too. We have two rooms

190

allocated to us, next door to the Director, somebody called Marc Chagall.'

I swear it grew suddenly colder as he spoke. The wind dropped, yet the air grew chill. Even so, I began to sweat all over my body. I thought of Bella, both as talisman and because I suddenly apprehended all her nameless fears.

None of us moved or spoke. Over the tableau of the three of us, it lightly began to snow.

I remembered Malevich's self-portrait and the portrait of his wife, both painted before he started the Suprematist movement, which was soon to dominate my life. In the self-portrait, Malevich's riot of colour evokes Expressionism, yet there is an over-controlled, rigid feel to it which denies its Expressionist birthright. Careful swirls of red against darker red in the background allow us to imagine what Matisse might have produced had he become an accountant. A green jacket is nailed in place by rigid shoulders.

Malevich shows himself square-on to the viewer, both eyes equally visible. It is a handsome face with chiselled planes, the young man's hair a complementary block of strength.

But we return to those eyes. They suck you in, as his Suprematist black square was to suck in art. They are bright blue, Cobalt blue, those eyes. They would be glacial, except glaciers have a life, albeit frozen. Malevich is a good-enough painter (just) to sum up his own essence. That essence is nothingness.

Those eyes are dead.

It is intriguing to see what this still-life of a man made of his wife, when he painted her. The answer is, he painted her as a servant. Sophia Mikhailovna Malevich, née Rafalovich, is painted holding the handle of a shopping basket in one hand and a scrubbing-brush in the other. She is wearing a bizarre outfit: a white servant's mob cap, trimmed with red, tops her head, and her red, white and blue dress – full white skirt with red inset, tight blue bodice nipped in at the waist – is reminiscent of an eighteenth-century servant's livery.

Sophia's face is rendered blankly business-like. It is a face of sharp points: sharp pointed chin, sharp pointed nose, slash-lips sharp at their ends. She is looking absorbedly past the viewer – none of the fixed challenge of Kazimir's pose, with its unnaturally open eyes.

She is on her way, Sophia is. She is ready to clean. She is ready to serve. Serve whom? Oh, need we ask?

When Bella and I arrived back from the baths, back at our shoe-box two-room flat, Ida was screaming in Chana's arms, defying her aunt's attempts to rock her to sleep.

'I don't know what's wrong with her,' Chana said.

Chana was edgy, though not as fearful as Bella. She was dark, too, like Bella, but bonier and not so pretty. She was much older than Bella and because she had left the family home so early, Bella thought of her as more like an aunt or even a distant cousin than a sister.

Bella took the baby. She started to coo at her. Ida continued to scream. If anything, her screaming grew louder.

'I was talking to Thea Brachman the other day,' Chana said. 'She said she'd be happy to come and babysit for you.'

Bella shot her a sharp look. Chana met her gaze.

'She's cold,' Bella murmured. 'Little Ida is cold. It's so hard to keep the blood flowing, these days.'

'I know,' Chana said.

'Can't you and David do anything?'

There was an edge to Bella's voice at this familiar refrain. David Rubin, Chana's husband, was a Bolshevik of long standing. The Rosenfelds had rescued him from gaol more than once, before the revolution. Chana followed David in politics, I think from conviction, though who knew, exactly?

Anyway, now we were living the revolution, Bella

expected her sister and brother-in-law to solve all our problems as they were so well in with the victorious Bolsheviks. So far, this wish had not been met. David Rubin worked at the town hall and was Commissar for the Spread of the Revolution. But our flat was as cold as ever; we still did not have enough to eat; I still had not been paid.

Chana left without another word. Bella resumed trying to pacify Ida. I went to bed to get a couple of hours' sleep before working on my paintings for the rest of the night.

Kazimir and Sophia Malevich arrived at their flat, next door to ours, after Bella and I got back from the baths. I can only assume they went to see Lissitzky, to whom Malevich owed his appointment, before moving in, otherwise they would have got back to the school first.

At any rate, as soon as Malevich and his wife arrived, Sophia started cleaning, first their flat, then the corridor outside. She used Argyrol to clean. The same stuff Indenbaum's wife once used to clean the corridors of *La Ruche*. The same stuff that would make Chaim Soutine's fortune when Barnes, the Argyrol king, bought all his paintings.

I fell asleep to the smell of Argyrol and dreamed a dream of The Hive. The Hive was being attacked by wasps. It was to be the beginning of a New Order, the overthrow of the bees. The Hive Mind, that unconscious repository of accumulated being, had called out the denizens in defence of our dwelling, our way of life, our morality, our lives.

Old Mme Segondet, as the Queen Bee, was leading the fight. In the guise of drones were Soutine and Modi, Mané-Katz, Kisling and Krémègne, Indenbaum and Osip Zadkine, all the Jewish painters and sculptors at The Hive. And there I was, Moyshe Shagal, young again, hovering on the edge, still with traces of make-up, transformed into a bee.

The attacking wasps were led by Kazimir Malevich, quite recognisable as a wasp. Behind him, El Lissitzky, then Ivan Puni and his lover Ksana Boguslavskaya. Behind them, nameless faceless countless wasps all the same, all thinking the same, all doing the same – a great thick swarm of them; a majority of them, a majority of the Ma-le, meaning The Bad, justified in any evil by future dreams, by their numbers and the implicit threat of *force majeure.*

And then I was not with the bees any more, though still a bee. I was on the outside, as ever, watching the wasps. I watched them, the dark swarm, just passing La Rotonde in enviable sunshine and warmth. The customers were sitting outside, as ever, drinking, eating, talking, laughing.

Patron Libion looked terrified as the swarm flew over his café. He flapped at them, bare hams of arms, a dancing apron, twisting this way and that. Some of the wasps stopped, bothered the flailing patron, swooped at him, others flew at the exposed sweetness of the food. But most continued on their mission, not to be deflected.

Led in a straight line by Kazimir Malevich, to whom a curve would be alien, as a thing of beauty, they swarmed into the wild Eden gardens of number 2 passage de Danzig. They were in view of The Hive.

At the gates, there was an old Jewish peddler. He swiped at the wasps with both hands, protecting the food on his cart. As with patron Libion, a few were temporarily deflected from their mission. This time two of them stung the peddler, who screamed. But the main body, one body with one mind, Malevich's, flew on in formation.

With me still watching from the outside, still a bee, they passed the sculpture of *The Spirit Shackled* in the gardens of The Hive. A few, again, broke off to swarm angrily at the impassive stone face of the angel of the free spirit. Malevich, however, flew determinedly on, in the lead, not to be deflected.

I caught myself admiring his single-mindedness. Why

am I so impressed by my enemies? We seek something to admire in anything, even evil. Why?

And on the wasps flew, blotting the sun from the garden I used to call my run-down Eden. They landed on, and defiled with their yellow toxic waste, the fruit trees, chestnut trees, linden trees and lilac bushes I knew so well.

The animals ran for it – the goats, ducks and hens in the garden. Even the rats ran for it. I saw a black cat running the same way, but whether it was the same black cat I knew, Matou, I could no longer say.

The wasp swarm ignored the bust of the Queen of Romania, there in the gardens. They were arrowing in. Their buzzing was growing louder, enraged by the stench of blood from the Vaugirard abattoir. They wanted blood of their own. Bee blood. They wanted The Hive wiped out and the last bee dead.

The wasps flew in formation along the pathway known as the Boulevard of Love, then they were in, through every crack and fissure. The bees had smelled them coming, even before they heard them. They began to fan their wings.

The defending bees, with me among them, engaged the wasps at the top of the corridor, outside the Queen Bee's area. The stench of propolis, the bee-glue from tree-buds holding The Hive together, was suddenly great as The Hive's very existence was threatened. The wasps were bigger than the drone bees; only the Queen was as big as the wasp leader.

The bees grew hectic as they faced the alien vibration from the wasps. They dug into the wax of The Hive walls for traction. Their buzzing grew louder. The first of the bees to attack was Modi, that face still handsome in the guise of a bee. He was instantly surrounded by wasps, their slashing claws cutting him to pieces in seconds. Kikoine and Kisling carried his body away, what was left of it, before the wasps could devour him completely.

I knew what was going to happen next. With a crack of his powerful jaws, the Malevich wasp bit Soutine's head off. Soutine looked bewildered for a second, then died. His fragile chance at life came and went in a day.

The wasps were trying to crush the bees against the walls of The Hive with the weight of their bodies. When wasps in gangs of two or three broke free, they slashed with their claws or bit at the bees. One bee, a sculptor called Alexandre Archipenko, managed a sting and then died.

Some wasps diverted to the stores of pollen and nectar, which gave the bees a chance, heavily outnumbered as they were. The hairy drones were using their weight against the wasps. Then the Queen Bee engaged the wasp leader in the narrow passageway, while around them fighting paused.

The Queen Bee was an imposing sight with her long abdomen, broad thorax and powerful orange-brown legs. She unleashed her curved sting. Some of her followers screamed 'no', fearing she would die if she used it. The wasp leader edged towards her, pushing each of his six elbows forward, one by one. Faster than sight, the Queen Bee shot forward, breaking an antenna off the wasp leader's head with her powerful mandible. I saw my chance, as the wasp leader screamed, and broke off another of its antennae.

The wasp leader was screaming, pouring vile green blood from its head. The other bees bravely held the wasps off while the wasp leader died, finally subsiding in a writhing heap. We had won. Not without terrible cost, but we had won.

As we cleared the body of the dead wasp leader from the corridor, it turned back into Kazimir Malevich and I woke up screaming. I was gasping, sobbing uncontrollably.

'Moyshe!' Bella was shaking me. 'Moyshe, wake up!'

'Bella, Bella. I was dreaming.'

Bella's gamine face swam into my view above her grey, once white flannelette nightgown. 'You woke me up,' she said. 'The first sleep I've had in days and you woke me up.'

'I'm sorry. I think I'll go and paint now.'

196

'Yes. That's it. Go and paint. You don't even put your arms around me any more. You leave me to the cold.'

'I'm sorry. If I could make everything right for you and for Ida I would.'

'But you can't, can you? Moyshe, I'm so afraid, so terribly afraid. Sometimes I want to die, just to get away from the fear. And the cold.'

I thought to myself that bees die below eight degrees. How cold does it have to get here before we die?

The first Suprematist painting I ever saw was Kazimir Malevich's *The Black Square*. It appeared out of nowhere hanging malevolently high over the door to Malevich's office.

Malevich's *Black Square* is a square painted in uniform black. It represents nothing, it evokes nothing but nothingness. It was consciously intended to destroy earlier ways of picturing the world.

Monet said black does not exist in nature. That, to Malevich, was the whole point. *The Black Square* was a revisionist assault on nature as much as it was on art. It was an attempt to destroy all that had gone before, artistic Hour Zero, a square black hole into which all preceding life would be sucked to its destruction.

It would all be replaced by a movement whose rules were to be determined by Malevich and his committee – UNOVIS (Exponents of the New Art). Malevich and UNOVIS called the new movement Suprematism, a term which lays bare its pitch for artistic and personal power. Under Suprematism 'constructions on a single plane' comprising 'geometrical relations' would reflect the 'utilitarian perfection of the coming concrete world'.

These quotations are from the UNOVIS Manifesto, written by Kazimir Malevich and printed on the lithographic presses of the Vitebsk artistic workshop in my school. The manifesto makes no mention of dreams or beauty in 'the coming concrete world' to be ushered in by the revolution, but colour does get a mention. It is banned: 'The town as a form of energetic combination of materials has lost its colours and become tonal. Black and white predominate in it.'

Our manifold visual perceptions of the world are to be replaced by the central icon of the spinning disc, blurring all colour. Indeed, even the world itself is to face relegation – 'The earth will be abandoned like a house eaten up by termites.' Suprematist fascination with the cosmos and space travel always implied finding a more perfect – meaning regular or uniform – alternative world out there somewhere.

Where art goes, humankind will follow. The revolution is to create its own new human beings for the coming better world. The title of one of Malevich's Suprematist pamphlets is 'We, as Utilitarian Perfection.'

Soon, Malevich's *Black Square* was joined on display by the second Suprematist painting I ever saw. It was called *Cross (Black)*. It was a thick black cross against a grey background.

The first change brought by the revolution in Russia was the inner lift of hope and belief brought about by the breaking of all Tsarist restrictions on the Jews. That lasted a few weeks, at the most. Bella was among the first to lose hope. Her belief in a better future was replaced within a month by underlying anxiety and surface fear.

The reason for such speed of vanishing belief was the next most obvious effect of the revolution. Throughout that first bitter winter, we were short of food and fuel. It was a struggle to ever get warm, to get nourishment for baby Ida or food for ourselves.

After that, the most noticeable change was the soldiers. Soldiers were everywhere. The Fifteenth Red Army was quartered in Vitebsk. They were based in an old Tsarist barracks in what was now Karl Marx Square, right near the main bridge over the Dvina River.

Their aeroplanes flew like moths in the sky, the first aeroplanes I had seen. David Rubin, my well-placed brother-in-law, who suddenly knew everything, told us that this army had twelve aeroplanes. *Twelve!* Such mighty power was unimaginable. How could it ever be opposed? We had better behave, had we not? Behave all over again, with new masters.

When the soldiers and their aeroplanes came, the animals left. Maybe they knew something, animals usually do. When I went back to the Small Side to visit my ancient mother and my remaining sisters I kept asking myself where the goats and the roosters of my childhood had gone. Sure, there was the occasional emaciated goat. A couple of donkeys, even. But the roosters had either flown off or been boiled down for soup.

These changes were the most immediate because we experienced them with our senses – hunger with the belly, soldiers with the eyes and so on. But then came the changes that affected the soul and the psyche. These were caused by the preponderance and dominance of organisations.

The most important organisation was the Cheka, the secret police. In the early days this was just a curiosity. The omniscient David Rubin, who looked a bit like Lenin himself with his bald dome, goatee beard and slight frame, told us to be careful what we said to whom. You never knew who was reporting.

This was over a meagre dinner, back at my family home on Pokrovskaya. I must admit I thought David was just trying to frighten the women, that and be the know-all. You know, the town hall man, our man on the inside of events? Trying or not, he certainly succeeded. Bella took to her bed for three days after David's advice.

David also advised me to learn to work through organisations. As well as the Extraordinary Commission to Combat Counter-Revolution, Sabotage and Speculation – known as the Cheka – there was also Glavproforb, the

Central Administration of Professional Education, which was quickly taken over by Glavpolitprosvet, the Central Administration of Political Education.

Then there was Narkompros, the Commissariat of Public Education; Obmokhu, the Society of Young Artists; and Posnovis, Young Followers of the New Art.

I was and remained bewildered by these organisations, constantly mixing them up. The air was thick with initials. Malevich, however, sat in the sluggish stream of acronyms like a basking alligator. He was so at home in his own organisation, Unovis – Exponents of the New Art – that he called his newly born girl-child Una, after his organisation.

Unovis itself eventually gave birth to Proun, Project in Affirmation of the New; Sorabis, the Union of Workers in the Arts; and Volfila, Free Philosophers, possibly the most misnamed organisation in world history.

And me? Well, if Malevich was born to be part of a committee, I was born to be alone. Me, I'm Moyshe Shagal, later promoted to Marc Chagall, and that's it. In my battles with Malevich I was a lone soldier taking on cohorts of highly organised drones, all flying in formation.

So who do you think won?

Kazimir Malevich arrived in Vitebsk with a title and a ready-made programme. The title was 'Studio Leader at the People's Art School'. The programme, developed to put Suprematist principles into practice, was one he had developed originally in his days in Moscow, but here it quickly became the Unovis Unified Painting Course.

The introduction and implementation of this course was an attempt to take over my school. It was led by Malevich, with El Lissitzky, and principally supported by two women teachers, Vera Ermolaeva and Nina Kogan, both of whom were besotted with Malevich.

Sophia Mikhailovna, Malevich's wife, had been sent out on cleaning work within days of giving birth. Baby Una was given to a wet-nurse on the Small Side, near the docks.

200

This left the Malevich flat, next door to us, conveniently vacant for Malevich's trysts with both Ermolaeva and Kogan.

For Malevich possessed a demonic fascination for females. What means he used to attract them I do not know. But it seemed he could, and did, possess any female he desired among the teaching staff and the students. On occasion, he diversified to the more labile among the male students, including my student Lev Zevin, who was among the party I had taken up to Yurieva Gorka (Yury's Hill) that day.

Bella is no prude. I, perhaps, am. Though even Bella grew tired of having to listen to the triumphs of Malevich's desires through the thin partition between our two flats. Somehow, it was clear to me that Malevich's sex with women was totally unlike Modi's, back at *La Ruche*, which I could also hear through the wall. To Modi, sex was joy and he brought joy-in-bliss to his partners, even if heartbreak sometimes followed.

To Malevich, though, sex was conquest by superior power. It was not centred on his own pleasure, let alone the partner's. The screams we heard in our flat were pleas for mercy, not cries of ecstasy. That much was clear even to an ingénu like me. And yet his partners came back for more. All of them did.

Sad though this was, what was more important to me was the ease with which this black technique of Malevich's was bringing the women teachers over to his side.

Vera Ermolaeva had had polio as a child and dragged one leg behind her in a caliper. She was well-read, from a rich family and pretty – I used to call her the Giaconda of Vitebsk. We were friends, yet that counted for nought against her enslavement by Malevich.

Nina Kogan was a converted Jew, the daughter of a military doctor. She was a highly cultured person, but Malevich polluted the well-spring of her artistic being so everything came out in his image.

For example, Nina produced a ballet, but it became a Suprematist ballet in which the dancers' movements had to echo approved Suprematist forms: Form 1 was a line; Form 2, a cross; Form 3, a star; Form 4, a circle; Form 5, a square, a black square. It was a series of Malevich paintings made flesh, springing from Malevich's member, just as Una was Unovis made flesh, springing from the same source.

Already intimidated by the man who was notionally my subordinate, I hatched a plan to know him and his work better. I did not know myself whether my intention was to accommodate him, find common ground, or oppose him with the weapon of better knowledge and understanding.

At any rate my suggestion was this: 'Kazimir Severinovich,' I shouted to him with false bonhomie as we ran into each other in the joint corridor outside our flats – already it reminded me of a black parody of the happy chance encounters I used to have at *La Ruche*.

He stared at me through blank blue eyes. He stared into me and through me.

'Kazimir Severinovich,' I started again. 'I have an idea whereby we can get to know each other's work and … er … ideologies better.'

'I do not have ideologies. I have only one ideology. Suprematism.'

'Er … Y-y-y-yes.' To my intense annoyance, my stammer came back, full-force.

He just stared at me. Was he about to command me into his flat for sexual subjugation?

'My idea is that I visit your lessons and you visit mine. In that way we …'

'I agree.'

And with that Kazimir Malevich strode past me in the corridor, as if I were not there.

My intention was that I visit *one* Malevich class and he *one* of mine. However, this was clearly not what Malevich had understood. He came to all my sessions with the students and somehow I found myself going to far more of his than I had intended. As I admitted to myself at the time, there was something hypnotic about being drawn into Malevich's orbit. It was like being sucked into a spinning black maelstrom; unknown, not safe, the outcome frightening, yet exhilarating.

Malevich's part of the Unovis Unified Painting Course took place in a huge room which had once been the banker Vishnyak's dining room.

Incidentally, there was much righteous congratulation at the fate of the former owner of the sometime mansion, now the school. Ivan Vishnyak, word had it, had fled the revolution and was now starving on the streets of Vilnius. He was universally assumed to deserve this fate, a triumph for the revolution. I never met the banker – presumed evil by virtue of his occupation – but my friend Viktor Mekler spoke well of him. He had loaned Viktor the money to start his business. The terms had been fair, though it was more than Viktor's life was worth – literally – to admit that now.

All that remained of the banker in his dining room was slowly being exorcised by the Unovis Committee. This exorcising of the past took the very practical form of burning all the banker's furniture, bit by bit, partly on class grounds but also because there was no other source of fuel in what was turning into a morbidly freezing winter. First the dresser went up in flames, then the sideboard, then the huge oak dining table, then the chairs.

When I first visited Malevich's lectures, some students sat on chairs and took notes on the table. By the end of my time as Malevich's observer – I felt like a student even if I was nominally his boss – all the packed-in students sat on the floor and took notes on the floor, swathed in overcoats, scarves and all the layers of clothing they possessed.

Outside the dining room, nailed to the banker's coffered

and once polished door like Luther's Theses on the door of the church at Wittenberg, was the following notice:

Presently, all artistic tendencies are represented at the school: students are free to choose among the teachers the one whose orientation best suits them.

I used to stop outside the door to Malevich's lectures and read and re-read that notice every time, before I went in, with Malevich's disciplined throng marching past me; they even mobbed in straight lines. I do think that word 'presently' in the notice was the most concise threat I have ever received – concentrated menace. It was aimed at me, everybody knew that. Anybody choosing me and my 'orientation' would be making a strictly temporary choice. The norm, the comforting, crushing norm had been established and I was outside it.

Now and again, trucks full of Cheka drove past outside on Bukharinskaya, which I still thought of as the old Voskenskaya, their rattling engines, puttering the ancient vehicles through the snow, reinforcing in sound the threat made by Malevich's words. And while the word-threat was still only implicit, the sound-threat certainly was not.

After I had read Malevich's notice, I would make my way in and sit on the floor with the others – sitting to one side would have been viewed as bourgeois elitism. Then I listened quietly to the master.

Malevich harangued them in front of a portable blackboard, furiously scribbling on it in chalk, wiping it with his sleeve, then scribbling on it again. He was listened to in silence shrouded in respect, awe and reverence. Nobody ever drew as much as a line, nobody painted. We listened. We imbibed. We were changed.

According to Malevich's lectures, all art and the voyage of each artist, without exception, must be from Cubism to Suprematism. Or as I thought of it, from art with no soul to art which made the soul impossible for all time.

The passing from Cubism to the new ultimate, Suprematism, was to be marked by a series of set, fixed, mechano-biological stages. Specific stimuli in the drawing or painting create genes in the viewer which remake the way the viewer sees. The aim, then, was to redesign the viewer to fit the picture.

Much of Malevich's lecturing consisted of illustrating the stages of this redesigning process and how the 'stimuli', that is the artwork of squares, rectangles and so on, would vary at each stage.

Each new stage would be marked by 'additions' (*dobavki*, in Russian). This term was then changed to supplements (*pribavki*) and finally the stimulus for the redesign of the viewer was known as the 'surplus element' (*pribavochnyi element*) as that brought it closer to the Marxist-Leninist term 'surplus value', thus bringing art neatly and totally in line with the correct political theory.

All this was received in reverential, concentrated silence by the students. Eventually, over the days and weeks, there were only a few left taking notes, as there was hardly any paper of any sort in Vitebsk, but all of them absorbed what they were told. The respectful silence continued even after three hours of Malevich talking. Nobody moved a muscle until told to disperse. Their faces were uniformly hard and blank.

Outside, Cheka trucks continued their apparently continuous throat-clearing roar, while occasionally military aeroplanes were visible through the now grimy picture windows, all reinforcing the Malevich message, in case anybody had any doubts. Though by and large, except for me, they did not.

And I kept my doubts to myself while I listened to his lectures. I certainly kept them to myself when I endorsed Malevich's claim to Lunacharsky via Glavproforb (or it may have been Glavprolitprosvet or even Gubispolkom) for payment for sixteen lectures of three hours each on

'The Theory and History of Painting'.

The payment came through promptly. At that point, none of the rest of us had received as much as a kopek.

Apart from my large paintings for the school, I was doing a lot of work for the theatre around this time. I was doing a design for the curtain of the State Jewish Theatre. I was doing the stage sets for a Sholem Aleichem play called *Mazeltov* which starred the best-known actor of the day, Solomon Mikhoels. I was even moving into costume design, with Bella and Chana's enthusiastic help and support. Even Thea Brachmann popped back into my life to help out.

I was enjoying all this collaboration with artistic people. I would have been happy without my duties as Director of the School and Commissar for the Arts. I had to schlep to Moscow to plead for funds, which I hated. I had to do administration for the school, which I hated, and could not do. And then there was the constant malevolent Male-threat.

But at any rate, at the beginning, my teaching was going well, after that shaky start on Yurieva Gorka. It was going so well I even contemplated bringing my own teacher, the 'reactionary' Yury Pen, back onto the staff.

Bella wanted me to, so did Viktor Mekler – they tended to agree on everything. I told them 'wait and see'. I was hoping to gain strength, overcome the Malevich-Lissitzky faction. After that, bringing back Yury would be my 'thank you' to him – perhaps overdue.

At first, my classes were oversubscribed. Everybody wanted to be taught by the famous Marc Chagall, who had sold paintings in Paris. They all knew of Efros's book about me; some had even read it. In those early days, the printed word was still respected.

Malevich came to the first of my art lessons in the school building – it was now too cold for any more *plein air* excursions. Fortunately for me, it was a howling success, though perhaps that gave me too much false hope. I don't know.

But when he came to my lesson, that day, I was soaring, soaring above Vitebsk. Perhaps a bit too hubristic, on reflection. But then I have always been very self-critical. Anyway, I enthusiastically explained my teaching methods and what I was doing, with Malevich listening.

We were on the second floor, in what had once been one of the banker's many bedrooms. There was a lovely view out over the rooftops. All my students were drawing or sketching. They had been asked to work on similar projects to me, but not exactly the same. So they painted stage sets, but not exactly the ones I was painting. Ditto the costume design. Some painted landscapes, scenes from around Vitebsk.

I went from one to the other, helping, encouraging, or so I hoped. Teaching!

'You are looking for beauty,' I said to Anastasia. This was Anastasia Ivanovna Berberova, who had been part of the party at Yury's Hill. She was painting a pretty market scene, prettifying it further.

'Don't do that,' I said. 'Don't look for beauty. You must find something ugly and make it beautiful. That is adding art to nature.'

Anastasia nodded hard, giving me a dazzling smile. 'Is it good?' she said, nodding at her canvas.

I smiled back, conscious of Malevich watching me. 'Not bad. Not bad!'

I felt like a woman in revealing clothes, being watched by a man about to possess her as I moved from easel to easel with Malevich's eyes boring into my body, listening to what I said.

Then, in the second half of the lesson, I stopped my students – I had about forty in the class, fewer than Malevich. I instructed them to gather round and watch me paint.

207

I was painting *The Wedding Feast*. *The Wedding Feast* was a celebration of marriage and food, eating in love and joy, painted for a theatre. It showed the family herring on a borrowed blue plate as the centrepiece of a feast of joy.

I had deliberately chosen a still life because the subject is uncomplicated but resonates deeply. While I worked, I talked about the choices I was making. How near can the blue of the plate come to that yellow circle top right? If you have a herring on one plate and a little man on another plate, what messages does that send?

It was like being back at *La Ruche*, learning from Chaim Soutine, from Modi, but also teaching them. I was teaching well, I knew I was. I caught myself wanting Malevich's approval. I felt myself soaring, floating again. Dangerous.

The door burst open. Nobody knocked since the revolution, knocking was bourgeois, privacy was outlawed. A woman member of the administration burst in. As Director I should have known her name, but I did not. Even indoors in the middle of the day, she was swathed in an outdoor coat, against the cold. Behind her, I recognised the tubby figure of Ivan Poporillo, saddlemaker and former mayor of Vitebsk, before the revolution – obviously, there were no mayors now.

'Comrade Malevich,' said the woman. 'Here is Comrade Poporillo. He wishes to make a complaint.'

Ignoring me altogether, she then swept out of the room again.

'What is the nature of your complaint, Comrade?' said Malevich, in that dry, even tone of his, as if he is forever reading out instructions to assemble a machine.

Poporillo looked round the room, bewildered. He caught sight of me and beamed. He had lost what I estimated as half his previous weight, but he was still the last fat man left in Vitebsk.

'Moyshe Zakharovich,' began the tubby saddler. 'We were asked, in no uncertain terms I may add, to loan property for the revolution, to be painted, as I understand it. And I did. But if it's all the same to you, I'd like it back now. We need it. It's my wife's ...' He added this last bit apologetically, the steam of his indignation evaporating from him in this strange room with such a large audience.

I played to the gallery, always a weakness of mine on the rare occasions I found myself in a large gathering.

'What is the nature of this object of yours, Simeon Fyodorovich?' I asked with mock solemnity. I was rewarded by laughter from my group and the huge brown eyes of Anastasia wide on my face.

'Why, Moyshe Zakharovich, it is a most valuable plate. The crown jewels, so to speak, of my dear wife's dowry.'

'Not a blue plate?' I spoke with mock seriousness. The students were hooting laughter, even Malevich was smiling.

'Yes! That's the one. A blue plate. Yes. Aaaagh!' The tubby saddler actually jumped in the air. 'I see it there. There it is.' He pointed dramatically to my carefully posed still life, with a herring on a blue plate at its centre.

'That blue plate?'

'Yes, that blue plate.'

'You cannot have that blue plate.'

'But it's miiii-ine.' The tubby former mayor hoped from foot to foot in anguish.

I thought of mocking the revolution by saying that all private property was theft, but thought better of it (fortunately). Instead, I said, 'Simeon Fyodorovich, your blue plate is no longer a blue plate.'

'It's not? Then ...?'

'Simeon Fyodorovich, your blue plate is now *art*!'

There was a crash of laughter engulfing the entire room.

I eventually made arrangements to return the plate to its owner – though one must no longer use that word. But more importantly, for me, I made a short statement to the students after Ivan Poporillo had gone.

Staring hard at Malevich, I said, 'We must be careful not to erase the individual peculiarities of each person, while working in a collective.'

Malevich remained impassive, blank blue eyes, as ever, unblinking, but I could see he had taken in my words. They were not to be forgotten, not by him, not by me.

Another Suprematist painting by Kazimir Malevich appeared on show on high in the corridor of my art school. I had a mad fantasy that they were breeding, like wasps. This one was actually called *Suprematism*. It showed an arrangement of shapes which was intended to evoke the working of a machine.

A few weeks after Malevich's visit to my lesson, I was in our little two-room flat at the school, close to tears.

Bella was close to tears, too. Her anxiety attacks were becoming more frequent. She would say things like 'I check all the parts of my body to make sure I am still there.' So I reproached myself for heaping my troubles on her, even while I was doing it. All my life I have blamed myself for whatever it was I was doing, but all my life I have gone on doing it.

Just as I started to speak, little Ida started screaming. Bella crossed the room to her, picked her up and began to hum a lullaby into her ear. It made no difference.

'She's hungry,' Bella said. 'When are you going to earn enough money to buy milk? And nappies. I can't keep asking my father.'

I went pale. We had asked Shmuel Noah for money at the beginning, but I thought we had stopped. The shame of it. And I was supposed to be a big shot around here. Though maybe not for much longer.

'Bella, I've got some bad news,' I said.

Bella actually howled, a visceral noise like an animal, a wolf maybe, foreseeing its own death.

She did not ask what the news was. She would not have asked, fearing herself unable to bear the burden. But

I could not bear the burden either, at least not alone. So I told her.

'I have come from Malevich's office. He has an office now.' Bella's huge dark eyes were pools of terror, growing wider, rounder.

'I have been told how to paint,' I said.

'By Malevich?'

We both looked at the thin wall behind which Malevich, his wife Sophia and baby Una lived, at least now and again. The wall was blank and thankfully silent. I remembered that Malevich was lecturing now, so there were no sounds of female ecstasy-in-agony coming through into our flat.

I nodded, blinking. My stammer was back in force these days. 'M-M-Malevich says, and I quote, "The artist must penetrate into his subconscious, select there his material, and circumscribe it with a line."'

Bella laughed. 'That's not so bad. Tell him your subconscious has goats in it. His presumably doesn't.'

'Ah, but he went on to say, "The Revolution can only be painted Suprematistically and in no other way." He has got this in writing in a *ukase* from one of these committees. From now on, only abstract art is to be allowed.'

'But that's ...' Her bravado flickered, then went out, like a candle in our freezing air.

'There's more.'

She put her hands over her ears. 'No, Moyshe. I can't take any more.'

I sighed. 'More is what I've got. All right? I'm sorry. Malevich gave me this.'

I held out the piece of paper towards her. I had been clutching it in my hand the whole time. It was creased. She recoiled from it. Then she put Ida down and took it. She read it aloud, which I had not intended her to do.

'The former apprentices of the "individualistic" studio announce their desire to follow the way of the Unovis collective, acknowledging it as "the only path to creativity". Moyshe, what in God's name does that mean?'

'It means all my students have left me and gone over to Malevich.'

'Moyshe, that's terrible! Is this true? What are we going to do?'

Such is the power and aura of Malevich; those blank blue eyes, that steady drone, a man whose every utterance had the force of a decree expressing the majority will, such was the sheer inevitability of the man that I had not thought to question the veracity of the order now in Bella's hand.

'Well, Malevich says ...'

'Malevich says. Malevich says.' Bella was screaming. 'What is this man? Is he the *meschiach*? The messiah? Is he God himself?'

'No,' I said, miserably, just as Ida, sensing our unhappiness, set up renewed wailing. 'No, he's not the messiah and not God but ...'

'But but but! You weak man! You *schlapschwanz*!'

I fought back tears as she brought *that* up again. My floppy penis.

'Moyshe, I'm sorry.' Abandoning Ida on the floor, she threw her arms round me. She spoke rapidly into my ear. 'It's good enough. I've always told you that. And anyway, after Ida, I don't feel like it any more.'

'I'm going back to my office.'

'No, Moyshe, wait. Don't run away. Please. Not this time.'

'What do you mean, not ...?'

'We're going to fight this, Moyshe. You and I and ... any allies we can find. You must have some. For a start, is what Malevich says even true? Have you contacted your students?'

'No.'

'No! Then get hold of them. Talk to them. If they've been bullied into leaving you, get them back.'

'But that's humiliating. I can't go round my own students, humbling myself, begging them to take my class, let me teach them. I ...'

'You are the great Marc Chagall. Efros wrote a book about you. I know.'

'I didn't say that.'

'What about Anastasia? Has she stayed loyal to you?'

'How should I know? Why her?'

'Because she wants to go to bed with you.' Bella gave a bitter laugh. 'You could try that. It might work. No, on second thoughts ...' She looked at the misery contorting my face. 'Moyshe. I'm sorry! I didn't mean that.'

'I'm not doing it, Bella. If they get rid of me, let me at least leave with some pride.'

Bella screwed up her face, puckered it. It was an expression I knew well, every line and crease of it. Bella was thinking. I let out a bitter laugh. The laugh did me more good than anything she'd said.

'You need allies,' Bella said, firmly. 'They have a gang, you need a gang.'

'They were born in gangs. I wasn't.' And then something occurred to me. 'Wait a minute,' I said. 'There is one person. Yury. Yury Pen. I'll bring him back in as a lecturer. I can still do that. He will be my ally. I'll organise an exhibition for him. The old guard, eh? Maybe we can fight Malevich and his revolution, after all.'

As Director (still!) I could at least recommend who was to be employed as a member of staff at the art school. Naturally, I had no idea how to work the system. I filled in myriad forms wrongly to the wrong bodies before a secretary took pity on me and booked me an appointment with Lunacharsky.

After a bit of resistance, Lunacharsky came round to my idea that the famous Vitebsk realist school of Judeo-Russian painting should be represented at our school. I had to concede that the style would be presented as an example of pre-revolutionary error, making clear what had been replaced by the improvement that abstract Suprematist art represented.

I agreed to all this rubbish gladly, so keen was I to have Yury Pen back at my side, after all he had done for me. In my hour-long talk with Lunacharsky I would cheerfully have agreed to herring being an erroneous forerunner of pork, if that had been necessary.

But having got Pen on board, an exhibition of his work proved surprisingly easy to arrange. I managed the administrative actions necessary to book rooms at my own school, found a friendly printer in town for the posters (Pen paid) and Pen and I did the hanging of his paintings ourselves.

Our excitement was tempered by the complete lack of any students coming to my art lessons or to Pen's. Malevich had been right when he said that every student had deserted us, though Anastasia Berberova and, more surprisingly, Lazar Khidekel and Moyshe Khunin, from my first *plein air* trip, were among the handful of students who literally whispered in my ear that they would have come if they could.

Lazar Khidekel went further. During a walk in the snow outside – he refused to say a word in the building – he told me that the Cheka would be mounting a counter-revolutionary drive soon. Property would be seized, he said. It was likely that counter-revolutionary elements would be taken and imprisoned in camps far away, so they could not damage the purity of the revolution.

That was all he would say. If he knew any names he refused to tell me. I checked this with David Rubin, my brother-in-law, with his town hall insider knowledge. David looked shifty at the question. He shrugged.

'Does that mean it's true?' I asked him.

He shrugged again. 'Yes.'

The revolution was a constant threat of something worse. That had the effect of concentrating the mind in the present as never before. You are happy? Enjoy it! You are alive? Treasure it, because tomorrow you might not be. You have a full belly, you are warm? I don't believe you.

But at Yury Pen's exhibition, black thoughts were far from my mind. There Yury was, in a red velvet jacket from the Tsar's time, looking like a star actor playing a rabbi in a play by Isaac Peretz or Sholem Aleichem. His paintings festooned the walls of the erstwhile banker's erstwhile dining room, four rows of them, all the way around. Yury beamed at them, his life's work.

There was Russian tea, kvass and ordinary milk to drink, on a surviving table down the middle of the room. There was even a handful of rolls, some gefilte fish, herring and some meats, though none of that lasted more than half an hour before the early visitors wolfed everything – some of them unashamedly blocking the table and stuffing their faces for all they were worth.

To my amazement, most of the guardians of the revolution put in an appearance: Malevich came, saw, nodded, left. Lunacharsky was there. Lissitzky stayed awhile. Ivan Puni came, ignoring Ksana Boguslavskaya, his wife, or perhaps she was not his wife these days. I have no idea.

Ksana stayed for the whole evening, asking a delighted Pen about his paintings, with apparent interest. Malevich's other women, as I thought of them, were there: Nina Kogan and Vera Ermolaeva, quite friendly with each other, making polite noises within revolutionary parameters.

More students appeared than I expected. Anastasia chatted to me for a long time, much to Bella's amusement. But frankly, Bella, in a blue dress, bravely on display when she removed her coat despite the freezing cold, was the most beautiful woman in the room and I was mesmerised by her all over again. I even kissed her in public – in front of Anastasia, actually.

The high point for Yury Pen, on this the evening of his triumph, was a surprise we had arranged for him. To be honest, it was Bella's idea. And to be very honest she also made all the arrangements – I was working hard on my paintings for the Jewish School.

Midway through the evening, with the room packed, everybody appreciating the paintings, I made Yury Pen close his eyes. When he opened them, the guest of honour was standing in front of him, wheezing slightly. There he was, fine-featured, bald-domed, with an unruly grey beard. He was one of the most important painters in the great realist tradition of Russian art. He was Yury Pen's teacher, Pavel Petrovich Chistyakov.

Yury gave a sort of spluttering howl and fell like a child into his old teacher's arms. The frail old man staggered back, but kissed Yury delightedly on the forehead, then on both cheeks. Both of them were crying.

Yury was ecstatic. 'Moyshe! Moyshe! This man … Pavel Petrovich taught Repin, do you realise that? He taught Repin himself.'

Yes, I knew that. Repin – the great Repin – Askenasii, Rubel, all the giants of the mighty Russian realist tradition in art. Here they all were in the room – in spirit at least – throwing a last party before the revolution smashed them. I cried with Yury and his teacher, but they were tears of joy and relief and release. This was *our* moment.

Meanwhile, ignoring my tears, Pen and his old teacher were hugging each other, both gabbling away, words torrenting over each other, reliving an entire past. I listened to them.

Chistyakov was teasing Yury about his failure at the entrance exams to the Academy of Arts in St Petersburg.

'They were right to fail you,' Pavel Petrovich Chistyakov proclaimed solemnly.

'No!' Pen's mouth was an open red circle of horror, fringed all round by fronds of grey and black beard.

'Yes! You hadn't met me yet! I taught you all you know!' Chistyakov's booming voice sounded as if it was coming from someone much bigger than Chistyakov.

It dawned on Yury that he was being teased. 'True, true,' he said with mock solemnity. Then, in a rush, almost panicking. 'But I passed the second time. I stayed in Petersburg for a year. I …'

Chistyakov, who knew all this, doubled over with laughter.

Their arms still round each other, Yury Moiseevich Pen and Pavel Petrovich Chistyakov went to look at Pen's paintings, walking slowly round the walls. I followed them. To my delight, half a dozen of the students followed me. So Pen was like a Pied Piper again, leading the dance along his work.

And as we passed, Pen's people looked down at us from their place on the walls. They were my people, too, even if I celebrated them in a different way. There they were, the Talmud scholars, the synagogue beggars, the Jewish craftsmen – all in their surroundings, all evoking their own world.

There was the old clockmaker, reading his Yiddish newspaper, perhaps Pen's masterpiece. There was the burly farmer; there the fellow artist, Turzhakansky, painting; there was the Jewish baker, an old man absorbed in his work, in his bakery – I knew him, his name was Yefim Jakovlevich Bertels. There was the glass seller, there the matchmaker, there the seamstress.

But the one I remember most vividly was *The Rabbi's Visit to a Merchant*. This was to be Yury Pen's last painting. The figures are depicted with a satirical touch. That and the rich colouring are strongly reminiscent of my early work, when Pen was teaching me. The Master was now at the feet of his pupil.

I took some pleasure at that but not much. There were bigger forces at work here. Yury had painted the last gasp of a lost world.

Outside in the corridor of the school another Suprematist painting had added itself to the soldierly line. *Dynamic Suprematism* by Kazimir Malevich showed a large triangle and a small triangle against a uniform background. There

217

are other small shapes against the larger triangle: a square, three or four rectangles, a few lines, a cross.

I stared at it blankly. It evoked blankness. I couldn't even bring myself to hate it.

Bella was in bed, where she had been for a week, paralysed by the crab anxiety which had its claws in her soul. She dribbled at the mouth with fear and hardly slept. Her sister, Chana, was looking after baby Ida at her and David's place in Putnaskaya, in the Small Side, a semi-permanent arrangement.

I was pacing up and down in front of Bella's bed – I mean in front of *our* bed – declaiming like an actor in the theatre. Malevich was away from his rooms, lecturing. These days we always knew where Malevich was – it coloured what we said and how we said it, especially how loudly we said it, as if he were actually in the room, instead of a baleful imagined presence, invisibly shrouding our lives.

'Now he's over-reached himself,' I gibbered in mid-stride, waving my arms about as if forlornly summoning aid. 'You see before ... before it was all, what? Insubstantial. Nothing concrete. He takes all my students away, but he can say they all wanted to leave me. Even if I got them to state, in writing, that they had been pressured it wouldn't work because ...'

Bella put a pillow over her face. 'You've gone over all that a hundred times,' she snuffled through the pillow. She was wearing a pair of my trousers, one of my shirts, a woollen nightdress and a dress and she was still cold under our meagre two blankets. The hunger made the cold even worse.

She emerged from the grey sagging clouds of pillow, spoke, then reburied herself in it.

'Tell me what's actually happened,' she said.

'I told you.'

'I don't understand a word you're saying these days.

218

You're in such a state, nothing you say makes sense. Tell me again. Clearly.'

'All right, all right. All right.' I addressed the pillow she had once more disappeared into. 'As I just said …' A groan came from the pillow. 'Right. You know the grants, the artist's grants we live on, instead of a salary? At least mine has come through, finally. But it appears that Malevich is on the committee which decides the grants. A committee in Moscow. I have been given a third-class grant.'

She emerged from the pillow, all huge scared dark eyes, circled by black from lack of sleep. 'Less than we had before?'

I snorted. 'Much less.'

'So … We have … even *less* … to live on …?'

'Yes. Yes. Yes. That's what I'm telling you.'

She started to scream. She screamed and screamed and screamed.

'Bella, stop that. Bella, this is good, that's what I'm telling you.'

'Good? Good? Good?' She threw the pillow on the floor and pushed herself up on one elbow, a bizarre figure in all those clothes. 'You've gone mad. You've finally gone mad. I'm leaving you. I don't have to stay with a madman.' She started to heave herself out of bed. 'I'm going to stay with Viktor.'

'Oh God, woman!' Now I was screaming. 'Oh God, oh God, oh God. Will you just listen?'

She climbed – thankfully I thought – back into bed under blankets and pillow.

'I am going to see David.' I was speaking unnaturally slowly, as if to a child. 'I am going to enlist his help to make a formal complaint against Malevich. I have a … a cause now. I mean a case. Something definite. I'll get him out. And then … And then …'

Bella stared at me, wide-eyed, dribbling. 'Don't just stand there, twittering away. Do it. Do it if you think it will work. Do it *now*, Moyshe. Don't say anything else. Don't paint anything else. Act. For once in your life. *Just do it.*'

So I went to see my brother-in-law, David, then and there. I walked all the way to the Small Side. Then I remembered I had meant to gather some papers, documents, evidence. You had to have papers these days. We had hardly any paper for anything else, certainly not for drawing on, but it seems we always had paper for papers.

I knocked miserably on the green wooden door of their *izba* in Putnaskaya, not knowing even if David was in. Chana opened the door, greeted me warmly, led me to a room exactly like the one I had grown up in, down the road in Pokrovskaya. And there was my Ida, my little Idotchka, playing on the floor.

I swept her up in my arms, smothering her with kisses. Ida gurgled.

'How is Bella?' Chana said.

'Could be better. Is David around?'

Chana shot me a sharp look. 'He's out the back, chopping wood. I'll fetch him.'

I felt soaring optimism at the success of my errand. David was at home! It was an omen! I put Ida back down on the floor and savoured my coming victory over Malevich.

David came in and embraced me solemnly. Chana took Idotchka off to the kitchen, leaving us to talk.

Over sweet, black tea, I told David what had happened.

'How can I have a third-class grant?' I said. 'I am the Director of the School. I am supposed to be Commissar of the Arts for Vitebsk, though everybody seems to have forgotten about that. I bet Malevich hasn't got a …'

David waved me to stop. He was sitting at the head of the table, compact little Lenin-figure, Buddha wisdom, solemn. I had abandoned my tea, and was pacing up and down in front of him, as I had been doing in front of Bella. David frowned. I felt a sinking feeling, then I felt sick. He was not going to help me.

'David, please …'

'Your best bet is not to attack Malevich, but to appeal the decision as an error.'

'Yes! Will you ...? David, I'm not good at this kind of ... I hate conflict. I hate procedures and documents and ...'

'You want me to see to it for you?'

'Yes! Please David.'

David nodded that head which was too big for his body. I thought of the Russian phrase which translates as 'all brain'.

'Thank you, David.'

'That's all right. Anybody can make an appeal against error. You can appeal on behalf of others. Leave it to me.'

I went over to the table and embraced my brother-in-law. I was crying. I felt, deeply, keenly the knowledge that David had been imprisoned in Tsarist times. I do not know how long for, but for years. When the Rosenfeld parents, Shmuel Noah and Alta, finally got him out, the cost of the bribes nearly bankrupted them. They managed to hang on to the jewellery shop but it was a close-run thing.

Such an experience of a Tsarist prison would have broken many men; it would have broken me. But here was David still fighting for what was right and just. I hugged him again and kissed him until he gently pushed me away, under the pretext of offering food.

Two weeks later, Chana came to see us at our flat in the school, with Ida in her arms. She was dry-eyed and calm. She spoke in a flat monotone. David had been denounced as a counter-revolutionary. His job as Commissar for the Spread of the Revolution had not saved him. The Cheka had taken him away in the middle of the night. He had been executed by firing squad the next day.

We never found out the reason for his arrest, so I never knew if it had anything to do with my case, and my visit to him, or not. My artist grant continued at the same third-class rate as before.

Even though I had no students to teach, I still went downstairs into the school every day, looking for something to do as Commissar of the Arts. I was still trying to set up a museum in Vitebsk, for example.

One day, I came into work as usual and found a new banner hanging across the elegant façade of the school. The banner said 'Suprematist Academy'. When I enquired from my own secretarial staff what was going on, I was told that Malevich and his henchmen in some committee or other had simply fired all the teachers who were not teaching Suprematism.

This included Pen, who had only just started. I had been dismissed as a teacher, but remained Director as well as Commissar of the Arts, presumably because Malevich had not yet found a mechanism to dismiss me from these roles.

I tried to resign on the spot, but the secretaries suddenly disappeared, leaving nobody around in the office. When I went back to our rooms, Bella persuaded me to at least delay my resignation. She did not want me to act in anger, and anyway we had our little mouth to feed, our Idotchka. Bella thought I should have a plan ready, at least, before I jumped into the void.

My wife was as skittish as ever, but what she said made sense. I resolved to do as she said. Another factor saving my sanity at this time was that, incredibly, I felt my painting was going well. My commissions for the Jewish School, my work for the Jewish Theatre were all received with enthusiasm and praise.

I harboured a deep longing to be a painter again, a painter and only a painter, which I would be if I could resign in peace. Something told me, however, that this would not be possible. You are either for this revolution or against it, they made that very clear. And further, anybody not actively, loudly, demonstratively for it was assumed to be against. Like me.

Very few people spoke to me. I carried the mark of Cain on my forehead, as clearly as if I had made one of the banners now hanging on every public building and painted 'I am a bourgeois individualist' on it.

So nobody told me that all Vitebsk's synagogues had been closed down. I was walking aimlessly in Governor's Square, trying to control my thoughts and fears, trying to calm down, as everybody kept telling me to do. The Little Lubavich Synagogue was closed and shuttered.

Shaking with apprehension, I hurried to the Big Lubavich Synagogue. There, it was even worse. The Torah scrolls, the words Jews regard as holy, the word of God, as precious as human life, were piled up in the slush outside the synagogue.

The big double doors were barred shut. I walked round the side of the building, this building where I had been barmitzvah, another me in another life. I looked in through the grimy window.

The holy place had been gutted. The *bimah* platform, where the service is read, was still standing, but the ark, where the holy Torah was kept, had been hacked to pieces. The chandeliers were gone, the pews smashed; the place was a scarred shell. It looked too desolate to cry for itself. I tried to cry for it but could not summon the tears. I retched a couple of times.

So much for the revolution freeing the Jews from oppression. They had ended the ghettos, the Pales of Settlement, but the ghettos had at least afforded us a protective fence, of sorts, to huddle behind. Now we were like clucking chickens out in the open, waiting to be picked off one by one for counter-revolutionary activity.

When I got back home, rehearsing my sad tale in my head to Bella, there was no Bella there. Chana was there. She told me Bella had been denounced and arrested.

It was late in the day, dark and snowing outside. Chana did not know where Bella was, only that she had been 'taken'.

She would not tell me who had told her about Bella. It was safer if I did not know, she said.

I was stunned. I sat down heavily, unable to move, while Chana tried to stop Ida screaming.

'We must go to her,' I said. I could hardly speak, my jaw was locking. 'Where is she?'

'I don't know,' Chana said. 'If she is at the Cheka barracks, where they took David, there is no hope. But …' she went on quickly, seeing my face dissolve before her, 'but that is unlikely. Bella won't have done anything political. She's probably at the police station.'

'What shall we do?' I felt helpless. I was helpless.

Chana thought a moment. 'Nothing today. I must speak to my father. He always knows what to do. We will all go to the police station tomorrow.'

I nodded, miserably.

'Let me take Ida,' Chana said. 'She can stay with me overnight. We can meet at the police station first thing tomorrow.'

'Would you? Chana, thank you. I'm so grateful.'

Without another word, Chana bundled up Ida's things and walked out into the snow, carrying the baby swaddled up against the cold. I slept for a couple of hours as the shock seeped through my body. Then, excited, I lit a kerosene lamp and began to paint.

I painted like a dervish all night, working on three paintings at once, two for the Jewish School, one a backdrop for a forthcoming theatre production about the trial of Danton. I felt a massive freedom and release. I swung from one painting to another, my mind so clear it was beyond thought, like an animal moving by instinct in a jungle. I was not exactly happy, but I was not unhappy either. I was beyond feeling.

The next morning, I was at the main police station on Padlo, the little market square, before it opened. I swung my arms around myself to try to get warm, peering anxiously along

224

the snow at the side of the square, looking for Shmuel Noah Rosenfeld and Chana. The police station had been open over half an hour before they appeared. I was tense and desperate by then. I have never been a patient waiter upon events.

Shmuel Noah greeted me solemnly, shaking me by the hand then embracing me. Chana was much cooler. She assured me that Alta – her mother – was looking after Ida, so I should not be worried. To be honest, I was not. I had forgotten all about Ida since last night. But Bella! Bella I was worried about. Worried frantic.

Shmuel Noah led the way into the police station, his portly full-bearded figure radiating authority. The young uniformed constable at the desk spoke respectfully to him. Yes, Bella was indeed in a cell at the police station. I met Chana's eye, sharing relief. The police had got her; not the Cheka. There was hope.

'May I know the charge against my daughter?' Shmuel Noah spoke with sonorous dignity.

'Probably petit-bourgeois counter-revolutionary activity.' The young constable spoke wryly, rolling the neologisms of the recent ruling jargon round his mouth, as if testing their taste. 'I'll call the custody sergeant.'

'Can you call an inspector?'

Shmuel Noah was superb! I felt so relieved he was here, so I didn't have to do all this.

The young constable shot him a glance that was almost complicit. 'Just a moment.' He disappeared but within minutes he was back, waving us through to a back office. 'Come this way.'

A middle-aged bearded man sat behind a desk, in the bottle-green trousers of the Tsarist police force with a *moujik* blouse over the top.

'Inspector Wengeroff,' he introduced himself.

I had the impression he was pleased to have something to do. The Cheka did most of the arresting these days, even petty larceny had been brought into politics as 'looting' and carried the death penalty, with the Cheka doing the arresting and summary execution.

'I am Shmuel Noah Rosenfeld, Bella's father.' Shmuel Noah did not introduce Chana or myself. He came straight to the point. 'What is the charge against Bella?' Then, cleverly 'I'm sure we can sort it out.' That opened the way for a bribe, but cautiously.

'You are the jewellery-shop owner?' Wengeroff said.

Shmuel Noah nodded his full-bearded head gravely in acknowledgement.

'Perhaps that explains your daughter's crime. She tried to pawn some jewellery. That is black market trading, counter-revolutionary activity.'

'May I see the pieces?' Shmuel Noah was all professional interest.

'You may.'

The inspector opened a drawer in his desk, rummaged in it and pulled out two necklaces, a brooch and, after a further rummage in the corner of the drawer, two rings. There did not seem to be much else in the drawer, reinforcing the impression that not much else was happening at the station.

'Those items are her personal jewellery,' Shmuel Noah said. 'They are not from the shop. My son-in-law's salary has not come through yet. Though I am sure it will,' he added hastily, before some criticism of the revolution could be understood. Shmuel Noah acknowledged my presence for the first time. 'This is Bella's husband, the painter Moyshe Shagal.' Not Marc Chagall, too foreign. I shot Shmuel Noah a look of admiration.

Then I shook hands solemnly with the inspector. But I continued to leave the talking to Shmuel Noah.

'My daughter is prone to … overreaction, shall we call it. I know they needed milk to feed the baby. Which will be available soon,' he added hastily. 'But she made an error of judgement, for which she, or I, will *pay*.' Shmuel Noah emphasised the last word just enough.

The inspector nodded to himself. Chana and I were asked to wait outside. Shmuel Noah told us afterwards there was some haggling, though not much. Bella was led up from the cells, frightened, thinner than ever but not physically harmed.

The incident, though, could only make her fears worse, which indeed it did. My poor dear Bashenka – Belloshka of Vitebsk on the hill, mirrored in the Dvina with its clouds and trees and houses.

My poor dear Bella, in terrible times.

I found a piece of paper from somewhere – I can no longer remember from where – and dashed off a pencil drawing entitled *The Rosenfeld Jewellery Shop in Vitebsk (interior)* for all the world as if I were back in *La Ruche* sketching in peace and happiness.

Mme Segondet always used to say I was time-bound, and perhaps I was. At any rate, my drawing shows no fewer than twelve clocks along the wall at the back. Alta, Bella's heavily built mother, is serving a whole shop full of customers, eleven of them.

Prominent is Abrashka the Hasid, the holy man, with his high hat, full beard and rich, pursed lips. Abrashka the Hasid is about to buy a necklace in its rich box from Alta Rosenfeld. Aiga Levant, round-faced, portly, middle-aged, stands at the end of the counter, half pushing in ahead of Abrashka. She was a cleaner at the Hotel Brozi. Right at the back is the beadle, Laizar, looking angrily behind him.

We received a warning that the Cheka were about to pay a visit to the Rosenfeld jewellery shop. The warning came from a former colleague of David, my late brother-in-law, may he rest in peace. There was talk of a raid.

Shmuel Noah's idea was to face them alone. But Alta and Chana would not hear of it. They wanted to be there. Bella, her voice creaking with fright, said she would be there too.

227

'Don't be silly,' I said. 'Let me do it. I'll stand with Shmuel Noah and Alta and Chana. You stay here and look after little Ida.'

I think she was relieved.

We stood in a little knot, me and Shmuel Noah and Alta and Chana. Rivka the cashier of the Rosenfeld shop was there, too. And Avramel Bernstein, the Chief Clerk. We stood there in silence, waiting for the Cheka to arrive.

I thought they would come by truck, but in the event six or seven cars pulled up on the wide boulevard where the Smolenskaya met the Podvinskaya, where the elegant façade of the Rosenfeld family jewellery shop stood proudly with the once elegant café Jeanne-Albert above it.

I was determined to show no fear as the Cheka piled into the shop – about ten of them. We did not know exactly what they wanted of us. Shmuel Noah had been denounced, that much was clear.

The Cheka leader, a young, fresh-faced fellow I had never seen before, went through the routine of accusing Shmuel Noah of counter-revolutionary activity. He told him this establishment no longer belonged to him. Then they began to throw the entire contents of the shop into jute sacks they had brought with them. All the clocks, the watches, the precious stones, the gold, the silver – all booty now.

They took the Rosenfeld family kitchen silver from the flat, too; the very knives and forks off the tables. They waved a revolver under Alta's nose, speaking to Shmuel Noah without looking at him: 'The keys of the safe, or else ...'

Shmuel Noah handed over the keys of the safe.

But they were not finished yet. The Cheka squad ripped up the floorboards in the shop and the flat. They made holes in the walls. They were looking for hidden treasure, but found none. The shop was wrecked.

Finally, we were all ordered to leave the family shop the Rosenfelds had owned for thirty years but no longer owned. They were told their house was forfeit, too. Shmuel Noah and Alta stayed with Chana for a few days. Then the three of them caught the train to Moscow, with Bella and Ida and me seeing them off at the station.

They never returned to Vitebsk.

The Rosenfeld shop was one of many 'bourgeois' businesses ransacked and seized by the Cheka. It became clear to all the frightened inhabitants of Vitebsk that anything at all of value was under threat for the furtherance of the revolution.

I feared for my paintings. I had no idea what they were worth, on the market, because there was no market in Vitebsk and contact with dealers in Paris or Berlin was impossible. But I did know that by now I was the famous – even world-famous – Marc Chagall, the subject of books, of interest to any gallery owner. This afforded me a measure of protection, personally. It also made my paintings even more vulnerable to seizure.

I discussed the situation with Bella, who was in bed, where she spent most of her days, now.

'I need to hide my paintings,' I said. 'They can be seized any time from here. Only the work for the theatre is really safe.'

Bella glanced at Ida. 'Yes, hide them. You could take them to Feiga-Ita.'

I grimaced. I saw little of my mother these days. With her peasant cunning she was keeping her head down, trading in food on the black market, trying to protect those of her more vulnerable children still alive (apart from my brother David, one of my sisters had also died).

'That's the first place they will look,' I said.

She glared at me. 'Most people in this situation would hide valuables with a friend. But you can't do that, can you? You haven't got any friends, only paintings.'

'There's some truth in that,' I said, sadly. Then I thought of something. 'I could give my paintings to Yury Pen for safe keeping.'

I went to see Yury at his flat, above what used to be his school. I stood in the same place, then sat in the same armchair as I had when I was a boy learning art. Now I had overtaken my teacher. But I was still the boy asking for help.

Yury, as ever, was alone in the still, dusty place, dressed in the Jewish gabardine which the revolution had made look more old-fashioned than ever, though not yet dangerous to go out in. Not yet.

He welcomed me warmly, served me black tea and little sweet cakes. We sat, talking amicably enough. He knew I wanted something, or I would not have come. But as ever he let life come to him. The request would be made soon enough, would it not? What's the hurry?

'My paintings and drawings, Yehuda Moiseyevich ...'

'Yes, you can leave everything here. I will hide them under the floorboards.'

Tears sprang to my eyes. 'Thank you, Yury.'

A few days after my visit to Yury, I came back to our rooms after a pointless time achieving nothing in the offices downstairs. Bella was out of bed, she met me at the door.

'Your girlfriend is here,' Bella said, dryly, as I walked in.

Anastasia Ivanovna Berberova shook her head, impatiently. She was dressed in a high white blouse, just visible under her thick coat, and a long plaid woollen skirt. 'Oh, please,' she muttered.

'She won't tell *me* why she's come,' Bella resumed in the same dry tone. 'She will only speak to the master. I'll leave you two alone then, shall I?' Bella picked Ida up. 'Come along, Ida, we'll go for a walk along the river, eh?' She shot Anastasia a look. 'The bedroom is through there. But you probably already know that.'

'Bella, for God's sake!' I shouted.

Anastasia shook her head, more impatient than angry. 'Mrs Chagall, I have come here at some personal risk

230

to myself to speak to both of you. I have some news,
unfortunately not good news. Now, do you want to hear it
or not?'

'Yes, we do,' I said. 'Anastasia, do you want some tea,
some …'

'Nothing, thank you. Please sit down.'

I did as I was told, catching Bella's amused bitter
glance at my obedience.

'Before I give you my news, there is something I want
to say about your classes, Marc Zakharovich.'

'Oh dear!'

That attempt at levity failed with both women. Ida
began to howl.

Anastasia looked serious. 'To be frank, Marc
Zakharovich, most of your students found your classes
chaotic and confusing. They could not understand the
limitation to three colours, for example.'

'I see.'

'Most of the students believe in the Suprematist
mission and their vision of the future. But a few, like me,
feel we learned something from you. I would have stayed,
but once your lessons were no longer accredited, no longer
counted towards our degree …'

'I'm glad … I was of some help while you were with
me.'

There was a long pause. 'You can't stay here,' Anastasia
blurted out, finally. 'Travel is possible again now. Get back
to Paris if you can. Or Berlin. London. Anywhere but
Vitebsk.'

'Why?' Bella said.

Anastasia ignored her, speaking to me. 'Yury Pen is
dead.'

The tears pricked my eyes. 'What?'

'What happened?' Bella spoke in a thin shocked voice,
but did not sound surprised.

Anastasia glanced round the room. There was no noise
from Malevich's rooms, next door. 'The Cheka murdered

him. They didn't even try to hide it. They don't have to, these days. They drove up in their cars, burst in and took everything. Pen's flat was wrecked, apparently. They took the floorboards up, drilled holes in the walls ...'

'I know,' I said. 'That's what they did to Bella's father's shop.'

Anastasia sighed. 'People are saying that poor Yehuda Moiseyevich refused to tell them where certain valuables were. They beat him up, but he still wouldn't talk. I don't know what they were looking for, though.'

'I do,' I said.

'Shut up, Moyshe!' Bella screamed. 'Don't say another word. Don't trust her. She's a spy.'

I made sure Yury was buried with honour on Yury's Hill, where we had painted together. I never found out whether or not the Cheka found my paintings, hidden under Yury's floorboards. I did not go back to Yury's flat to look for them.

An exhibition of Vitebsk artists held in Moscow did not contain a single work by me. It consisted entirely of Suprematist paintings and was hailed a triumph. Unovis works found their way into every art gallery and museum in the country.

I handed in my resignation as Commissar for the Arts and Director of the School. Bella and Ida and I headed back to Paris. On the train to Moscow, on the first leg of our journey, we saw Malevich and his cronies. They were in the same compartment. They were on their way to Moscow to arrange another exhibition of Suprematist art, by popular demand.

Malevich ignored me on the train. He did not even crow. He did not need to.

The last work I did in Vitebsk before we left was called *Man with Marionettes*. It was inked in on a scrap of brown wrapping paper salvaged from the Rosenfeld shop under the eyes of the Cheka. I think it may have been the last piece of paper in Vitebsk which did not have a report on it.

Man with Marionettes shows a leering Malevich in profile, in a *moujik*'s cap, kneeling on one knee. He is whirling a tiny marionette in each hand, windmilling them about. One marionette is upside down, one the right way up. One is Yury Pen, the other is Marc Chagall, Moyshe Shagal.

Me.

PART VI: PARIS, 1922 ONWARDS

Back at The Hive. Back at The Hive. I am back at The Hive. Here I am, coming from the Gare du Nord, turning into the rue Danzig, as I did the first time, a lifetime ago. Back, but with Bella at my side holding our child by the hand, in her checked cotton frock. All is the same here, all is different.

There is no old peddler outside the gates, selling herring. I miss him. I go inside the gates, I walk along past the sculpture of *The Spirit Shackled*. I walk at my own pace; Bella and Ida drop behind me, out of sight. The garden is as overgrown as ever, the grass folding under its own weight, the trees bowed with blossom. Ida gives a cry of delight as a cat breaks cover, scampering along the path ahead of us. But there is no goat. What have they done with my tethered goat?

At the end of the Boulevard of Love I can see the Exhibition Hall, humming with the ghosts of dealers in art. I turn in the narrow doorway, leaving Bella and Ida to follow as best they can. Oh, Bella knows the way. As I think that, I think of Osip Zadkine, then banish him from my mind.

I take a deep breath outside the door of the concierge, Mme Segondet. Here, back at The Hive, my awareness of the visions comes back to me. It had been absent in Vitebsk. I apprehend that I will lead other lives, do things differently. I am excited.

I knock on the door, then turn the door handle. Locked. Silence. I knock again. Nothing. There is no light from under the door.

I stride along the corridor, look for the door with the big letter A on it. There it is! Nothing has changed. I even look for the wire I twined round the door handle to keep people out. There is no wire. But I open the door confidently, expecting to see everything all the same, my paintings against the wall, where I left them.

There are no paintings against the wall. There is a gentleman painting in the middle of the studio. At that

237

moment, Bella and Ida join me in the doorway of what used to be my studio. I recognise the painter, though he looks much older now.

'Foujita!'

'Who...? Oh, it's Marc Chagall. The famous Marc Chagall. Back here where you started. How wonderful!'

'I started in Vitebsk.'

'But you are world famous now.'

'Thank you. Clearly my old studio is now yours. Is Mme Segondet around?'

'She is visiting her sister, *maître*. Back tomorrow, I think. But the Ostrouns are here. At the back, in the restaurant. I'm sure they can help you.'

I feel a warm rush inside at the memory of the frame-maker and his wife who looked after us so well. After bidding Foujita farewell, I find the Ostrouns. They set my little family up with a large studio on the upper floor.

I started work that night, using canvases and paint the Ostrouns had provided. I painted *Cubist Landscape* in one intense session. Some kind critics later called it 'a defiant and brave painting'. Maybe. Maybe not. I have hated conflict all my life, but I blamed myself for my defeat and expulsion at the hands of Malevich, Lissitzky and the Suprematist faction. My response in art was this painting, *Cubist Landscape*.

In this painting, I incorporated Suprematist ideas into my own style, making a painting of beauty and worth from them. I had done this before, in the early days of my time at *La Ruche*, taking what I needed from Cubist techniques but adding a heart and soul.

Cubist Landscape shows the school on Bukharinskaya, where I had suffered my great defeat. The school is surrounded by Suprematist forms: segments, triangles, semi-circles. But I have used God's gift of colour to give them life and make them fly.

A theatre curtain sweeping towards the school has my

name on it. Outside the school, untethered and defiant, stands an archetypal Chagall goat, munching grass. The goat is quite content.

The next day Mme Segondet's door was still locked. I went to find my dealer, Charles Malpel, but his shop in the rue Montaigne had become a café.

I went round the other dealers, just as I used to in the old days, but this time seeking news of Malpel. I was warmly received. I was called '*maître*', invited to lunch – invitations which did not interest me. But nobody knew what had happened to Malpel, or to my other dealer, Herwath Walden, in Berlin.

I was suddenly miserable. I had come so far, I had achieved success, yet my early paintings were lost to me. Then, finally, a turn of luck. After two days of knocking at her door, I finally caught up with Mme Segondet.

The old concierge was much aged. She walked laboriously, using her stick all the time. She had developed a bronchitic cough. But the soup, the potato soup of my early days, was on the boil, just as it always had been.

'What happened to my paintings?' I blurted out, spooning potato soup into myself.

Mme Segondet shrugged, eating along with me. 'Malpel took them. He sold them, then moved out. Nobody knows where he is.'

'That's it, then. I'll have to start again.'

She nodded, heavily. 'In a sense. Although your work is turning up all the time in galleries and museums.'

I nodded, sadly. I suddenly and acutely missed Modi and Chaim Soutine. Modi was dead; Soutine away in the south of France, somewhere. In fact all my old crowd had gone, Mr and Mrs Indenbaum, the Bolshevik Kikoine, the bitter Krémègne, Kisling, even Osip Zadkine.

Back in my room I started painting *The Flayed Ox*. It was my homage to Rembrandt. As soon as I started painting I

239

was filled with that certainty of being controlled by another force, a force outside myself.

In my painting, the bright pink ox is suspended upside down, as it is in Rembrandt's version and Soutine's. But it is lapping from a bucket of water with a chilling smile on its benign face. This ox is still alive while it is being flayed, still joyous and optimistic.

This ox is the Jews of Vitebsk.

Then the Prophet appeared again.

The Third Vision

I was back in Vitebsk. The first picture I saw far below, as the Prophet and I looked on, was Smolenskaya, with the façade of the empty Rosenfeld jewellery shop and the cupolas of the Uspensky Cathedral in the distance. German tanks were rolling down the street at walking pace. Some had *Panzergruppe 3* painted in white on their sides. They had their hatches open as they rolled along, observers peering out, creeping forward on squealing tracks, cautiously conquering.

There were motorcycle outriders alongside the tanks. Outside them, soldiers on foot made sweeping, waist-high arcs with their rifles as they walked. The tanks kept dipping into shell holes in the road then up again. Vitebsk was battle-scarred. Some of the hotels and shops along Smolenskaya and Podvinskaya were burnt out and smouldering. Russian soldiers had set them aflame before they retreated out of Vitebsk.

It was late summer, but some of the invading Nazis were already shivering in their summer uniforms, which were all they had. The uniforms were mostly field-grey, just a few camouflage, a few black.

There were many faces at the windows but only a few figures on the street as the tanks creaked and squeaked past. The figures on the pavement were mainly old men. One of them, in a full beard and a cap, was peering curiously at the Nazi soldiers. His mouth dropped open in wonder; he was too old to be afraid.

As I watched with the Prophet, the tanks reached the spot where Smolenskaya widens out into its full elegance as a boulevard. There, the tanks drew level with the blackened façade of the Rosenfeld jewellery shop.

The next picture was on the outskirts of Vitebsk, right near Yuryieva Gorka, Yury's Hill, where I had painted *en plein air* and where my teacher, Yury Pen, is now buried. Male Jews had been formed into forced labour battalions; a group of them were hauling a German field kitchen out to one of the outlying camps.

The field kitchen was a strange-shaped contraption, with the chassis of a cart on large wheels. Above the cart-like chassis, it had a stove with a pipe which stuck up, black, like the periscope of a submarine.

The Jewish men schlepping the thing all had peaked caps, as I looked down on them. I glanced at the Prophet. I recognised one of the men doing the hauling: it was Avramel Bernstein, Avram the cashier, later the Chief Clerk, who had worked for the Rosenfelds in the jewellery shop. Avram, I knew, would not be able to cope with such work for long, especially on what were no doubt starvation rations. Even as I thought that, he looked up, attracted by the buzzing of flies. There were tears in his eyes.

We were invisible, the Prophet and I, in what had been the Town Hall under the Tsars and the District Administration building during the revolution. It formed almost one complete side of Governor's Square on the west bank of the Dvina River. This was the very office where I had been interviewed by Duma Deputy Maksim Moyseevich Vinaver when he had so mysteriously given me a small fortune to go and study art in Paris.

The once elegant room was now a shabby scoured shell. All the furniture had been burned for heating during the revolution. The Nazis had found a battered desk and some chairs; there was no other furniture. The elegant walls had been whitewashed over, the parquet had been stripped from the floor, leaving concrete. Most of the windows had been broken. The Nazis had boarded them up, making no attempt to replace the glass. The lovely Levitan painting on the wall had gone.

I watched as Petr Antonovich Shostak was sworn in by the Nazis as head of the local police force. The Nazis needed an obedient local police and a subservient local administration to smooth and speed up their dealings with the Jews. They now had a leader for their police force. The new administration was headed by the ferrety figure of Vsevolod Rod'ko, another local man, who was also in the room.

One of the police guards at the swearing-in was Nicolas Antonowich, who had worked at Gourevich, the Jewish bakery and pastry shop. This inside knowledge of the Jewish community, especially where they were likely to hide, made Nicolas Antonowich useful to his new masters. He had already been promoted twice and was now a lieutenant.

It was the local police who were responsible for the day-to-day enforcement of Nazi instructions to the Jews. Under Nicolas Antonowich, the police identified any Jews caught not wearing yellow stars on their clothes. These miscreants were publicly paraded before an assembly of all Jewish men between the ages of fifteen and fifty in Lenin Park, as it was still known, not far from the main bridge over the Dvina.

The Jewish men were formed into several rows in the park. Thirty men were arbitrarily selected, some from each row, and then shot. One of these men was

Zussy Javitch, a close neighbour whose family *izba* shared a courtyard with my family's. Zussy was the groom in my painting, *The Wedding*.

The man who killed Zussy was from a regular infantry battalion, so he was wearing a field-grey uniform. His name was Waldemar Haensch, from Bielefeld in North-Rhine Westphalia. He had originally been in the Social Democrat youth organisation, back home, but transferred seamlessly to the Hitler Youth when it took the Young Socialists over, in the year the Nazis came to power.

Waldemar was engaged to be married to a girl he had known since childhood, Jutta Blobel, but was having second thoughts after some enjoyable nights in the brothels in Smolensk, where his battalion was based before they took Vitebsk. When he shot Zussy twice in the chest with his rifle, Waldemar was thinking about what he was going to do that evening, after he got off duty.

Among the women caught not wearing a yellow badge on clothing was Mrs Bishowskaya. Mrs Bishowskaya, all flower-scented and white-gloved, once bought a diamond necklace in an elegant blue case from Mr Rosenfeld at the jeweller's shop. The smaller stones were not of the first water, as Mrs Bishowskaya had pointed out. I had drawn her in *The Rosenfeld Jewellery Shop Vitebsk (exterior),* which Osip had taken from my room at *La Ruche*, those many years ago.

Mrs Bishowskaya was shot at point-blank range in the head with a pistol, by Eduard Naumann, a Panzer Battalion captain. Naumann was from Essen, in the Ruhr. He was an enthusiastic Nazi, believing that Hitler had unified the puny warring factions back home and would soon unify Europe, then the world, behind an ennobling ideal – a racial ideal.

When Eduard Naumann shot Mrs Bishowskaya,

243

he wished to impress the idea of punishment onto the watching Jews, so that no further commands were disobeyed. He was also concerned not to get any mess – blood or brains – on his uniform, so he shot her from slightly behind. Naumann was a lean-faced, slightly built figure, but a bit of a dandy. He was meticulous about his clothes and used cologne when he could get hold of it.

Towards the end of the summer, the Feldkommandantur, from its headquarters in Governor's Square, ordered the establishment of a Jewish ghetto, as was standard practice in all occupied territories. The ghetto was to be on the western bank of the Dvina, defined by a stockade.

The main bridge across the Dvina, the Dvinski Bridge, had been blown up by the Russian army when it left Vitebsk. This was the bridge where I had stood with Bella to one side of me and Thea Brachmann on the other. It was also the bridge under which I had floated with Osip Zadkine and Lazar Lissitzky when Osip said I had a small one.

The Nazis had thrown up a pontoon bridge across the river, to replace the Dvinski Bridge, but no civilians, let alone Jews, were allowed to use it. It was strictly for military use only. So now the only way across from the Small Side was by boat or raft.

A deadline had been set for all the Jews of Vitebsk to enter the ghetto and nobody wanted to miss that. So, as the deadline approached, Christian boat owners did a holy old trade charging Jews a fortune for a boat trip across the river.

Nicolas Antonowich was one such boat owner, though he reduced the rate for a nephew of the Gourevich family, owners of the bakery and pastry shop which had employed him, as the Gourevichs had always been so kind to him. This nephew was Jakov Gourevich.

Another way across the river, much used by poorer

Jews, was the home-made raft, just like the ones I used to go rafting on. In fact, as I watched, I compared our old raft favourably with the ones the Jews had hastily put together, in order to get across on time.

Every day, when the boats or rafts full of Jews set out, the Germans launched every boat they could get hold of, including some motorboats, to fire at the Jews with machine guns and small arms as they crossed the river.

Another sport was to drive a speedboat very close to a homemade raft, so the Jews on it were tipped off into the water. This game was always accompanied by loud laughter, especially as many of the Jews crossing could not swim, and so drowned before the amused eyes of the German soldiers. My former teacher, Dyadkin the *melamed*, now a very old man, died this way.

Nobody among the Nazis ever pointed out the illogicality of hindering the Jews from obeying orders they themselves had enacted. For years, back home, Nazis had done everything in their power to drive the Jews out of Germany, while simultaneously making the procedure for leaving as difficult as possible. All the soldiers based in Vitebsk had experienced this in their own home areas, so this way of thinking was nothing new to them.

Among the Jews who perished in the Dvina River was Tanjka the *gonif* who appears in my painting, *The Wedding*. A group of soldiers in mufti on their day off, there for sport but heavily armed, laughingly stopped each other from shooting her because they were having such a good time watching her drown, as her heavy petticoats dragged her under the water over a period of nearly ten minutes.

One they did shoot was the beadle Laizar. He was the one looking angrily behind him in my drawing of the

Rosenfeld shop. He was picked off by a rifle fired by Walter Seibert from the side of a speedboat.

Walter Seibert was from Cologne. A religious Catholic, he had intended to become a priest, but put this ambition on hold to fight for Germany. Germany had been treated shamefully, in his view, but Hitler would make the guilty countries pay for it. Walter had rejoiced when the first Jews had left Cologne in sad little columns, carrying one suitcase each. He had leaned out the window to watch them as they passed. 'Now you can't be lawyers or doctors any more,' he shouted at the Jews, as they slunk away. 'Now you'll have to do the *Dreckarbeit* – the dirty work – like the rest of us.'

As he shot the beadle Laizar, Walter was concentrating on not missing, in front of the other soldiers, his comrades. But as the beadle's blood spread red in the water, he resolved with utter firmness to enter the priesthood after the war. It was an epiphany, this moment. It was a moment of exaltation, such as the saints experienced.

The ghetto was created by lashing together thick wooden palings cut from the nearby birch forests to form a winding stockade. It ran along the northern bank of the Dvina along that part of the right bank known as the H'inskii Embankment.

Its inhabitants referred to it not as a ghetto but as the 'pale of Jewish settlement'. They settled into it with a feeling of familiarity, if not inevitability, as this is all their collective memory had known for centuries. The ending of these pales of settlement, which I had greeted with such enthusiasm when the 'revolution' came, had been brief.

The Jews were not allotted habitations, as such, in the ghetto, but were herded and packed into various buildings. One was a former vegetable shop; there was also the former yeast plant; a tobacco factory; the old

246

flyers club building and some former patrician houses along the Komsomolskaya.

The Prophet and I noticed one exemption from this packing of the Jews like herrings in a barrel.

'The doctors,' I whispered to the Prophet as we swooped above the ghetto. 'There isn't a single Jewish doctor here.'

'That's right,' the Prophet whispered back. 'They need them on the outside.'

Pragmatic as ever, where their own larger interests were concerned, the Nazis let the Jewish doctors continue to practise in Vitebsk because the Aryan doctors were swamped by outbreaks of typhus, as well as pneumonia, rickets and other diseases of starvation.

We spotted old Dr Brachmann, Thea's father, still attempting to treat the sick until he caught typhus himself and died. Some of his family – his wife, Thea and one of her two brothers, Roman – had been herded into a large house at 30 Komsomolskaya, along with nearly a hundred others.

I had the notes of the *Pathétique* in my head, as I watched them. I heard it as I had heard it at their house.

The Nazis had established work columns. Every morning, groups of forced labourers were assembled at Engelskaya, near the main entrance to the ghetto. They were marched under armed guard across the pontoon bridge and set to clearing the city of the ruins and rubble left by the fighting, and to restoring some of the fire-damage left by the retreating Red Army.

Among these forced labourers, I recognised Bejline the *moujik*, the father of Chaja Bejline, the bride in *The Wedding*, and the now emaciated figure of Abrashka the Hasid, who I drew buying jewellery in the Rosenfeld shop.

One of the features of the existence of Vitebsk's Jews

behind the stockade was the evening gatherings at secluded spots in the fencing, where the palings had been widened. Here, enterprising Christian traders gathered to sell the Jews small quantities of often mouldy food in exchange for jewellery, cash or any other valuables the Jews had managed to smuggle into the ghetto.

A leading figure in this trade was Nicolas Antonowich. Years of kindness towards him by the Gourevich family, which included arranging his training and qualification in bakery at their expense, had turned Nicolas Antonowich into a rabid hater of Jews, on the grounds that these alien interlopers should never have been in a position to be kind to him in the first place.

Nicolas Antonowich turned up at one of the trading places along the palings, usually the one facing Kirovskaya, nearly every evening. He did his business, turned his profit, bought and sold, wearing civilian clothes. All the while he would watch carefully up and down the palings to see who was trading on the Jewish side.

A few days later, Nicolas Antonowich, now resplendent in Bylorussian police uniform, would lead a raid on the ghetto. He had a list of names of Jews who witnesses had seen engaging in black market profiteering – a typical Yid trick. Anything to make money. These Jews were seized by Nicolas Antonowich's men, placed against the nearest wall, usually the wall of the vegetable shop, and shot. Their meagre belongings were then divided up among the men of the firing squad, Nicolas Antonowich himself remaining loftily and generously aloof from such pickings.

Among the first to be shot under this procedure was a man by the name of Yitschak Segalovich. His wife, Dina, was shot with him – indeed they held hands at the last, even managing a statement of their love for each other as the bullets hit them. I had used Yitschak and Dina as models for the man and wife in *The Cattle*

Dealer.

The work of large-scale killing of the Jews inside the ghetto was left to specialist Einsatzkommando (Task Forces), as it always was. Einsatzkommando 9 had arrived at the rear headquarters at Smolensk in the early autumn, after their murder of the Jews in the Minsk ghetto. But it was decided to give them some well-deserved leave before embarking on their next task – obliterating the ghetto of Vitebsk.

The Prophet and I watched them arriving. They drove through the birch forest along the main Vitebsk highway in two jeeps, singing 'Heathlands of Brandenburg', an old SA marching song, at the tops of their voices. Most of them had been in the original SA, the brownshirts of the early days. They all had low Nazi Party numbers; true believers who had signed up early.

They were from various parts of Germany, those dozen men, but they had all trained together at the old Border Police headquarters at Pretsch. That was four years ago and they had been together ever since, operating as a unit with one brain and twenty-four hands. And what a good brain it was. Six of the twelve had doctorates, two were qualified medical doctors, another was a leading architect.

Their leader, Brigadeführer Heinz Jost, was a lawyer. He was sitting in the first of the two jeeps, in the front, next to the driver. He was not singing. He was asleep. He tended to drop off in vehicles, cars or trains. It was part of a lazy streak which had seen his career falter at the upper reaches, when he would otherwise have had a staff job, probably directly under Heydrich. Having not quite made it, he was here killing Jews instead. But he was content enough with his lot.

When the time came to murder all the Jews still left alive, Einsatzkommando 9 instituted well-worn procedures. The Bylorussian police, under Nicolas Antonowich, were told to tell the Jews they were about to be deported to Palestine.

The Einsatzkommando, aided by a detachment of thirty Bylorussian police, then marched all the Jews out of the Vitebsk ghetto. Those with any possessions left, and who had packed small suitcases, were allowed to keep them on the march, to maintain the journey to Palestine fiction. Small children were allowed to stay with their mothers, family groups were allowed to stay together.

This massive Jewish exodus was marched in convoy after convoy to the village of Sebiakhi, a few miles east of Vitebsk. There, there was a ravine. The Jews were made to undress down to their underwear and stand at the lip of the ravine, where they were shot by the machine guns and rifles of the Einsatzkommando and the Bylorussian police. No distinction was made between men, women and children.

I looked at the face of Heinz Jost while the murders were taking place. It was a small-featured, narrow-lipped, unremarkable face. If anything, he looked less intelligent than he was. You would have said 'stores clerk' or 'legal assistant'.

'What will happen to him?' I asked the Prophet, as the murder of the Jews of Vitebsk took place below us. 'Will he get away with it? Will they all get away with it?'

'By and large,' he said. 'Most of them, at any rate. Jost will spend a few years in Landsberg Prison, where Hitler was. After that he will work as an estate agent in the Rhineland. He will die an old man on a visit to New York.'

'Why?' I said, glancing down as Jewish bodies continued to fall into the ravine. 'Why will they get away with it?'

'The world was tired,' the Prophet said.

'Too tired for justice?'

'Apparently so.'

As we watched, Heinz Jost pulled out his pistol. An old Jew was struggling his way towards the ravine with a violin case in his hand. I recognised my Uncle Neuch, the original fiddler on the roof. Heinz Jost shot him through the head.

Before they withdrew from the area, the Nazis set fires in Vitebsk, more or less at random. The Big Lubavich synagogue, which the revolution had despoiled, leaving Torah scrolls outside the vandalised building, was torched and completely destroyed. The shell of the building which had housed the Rosenfeld family jewellery shop was burned to ashes, obliterated.

Back at *La Ruche*, I painted *The White Crucifixion*. I showed Jesus as a Jew wearing a Jewish prayer shawl as a loincloth. In the background Vitebsk is in flames. Jews in boats are being shot by Nazis, as they were when the Vitebsk ghetto was destroyed. The ghosts of past persecution float above.

There is also the figure of the Prophet Elijah, as an old Jew with beard and cap and with a sack on his back representing the Jews fleeing with their homes on their backs.

The Fourth Vision

When we got back to The Hive, after witnessing the murder of Jews in Vitebsk, I was furious with the Prophet.

'Why did you show me that?'

'So you could paint *The White Crucifixion*. Some consider it your masterpiece.'

I was crying. 'Show me something happy. I want another vision, to help me forget this one.'

'All right, I'll show you your death.'

'Do you ever listen to a word I say?'

And that is how we came to witness the retrospective exhibition of my work mounted by Pierre Matisse, Henri Matisse's son. This was in New York, where we lived. It was held when I was a very, very old man.

One of the minor pleasures of life, I have found, is eliciting the reluctant admiration of your enemies – even when they are faking it, which they usually are. It is no secret that I am no fan of the art of nearly all my contemporaries – among the major figures I respect only Henri Matisse, especially after his son helped me so much. And I am even less a fan of the company of artists.

But when a whole honeycomb from The Hive ended up in exile in New York, or the Babylonian Captivity as I called it, we naturally had a reunion. We had them all round to our flat on East 34th Street, with Bella and Ida as gracious hostesses. It was a pleasure to speak Yiddish again, rather than fight my losing battles with English and French.

Zadkine was there, Mané-Katz, Indenbaum, Jacques Lipchitz, Kikoine and Kisling.

And what of the changes? Most of them had travelled far to stay the same; some made small circles, some big. Mané-Katz still painted schmalz, Indenbaum still hacked away at life and stone, making his ponderous small impression on both.

The most changed was Osip Zadkine, who had become a fully-fledged *mensch* – a change indeed. He had something of his own –success, happiness – so he no longer wanted everything I had.

We all decamped from my flat to visit the opening of my huge retrospective at the New York Museum of Modern Art. And there I basked in their admiration and congratulation, while Bella and Ida fussed over me like hens over one of my roosters.

I was interviewed. I was photographed in front of my paintings alone. I was photographed in front of my paintings with Bella. I was photographed in front of my paintings with Bella and Ida. I was photographed with Bella and Pierre Matisse, in front of my *Double Portrait with Wineglass*.

That last photograph, taken by our beloved daughter, Ida, shows Bella and me at the very apogee of our happiness and my fame. *Double Portrait with Wineglass* is the painting which perhaps best captures our love and my need for Bella. I am photographed wearing a suit which cost as much as my father, the herring schlepper, earned in a decade. My Bella is wearing a mink coat with shoes and a hat which do not disgrace the coat.

The exhibition, the major retrospective, was timed to coincide with the publication of yet more books about the world-famous Marc Chagall.

I met a strange chap there, at the exhibition. He was an old Jew with a beard, in a cap, with a bundle on his back. He was a tall, broad-shouldered, very skinny man, with gappy teeth and a long beard. He was dressed in a much-worn Jewish gabardine.

I knew I had seen him before, but for the life of me I could not place him.

'Yes, that's right,' said the old man. 'I am Elijah, the Prophet.'

The old Jew looked at me benignly, then smiled. 'Listen to me, Moyshe. Listen carefully. You were not responsible for the death of your sister. Yes, Rachel ate the charcoal you gave her, but that is not what killed her. She had an epileptic fit.'

'Thank God! I mean ...'

'And the death of your teacher, Yury Pen. That, too, was nothing to do with you. The Cheka stole your paintings, but they did not know they were there when they started searching. Yury resisted them, they started

253

beating him. It was horrible, Moyshe, but you were not involved, not to blame.'

Tears sprang to my eyes.

'And your brother-in-law, David Rubin. You were not to blame for his death, either. He did not intervene with the authorities about your grant, as you asked him to. He never intended to. He deceived you. He was denounced because he had been in a Tsarist prison.'

'Oh, poor David!'

'The Cheka suspected he had collaborated to obtain his release. But they were wrong.'

'Such injustice!'

The Prophet smiled, grimly. 'And another thing,' he said. 'Your generous allowance from Duma Deputy Maksim Vinaver.'

'Yes. How did that happen?'

'Viktor Mekler arranged it. And Viktor Mekler arranged it because Bella Rosenfeld asked him to.'

'So … I owe everything …?'

'Yes. You owe everything to Bella and Viktor.'

'I will thank them.'

'No, you will not, because you will have no memory of this conversation after it finishes.' For some reason that struck me as familiar. 'And anyway you will not have time. You are about to die.'

I shivered at that but the Prophet spoke on.

'I have some more information for you.'

'I am ready,' I said.

'You remember the eighteen Jews who died in the terrible time?'

'Yes.'

'Can you name them? All of them?'

'I'm afraid I can't.'

'Very well, then. I will name them. And in their names we will honour them together. They are Chaim Soutine, Yury Pen, Dr Brachmann and his son, Roman; the cattle dealer Yitschak Segalovich and his wife Dina;

Avramel Bernstein, Zussy Yavich, Mrs Bischowskaya, Jakov Gourevich, the baker, Dyadkin the *melamed*, Tanjka the laundress, also a *gonif*, the beadle Laizar, Bejline the *moujik*, the father of Chaya Bejline, the bride in your painting, *The Wedding*. She died of typhus in the ghetto, so did her husband.'

I nodded, crying now.

'There is also Abrashka the Hasid and your Uncle Neuch, the fiddler on the roof.'

When he had finished, there was silence. Once again, I could hear the chatter of the visitors to my exhibition.

Then the Prophet spoke again. 'But what you do not know, is that eighteen, the number of deaths, is a magical number, a mystical number.'

'How so?'

'The letters of the Hebrew alphabet are the building blocks of the universe. Each letter has a number. Anything that equals eighteen has a connection to *Chai*, which means life. The words *Yehi Or, Vahehi Or* from Genesis, meaning "Let there be light, and there was light" have the first letters *roshei teivos*, that equals eighteen.'

'I understand but ... what does it mean?'

'It means you were chosen to bring light. And that light will preserve the Jews beyond death, even after slaughter. Your light in art will guide us Jews as we go on, as we survive everything they have done to us.'

I nodded, dumbly, unable to speak.

'What have you learned thus far from this meeting with me?'

I stopped for a second; all life stopped. A new experience befell me: what I said next was not said by me. Someone or something was speaking through me: 'I have learned that which was foretold in the vision of Jacob and the ladder to heaven. Our souls are reborn. I am about to be reborn.'

'Good. And?'

The experience continued. I spoke but it was not my voice. 'I have learned that life is like a plant that appears above ground only for a single summer, then withers away, but something endures beneath. That something grows again, better and stronger and always different from before, striving upwards.'

'Good. And what is the result of this knowledge?'

'That just as plants and flowers do greatest good by sharing, enriching others with their beauty, so we are put on this earth for the sake of others. But not all others, only those closest to us, from the same stem. Love of all mankind is a false messiah.'

'Good. Goodbye, Moyshe. My work with you is done.'

As the Prophet disappeared, his place was taken by a strange fellow, expensively dressed, a German who spoke to me in English. He said he was a collector, he said he knew Vitebsk, he said he wanted to buy one, maybe more, of my paintings of Vitebsk. I could not understand half what he said to me but I knew I didn't like him. He gave me the shivers.

He said his name was Heinz Jost.

On the way back down in the lift, I had a heart attack. All my life, I have survived by the skin of my teeth, but this time I did not. I died. I died with a smile on my face, please God you should, too.

And you know something? With my last scrap of consciousness on earth, I was made aware of the death of Heinz Jost. Just as I myself was dying, I saw Heinz Jost lying dead with an old Jewish peddler standing over him. In his hand was a sword, which I knew was the Sword of Righteousness.

Isn't life strange?

Further Reading

About Marc Chagall

My Life, Marc Chagall, Peter Owen, Modern Classics paperback, 2011

Chagall: Love and Exile, Jackie Wullschlager, Allen Lane, 2008

Marc Chagall: An Intimate Biography, Sidney Alexander, Athena Books, 1978

First Encounter, Bella Chagall, Schocken Books, 1983

My Life with Chagall, Virginia Haggard, Donald L. Fine Inc., 1986

Chagall, Franz Meyer, Harry N. Abrams Inc., 1964

Chagall: The Russian Years 1907–22, Alexandr Kamensky, Rizzoli, 1989

Marc Chagall and His Times: A Documentary Narrative, Benjamin Harshav, Stanford University Press, 2004

Chagall: A Retrospective, edited by Jacob Ball-Teshuva, Hugh Lauter Levin Associates Inc., 1995

Marc Chagall, Jonathan Wilson, in Jewish Encounters, Schocken, 2007

Tate Introductions: Chagall, Monica Bohm-Duchen, Tate, 2013

Chagall, Monica Bohm-Duchen, Phaidon, 1998

Chagall, Andrew Kagan, Abbeville Modern Masters, 1989

Chagall: Modern Master, edited by Simonetta Fraquelli, Tate Publishing, 2013

Chagall, Susan Compton, Royal Academy of Arts, 1985

Chagall: Love and the Stage, edited by Susan Compton, Royal Academy of Arts/Merrell Holberton, 1998

Marc Chagall on Art and Culture, edited by Benjamin Harshav, includes the first book on Chagall's art by Efros and Yugendhold, Moscow, 1918, Stanford University Press, 2003

Chagall: Painting as Poetry, Ingo F. Walther & Rainer

Metzger, Midpoint Press/Taschen, 2001
Chagall: Love, War and Exile, Susan Tumarkin Goodman,
with an essay by Kenneth E. Silver, The Jewish Museum
New York/Yale University Press, 2013
Marc Chagall: His Life and Work, Isaac Kloomok,
Philosophical Library, 1951

About Vitebsk

Vitebsk: The Life of Art, Aleksandra Shatskikh, Yale
University Press, 2007
*Masterpieces of Jewish Art: Artists from Vitebsk: Yehuda Pen
and His Pupils,* G. Kasovsky, Memorial Foundation for
Jewish Culture
Encyclopaedia of Camps and Ghettos 1933–1945, volume II,
edited by Martin Dean, United States Holocaust Memorial
Museum/Indiana University Press, 2012

About The Hive (*La Ruche*) And Montparnasse

La Ruche & Montparnasse, Jean Warnod, Exclusivité Weber,
1978
La Ruche, Jacques Chapiro, Flammarion, 1960
La Ruche, Cité des Artistes, Sylvie Buisson, Martine Fresia,
Art en Scène, 2009
The Circle of Montparnasse: Jewish Artists in Paris, 1905
1945, Universe Books, 1985
Montparnasse Vivant, J.-P. Crespelle, Hachette, 1962
Bohemian Paris, Dan Franck, Grove Press, 1998
Ambroise Vollard: Recollections of a Picture Dealer, Dover
Publications, 2002
Life with the Painters of La Ruche, Marevna, Macmillan, 1974

THE AUTHOR

Michael Dean has a history degree from Worcester College, Oxford, an MSc in Applied Linguistics from Edinburgh University and a translator's qualification (AIL) in German.

His novels are *The Crooked Cross* (Endeavour Press, new edition 2018) about Hitler and art; *Thorn*, (Bluemoose Books, 2011) about Spinoza and Rembrandt; *Magic City*, (Odyssey Press new edition 2017) a Bildungsroman; and *I, Hogarth* (Duckworth-Overlook, 2012), which set out to unify Hogarth's life with his art.

He has also written three e-book novels for Endeavour Press: *The Enemy Within* (2013), about Jewish resistance in the Netherlands in World War II; *Hour Zero* (2014), about Germany in 1946; and *Before the Darkness* (2015), about Walther Rathenau and the Weimar Republic.

His non-fiction includes a book about Chomsky and many educational publications.

Holland Park Press is a unique publishing initiative. Its aim is to promote poetry and literary fiction, and discover new writers. It specializes in contemporary English fiction and poetry, and translations of Dutch classics. It also gives contemporary Dutch writers the opportunity to be published in Dutch and English. .

To

- Learn more about Michael Dean
- Discover other interesting books
- Read our unique Anglo-Dutch magazine
- Find out how to submit your manuscript
- Take part in one of our competitions

Visit www.hollandparkpress.co.uk

Bookshop: https://www.hollandparkpress.co.uk/books.php

Holland Park Press in the social media:

http://www.twitter.com/HollandParkPres
http://www.facebook.com/HollandParkPress
https://www.linkedin.com/company/holland-park-press
http://www.youtube.com/user/HollandParkPress